Also by S. Renée Bess:

Breaking Jaie
Leave of Absense
Re: Building Sasha
The Butterfly Moments

The Rules

S. Renée Bess

*Regal Crest Books
by Regal Crest*

Texas

ISBN 978-1-61929-156-0

First Printing 2014

9 8 7 6 5 4 3 2 1

Original cover design by Donna Pawlowski
Final cover design by AcornGraphics

Published by:

Regal Crest Enterprises, LLC
229 Sheridan Loop
Belton, Texas 76513

Find us on the World Wide Web at
http://www.regalcrest.biz

Published in the United States of America

Acknowledgments

I thank Mona and Rosalind and trust they know why.

I owe a huge thank you to Patty Schramm and the Board of Directors of the Golden Crown Literary Society for all of the tasks they accomplish in order to present their conferences.

I thank the staff of the Endoscopy Department at Mercy Suburban Hospital for making me feel like part of their team.

Thank you, Cathy Bryerose of Regal Crest Enterprises, for giving my books a home.

I thank my editor, Verda Foster, for her skillful work.

Thanks to my friend, Lynette R., who read the unedited version of this book and shared her opinions.

I am grateful for my parents, Thomas and Lorraine, and my sister, Stephanie who has always been in my corner.

I have unending gratitude for my life partner/wife, Vivian. We continue to do what it takes to understand and accept each other.

Dedication

To every woman of color whose authenticity is challenged because she calls the shots in the boardroom as well as in the bedroom, enjoys the sounds of symphony orchestras as well as the tight syncopation of rhythm and blues bands, and trusts the promises whispered by white and black lovers alike.

To all these women who speak the King's English and parlay the Queen's dialect; who are comfortable looking at the world from their front stoop as well as regarding it from beyond America's shores.

To those who don't believe physical perfection equals skin the color of creamed tea and hair straightened by any means necessary.

To all women of color who pay the price of being different.

To all of us, of all colors, who understand the rightness of shredding the cords that bind hatred to ignorance.

To those of us who believe we don't have to be at war with each other for eternity.

To those of us whose lives form the bridges that link understanding to love.

This book is for us.

Prologue

LIFE PRESENTS US with all sorts of rules, many codified by law, others cast in cement by virtue of our passively accepting them over the course of several generations. I've come to believe the most strictly obeyed rules are those that we follow out of habit, without thinking or questioning them. When the rightness of certain rules remains unchallenged, we risk excluding experiences and people from our lives. This exclusion diminishes all of us except those who possess kind hearts, generous spirits, and the willingness and determination to crush those rules to dust.

Chapter One

London: That Was Then

EVERYONE NEEDS SOMEBODY in their life they can trust with their secrets. Roberta Baker may not have trusted me with hers, but I was sure she'd guard mine. For one thing, she never talked much. She shared little about her family and didn't blab any of the things she heard about the other kids in our class. I embedded my faith in her ability to keep a secret every time she vowed she'd never tell a soul the things I'd told her about myself. In return, I held on to each of the sermonettes she delivered during the two years we traveled together back and forth to school. The years when we were the only black girls riding in a school bus filled with the others, the powerful others.

At the time I didn't realize there was a third black girl on the bus. I would have taken her in my confidence had I known, but the combination of her silence, her gray-blue eyes, her golden ringlets, and near white skin fooled me. I'd seen Roberta shoot her a look and then make a sucking noise with her tongue and teeth, so I guess she'd figured her out. If she had though, she never breathed a word. That was Roberta. Even the passing-for-white girl's biggest secret was safe with her.

One afternoon I thought I was going to die on that yellow school bus. I was used to it hurtling down the narrow tunnel of a particularly steep road. That day, it felt like it was out of control. My stomach lurched two feet in the air when we hit a pot hole. I grabbed the metal bar across the top of the seat in front of me and searched frantically to make sure the driver was still in his seat. There he was, his upper arms flailed at a forty-five degree angle as his beefy hands grabbed the steering wheel in anticipation of the sharp turn that laid in wait for us at the bottom of the hill.

"If we crash we're gonna be rich," Roberta said.

"What?"

Roberta pointed her index finger toward the front of the bus. "That reckless jerk can't drive. He's gonna crash this bus, and our parents are gonna sue the crap out of the school district."

Roberta's steely gaze assured me she knew what she was talking about. All I could do was blink a frightened response. I split my attention between Roberta and the little bit of road I could see rushing toward the bus's windshield. The vehicle bounced so violently I could barely stay put on the slippery vinyl seat.

"Plus, he's a ackaholic," Roberta added.

"How...how do you know that?"

"His nose is always redder than Rudolph's. And whenever I ask, 'How you doin', Mr. Ralph?' he says, 'Fine, kid,' and his breath stops right in front of my nose. It stinks just like my father's does after he's been hittin' the bottle."

"Oh."

Oh was all I ever said when Roberta uttered something my ears weren't prepared to hear. Sometimes I'd ask her questions and then mentally record her answers for posterity. Lots of times I'd laugh at Roberta because she had a way of saying things that tickled my brain.

Roberta was simply the smartest girl I knew. Her plainly spoken declarations constantly surprised me. Often I tried to react to her dry, expressionless delivery with a certain amount of detachment, because I didn't want her to know how amazed I was by what she was saying. I wanted her to view me as an equal, not some little sycophant lined up behind her like a baby gosling following its mother.

If Roberta announced the next night's expected snowstorm would peter out and leave only an inch or two of slush on the roads instead of the predicted school closing eight inches or more, I believed her. If she swore she'd never go swimming in the recently desegregated local public pool because she'd have to knock out the first white boy who "called her out of her name," I knew she'd keep her promise. So, when Roberta declared our parents would win a lawsuit against the school district that hired a reckless bus driver, in my mind it was a done deal.

I was fairly certain none of the teachers at James Buchanan Elementary School were aware of Roberta's intellectual talents. They had the habit of skipping over her when they asked us questions and then calling on Brad, Eugene or cute little blondie-passing-for-white.

Roberta was far smarter than Brad and Eugene and blondie. I suspected she was too smart to let them and our teachers discover just how intelligent she was. I don't know why Roberta was pulled out of class twice a week and sent to Mrs. Stone who taught Remedial Reading. As far as I could see, Roberta didn't need that special group. She could read just fine, comics, books and people, especially people.

Once in a while Roberta was absent. When she wasn't in school, I'd hang out with Brad and Eugene. The three of us would speed through our assignments, have them approved by the teacher, and then busy ourselves drawing pictures of rockets. During recess, we'd trade our little artistic creations and add little details like U.S.A.F. on the fuselages, or multi-colored stripes emblazoned on the rockets' wings. Brad always named the spacecrafts while Eugene composed all kinds of speed and distance statistics and wrote them near the bottom of the drawings. I'd daydream I'd pilot the spaceships and make safe landings. Safe, smooth landings were paramount. I'd never crash the thing.

That's why the school bus's daily race down the hill with the winding turn at the end scared the stuff out of me. I knew one of these days we were going to end up among a million twisted pieces of yellow metal, smashed beyond recognition. What good would Roberta's plans for a lawsuit do us if we were paralyzed, or worse?

From the first afternoon's ride home when Roberta Baker plunked herself down next to me, I knew we were going to be friends. She eyed my outfit and my new book bag and uttered the first of her many proclamations.

"Coventry Village."

I nodded.

Then, she asked the first of the very few questions she'd ever pose to me.

"You get off the bus on Pinetree Lane?"

"Yes."

"Me too, but not the same corner as you."

I wasn't sure how she figured which stop on Pinetree was mine, but Roberta knew all sorts of things that hadn't yet occurred to me, like the bus driver's drinking habits. Often she'd blurt out her assumptions as if they were well documented truths. Then she'd narrow her eyes and focus on some faraway target, like she was leaving our conversation for a few seconds and gathering her facts.

I admired Roberta. I respected her knowledge more than I respected Brad's and Eugene's ability to draw rockets and calculate how long it would take for them to reach Mars or Saturn. I could tell Roberta knew things about people, especially adults.

When she compared the bus driver to her father and then got that faraway look in her eyes, my imagination tried to follow the trail her stare took. But it never succeeded. I never knew what she was thinking because she never told me.

That day we thought the bus was going to crash turned out just fine. The brakes moaned and although we were all sucked forward toward the seat in front of us, we arrived intact at the bottom of the hill. I imagined we were spaceship pilots and we'd made our fiery reentry from outer space with our heat shield protecting us from certain immolation.

A half mile short of my destination, the bus halted to discharge some kids. The door opener squealed and two girls clutched their light blue notebooks and pencil cases, bowed their heads in deference to the school bus safety gods, and descended to the sidewalk. I watched one of them flip her ribbon-ended pigtail, sending it airborne for a second until it came to rest on her shoulder. Her freckled companion grinned at her.

I turned to face Roberta.

"Hey, wanna come over to my house on Saturday and play some records in our rec room?"

"I don't know. I think I have to help my mother on Saturday."

"Okay."

It seemed to me Roberta always had to help her mother, no matter what day it was. I don't think she ever had free time. I continued to invite her to my house though, because I was eager to prolong the jokes and listen to the stories she shared with me during our bus rides.

The days and weeks sped by, filled with more invitations but without any after school or Saturday afternoon visits from Roberta. After a while, my persistence dwindled. I found myself synchronizing the invitations with the change of seasons, or at least with the changes in my wardrobe. Madras plaid cotton skirts became corduroy. Hand knit sweaters morphed into a favorite woolen blazer emblazoned with a rakish golden thread crest on the breast pocket. My winter parka covered me for a while. Then, it was back to a lighter weight poplin jacket, and finally pastel colored short sleeved blouses meant to coordinate with knife-pleated skirts.

Whenever the weather forced me to head to a different area of my clothes closet, I'd asked Roberta to come visit me some Friday after school or some weekend afternoon. Just as faithfully, she danced away from each invitation. She always promised she'd ask for permission and I always hoped she'd be granted dispensation from her chores and allowed to forge the dozen or so blocks that separated her house from mine.

At home, I boasted about Roberta's braininess. I'd spin around on one of the kitchen stools, my chest stuck out proudly, and quote her opinions about life in general. Borrowing her views made me feel smarter. I knew not to share everything she'd said about the adults in our lives, including the "ackaholic" school bus driver. I especially suppressed the portrait she'd painted one day of our two female gym teachers. That anecdote made me feel uneasy.

"She's just about the smartest girl in our class," I told my mother. I wasn't ready to cede "first brain" to Roberta. After all, I had earned nothing but A's on my last report card, and Roberta had one A, one B and two C's to show for her selective lack of effort.

"And she's the only one who's never made fun of my first name," I added.

"Is that so?" My mother asked.

"Yes. And we always sit next to each other on the bus."

"What does your friend look like, London?"

While she waited for my answer, my mother patted my head. She'd begun doing this more and more frequently. She'd start in the center where a carefully crafted part divided my thick hair into two hemispheres. Her fingers would smooth first one side and then the other, exerting increased pressure as she moved away from the dividing line and closer to each of my two fat braids.

I gave in to my mother's hair care technique and summoned Roberta's image.

"She's as tall as I am. And she's skinny. She wears her hair in braids, like me."

"Are her clothes as nice as yours?"

"I guess so." Even as I answered this question, I visualized Roberta the way I'd seen her so often this past winter, bootless and wearing a thin corduroy jacket. Each morning I'd blinked away the reality of her arm shivering against mine when she slid into the seat next to me.

"Where exactly does Roberta live?"

"On Jefferson Road."

"In Grantville?" My mother's voice became a clarion call of alarm.

"I think so."

There was no thinking at all involved in my answer. Roberta lived in Grantville, not Coventry Village. Grantville was directly across the street from Coventry Village's west entrance, but it might as well have been miles away. Grantville. My parents referred to it as "Wild Grantville" or simply "The Wild West."

"I think I should meet your little friend, London."

"I've invited her over but she always has to help her mother."

"Maybe that's for the best." My mother pressed her lips together tighter than a sealed offering envelope carefully placed in the silver plate at church.

"Why don't you invite a few of your other friends to visit?"

Dealing with my parents had forced me into bilingualism, so I found it easy to translate my mother's suggestion. What she'd meant was, "Roberta from Grantville is not the type of friend I want you to have."

Although I hadn't learned how to swim, I could dive underneath my parents' words, open my eyes, and understand what they were really saying. So I knew when my mother asked what Roberta looked like, she was inquiring about Roberta's skin color. The truth was, I didn't know how to describe Roberta's complexion. I might have noticed its hue the first day I met her, but after that, all I saw was Roberta. We were both black girls, weren't we? We were both different from the other kids in our mostly white elementary school and on the mostly white school bus. In my mind, Roberta's complexion was the same color as her personality: clear, compelling, clever, and wise.

My mother's interest in Roberta's skin tones failed to mute my admiration for my friend. It did convince me to hide some part of the truth though. Her inference that I'd crossed some invisible boundary that was meant to separate Roberta from me introduced me to the subversive stratagems with which I became familiar and in some sense comfortable.

I toned down my animated descriptions of Roberta. I mentioned the possibility of her visiting me less frequently. I pulled back so successfully from referencing Roberta, that I began to withdraw from her. I became aware of things I hadn't noticed before, like our differences, and I questioned exactly what had been so compelling about Roberta the two years we were friends.

Fourth grade galloped toward fifth, and Roberta never crossed my house's threshold. During two years of friendship we never spent a single Saturday playing records in my rec room and gossiping about the teachers and the other kids we knew.

One mid-June weekend I went to the local public swimming pool with a group of neighborhood kids. I walked through the gates, scared to death the rumors I'd heard were true. That the white kids, on seeing us arrive, would surreptitiously smash glass bottles against the sides of the pool and we'd cut our feet to bloody ribbons. They didn't do that, but I spent a couple of hours with my back plastered against the pool's walls, watching warily and wondering what Roberta would have said about my paralyzing fear had she been with us.

Two weeks later the school year ended and emptied us out to our respective backyards and summer camps. Despite the distance that had developed between us, I felt sad about spending the next two months without hearing Roberta's wise sound bites.

One July afternoon my father asked if I wanted to go with him to Grantville to buy bait and fishing lures for an upcoming trip he was planning. Thrilled to be able to enter the "Wild West," I forgot I was totally disinterested in anything related to fishing. On our way to a corner store that sold everything from popsicles to second hand furniture, my father drove his red and white Oldsmobile down streets and across intersections I'd never seen before. Everywhere we went I craned my neck and searched for a girl my age who wore braids and a smileless expression and uttered short declarative sentences that either took my ears by surprise or pulled a grin across my lips. That day I saw lots of kids in those streets and front yards, but I never caught as much as a glimpse of the girl I searched for.

After Labor Day, when the school bus stopped at Roberta's intersection, I didn't see her climb aboard. I didn't hear our new teacher call her name when the roll was taken. When I questioned a few of the other kids who lived in Grantville, no one knew where she was. Starting the year I spent in fifth grade, Roberta went missing from my life. I mourned her absence for a very long time.

Chapter Two

Roberta: That Was Then

ROBERTA L. BAKER stared at her reflection in the bus window. This was the third Greyhound bus she and her mother, Brenda, had climbed onto during the last twenty-four hours, and she was tired and bored. Philly to Richmond was a haul. Then came Richmond to Little Rock. Now they were headed to Mobile, Alabama, where her Aunt Lizzie lived.

Roberta looked up above her head and watched as her small suitcase moved almost imperceptibly whenever the bus rode over a bump. Exhausted, she remembered this was Labor Day weekend.

I'm supposed to start fifth grade on Tuesday morning, she thought. I guess I won't be going to James Buchanan Elementary School. I won't see London. Roberta bowed her head and let her chin touch the top of her chest.

"Sit up straight, gal. We're almost there." Her mother nudged her arm. "I want you to be alert and look smart when your Auntie meets us at the bus depot."

Roberta lifted her head.

"Why are we going to Mobile, anyway?"

Her mother looked down at her. She seemed to weigh her next words before she spoke them.

"Cause if we'd stayed in Grantville, I'd end up in jail for the rest of my life."

Roberta's throat tightened. She felt the saliva on her tongue dry instantly.

"Why would you end up in jail, Ma?"

Roberta knew the answer, but she wanted to hear her mother pronounce the sentence that would burst open the great secret and destroy the huge wall between them. She wanted absolution. She craved forgiveness from the only person in her world who could offer it along with a gentle smile or a gesture more tender than a tug on her pigtails or a nudge on her shoulder.

"They woulda put me in jail cause I'd killed your father."

There. It was spoken. The pus filled wound Roberta's father left when he'd touched her private area with his private thing was lanced. Now air would sweep over the wound. Acknowledgment of the lesion would lead to its cure.

Roberta turned toward the window and thought of two games she could play while the bus completed its journey to Aunt Lizzie's. There was the first one, the "Father Knows Best" game she played those times she was left alone with her dad. After he'd rubbed himself on her, grunted and then gotten up, she'd pretend her father was really James Anderson who always dressed in a suit or wore a sweater on top of his nice shirt and tie. Her mother, Mrs. Anderson, would soon call the family to dinner in the huge dining room where they would eat roast beef with gravy, potatoes, carrots and green beans. She'd have a brother, Bud, and an older sister, Betty, and they'd talk about the things they'd done that day in school.

But that night, in the darkness on the bus, there was something about the explosion of her great secret that made Roberta think she wouldn't need to conjure up the Andersons any longer. She shifted from that game to her stand-by activity. She began to list the things she'd never wanted.

She'd never wanted people to know she was real smart because everyone would pin their expectations on her. At school, she never wanted to win the spelling, science or math contests even though she figured she could win them all without breaking a sweat. Although she didn't want to let on how well she could read, she often wondered how come the smart, well-educated teachers never even tried to discover how intelligent she was, especially Mrs. Stone, the Remedial Reading teacher, who seemed dumb as a rock and determined to never really look at her.

She never wanted to have a best friend, only acquaintances. London was a good pal to her on the school bus. That was all. Roberta liked the name, London Phillips. From the first day she'd heard it, she pictured its large black letters written on top of a little green and brown colored island on the globe near the front of their classroom.

Roberta thought she'd never wanted to dress like London, except for that snappy blazer she knew would have looked better covering her thin torso than it did cloaking London's chunky one. And maybe she would have liked London's loden green winter parka. Its left arm always felt warm and cozy whenever she climbed aboard the bus and plunked herself down on the seat next to London.

Roberta moved each of her fingers as she kept score of all the things she never wanted. She never wanted to go to London's house and play records. She knew exactly where London lived. She'd walked by the large ranch style house with its perfectly trimmed shrubs several times when she ventured from the streets of her neighborhood and went to "Never-Neverland," the label her mother gave to "uppity Coventry Village."

Roberta hadn't ever seen London outside the house, but she had seen London's mother sitting on the white and yellow glider on the front patio. She'd sneaked glances at the woman and she'd felt Mrs. Phillips staring at her as she walked by. In those few seconds, she'd decided London's mother was probably as cold and hard as the metallic chair she was occupying.

Roberta knew although Mrs. Phillips might look at her, she'd never really see her, just like her teacher, Mrs. Stone, failed to really see her, but for different reasons. She was certain Mrs. Phillips wouldn't see anything more than her chocolate skin and her shiny hot-combed straightened but never faultlessly neat hair.

Roberta sensed the bus slow as it approached the Greyhound station.

"Get ready to stand up. I'll get our bags," her mother said.

Roberta nodded obediently. She had no idea what the next hour would bring, much less the next school year. As she waited for the bus to enter its parking slot, she rushed to conclude her things-I-never-wanted game.

I never wanted that ackaholic driver to crash the school bus, and he didn't. I never wanted my father to do those things, but he did. I never wanted my mother to believe I caused my father to do those things, but she might have.

I never wanted to be close to London, so I wasn't. I never wanted to spend Saturdays with her in her rec room, and I never did. I never wanted to be late for the school bus, especially on cold windy days when London's coat sleeve would keep me warm, and I wasn't. I never wanted to have a secret, especially the one about how much I liked girls, but I couldn't help it. I never wanted to skip entire chapters of my childhood, but I did. I probably didn't know half the things I skipped because I didn't know those things could exist.

Roberta and her mother stepped off the bus and into the arms of Aunt Lizzie.

"Oh my Lord. Brenda. Roberta, honey. It's so good to see both of you. Come on and give me a hug."

Lizzie's husband, Leroy, stood to one side and mumbled his greeting.

"The car's over there." Lizzie pointed to an old black Buick parked near the entrance of the bus depot. "You remember we live a good twenty minutes from Mobile, right?"

"Fifteen minutes this time of night," Leroy said.

"I remember." Brenda picked up her suitcase and gestured for Roberta to do the same.

Roberta took a couple of steps toward the car and sniffed the air.

"What's that smell, Mom?"

"That's nothin' but the odor of the sea mixed with the sweat of dead slaves, honey." Aunt Lizzie spoke before Roberta's mother could summon an answer.

Roberta had heard of slavery and she had a vague notion she had some connection to it, but exactly how she was connected, she didn't know.

The four of them got into the car. Aunt Lizzie turned her head so she could see Roberta from the front seat. "So how old are you now?

What grade are you in?"

"Nine. The fifth grade."

Lizzie chuckled.

"She don't talk much, huh?"

"Not much. And when she does talk, she's liable to sass you."

"Well, we can take care of that." Lizzie wagged her finger at Roberta. "Down here we don't brook no sassy behavior, young lady."

Leroy kept his eyes on the road ahead of them.

Roberta stared at the back of Leroy's head. She figured he was like her, smart but quiet. After one week she'd changed her mind. Uncle Leroy wasn't all that intelligent. She didn't know if he tended to grunt answers to questions instead of answering them with words because he lacked vocabulary skills or had acquired the habit of laziness. Maybe it was neither. Perhaps it was just easier to communicate with Aunt Lizzie without sentences. Roberta did know he seemed to look at her an awful lot, as if he expected her to change from one moment to the next.

As the oppressively hot Alabama days dragged by, Roberta acquainted herself with her new surroundings. She compared the little town where her aunt and uncle lived to the village of Grantville and found it came up short. It was mid-summer and school wasn't in session. Yet nightfall saw a dearth of kids playing in the streets. Most of the shops closed way before dusk. The only place Roberta could go if she wanted a soda or candy after supper was a little hole-in-the-wall store attached to the one-pump gas station. Here and there, once in a while, she would see a neighbor pay a visit to another one. She'd listen for their raucous laughter and instead hear fragments of conversation muffled between the pleats of handheld fans that had been discreetly pilfered from church.

In no time at all Roberta concluded she was bored. One morning, as she extended her daily walk to a new street she hadn't yet explored, Roberta discovered the place and the person who would rescue her from monotony. She practically vibrated with excitement upon entering the world of Miz Myjoy Henderson.

Chapter Three

London: This Is Now

"YOU LOVE YOUR job. You like where you live. You've got good friends and good health. What more do you need to make yourself happy?" My friend Theresa asked one day a couple of years ago.

"You sound like an old woman, Theresa."

Theresa leveled her gaze at me. "I'm not old, but I'm trying to be wise. Look at us, London. We both have a lot to offer but neither of us is ringing up sales in the romance department."

"I know, Tee, but I'm not getting stressed about it. With a partner or without one, I'm moving on with my life."

"But you have to admit, it sure would be better to move on with someone standing beside you."

Theresa and I had debated this point many times, usually right after one of us stopped dating a woman of interest.

"We've been looking for the ideal person, Tee, and she doesn't exist," I said for the umpteenth time.

"Speak for yourself. I think she does exist. She'll have an adequate income, a nice home, no habits that will harm her health or mine..." Theresa squinted and looked up to the ceiling in search of the rest of her "dream woman" description.

"Most of her own teeth, no one else's hair, and a decently funded IRA, right?" I asked.

"Now you're making fun of me, London. I don't have that many requirements or needs."

"Nor do I, Tee. The only thing I need is to see at least one miracle each day. Two miracles daily would be grand, but one is enough."

"Lots of luck, sis. Don't hold your breath."

I wasn't naïve. I was well into my forties and I'd had enough negative experiences with people to be able to appreciate positive encounters when they came my way. I knew if I'd decided to be open to seeing miracles, I'd see them. I wasn't talking about watching folks walk on water or witnessing the blind spontaneously regain their sight. I liked to notice ordinary acts of kindness or sightings of nature that helped me appreciate life. My miracles were simple things, like finding an earring I'd misplaced months ago, or listening to the gratitude in an elderly person's voice as she told me how fortunate she was to be able to feel the morning sunshine warm her face.

My miracle searches were in no way analgesics to mask the ache I felt after my lover, Paula, went on about her life without me. Nor were they meant to be a cure for the hurt that had settled over me after my father died. To take note of one miracle per day seemed to me a better deal than to remain straddled to the past, sitting atop a pile of regrets.

I was convinced being open to the smallest miracles meant I had dominion over some of the negative events that had crossed my path. It meant my faith in the inherent goodness of humanity was stronger than any sorrow I'd felt. Recognizing a miracle, no matter how small or insignificant it might be, symbolized my ability to be at peace with my father's dying and interpret my lover's departure as an opportunity to keep growing, not a liability.

My dad's death climaxed nightmarish months of illness and bought me my membership in the orphaned adults' club. Although his passing wasn't accompanied by the horrific surprise my mother's death flung at us years before, it hurt nevertheless.

My mother's sudden departure left me with a sense of things left undone, a never-ending series of reminders that I had to accomplish the great task of growing into womanhood correctly, promptly, and with decorum. And no matter how determined I was to do just that, I'd never be able to succeed perfectly. There would always be something amiss.

The morning after my father was eulogized and buried, I felt a specific kind of aloneness I never knew existed. Who would supply the other half of our father-daughter chatter when I dialed his phone number? Who would assure me everything was fine, even if we both knew things were far from fine?

No one other than my dad could have adored my mother so faithfully without giving that adoration a second thought. No one other than he would have tolerated her oft spoken intolerances and accepted them with gentle nods. No one other than my father would have supported her judgmental biases at the same time he offered me the emotional scaffolding I needed to help me stand erect and be a woman altogether different from the one my mother intended me to be.

My father's faith in my personhood supported me when I fell in love with Paula, and his belief in my strength sheltered me after Paula and I broke up.

"You'll be okay, London. You're hurting right now, but you'll get through the pain."

I was certain my dad would have affirmed my daily searches for little miracles, even if no one else would.

Each morning, I got out of bed, slid my feet into my slippers, and glided my way along the well-worn path between the bedroom and the bathroom, where I would stand in front of the window and expect to spot a miracle. Today for example, I stood there, my forearms propped on the edge of the breast-high sill, and began to count the Colorado spruce trees that defined the perimeter of my small backyard. Halfway through the census, I spied a hummingbird, the day's first miracle. The little thing hovered near its feeder, then darted closer to one of the nectar ports. The bird's long needle shaped beak penetrated the opening. Its iridescent bluish green back reflected a second's worth of a sunbeam before the tiny bird sped away.

I acknowledged the magic of the moment, left my perch by the window, and stepped into the bathtub, under the spray of the shower head. As I let the water cascade over my body, I thought about how I'd spent the previous day.

I'd used my time off from work to catch up with e-mails, read an endlessly long editorial about the President's successes and failures during his first term in office, and write a blog about all the angry people who'd plastered their cars' bumpers with "Take Back America" decals. For the life of me, I hadn't been able to figure out who'd absconded with America and where he, she, or they had taken it.

After I finished writing the blog, I set aside time to do what I'd really wanted to accomplish, read a submission a writer had sent to me in the hopes I'd accept it for the short fiction anthology I was compiling.

There were two things I hadn't done yesterday. One was to continue my search for Milagros Farrow, a favorite writer of mine whose contribution I'd counted on including in the anthology. My publisher's deadline was perilously close and I was determined to finish the collection on time. Hopefully I'd hear from Ms. Farrow before I had to send the finished product.

I'd been trying to locate her for months, but without any success. It's as if she'd dropped off the face of the earth immediately after her last book saw the light of day. She hadn't done the requisite promotion tour her mainstream publisher always arranged when her books debuted. I knew this because I'd searched for her appearance schedule the moment I'd read a preview of her latest book. Undaunted by my failure to find out where Ms. Farrow would do her readings and book signings, I'd continued to search for any information I could find about her. Surely she'd make an appearance in Philadelphia, either at the city's public library or its sole gay bookstore.

During these past few years I'd come to envy Milagros Farrow's life as I imagined it must be. I was certain she was always driven to airports, ticketed for a business class seat, and booked into first class hotels. I just knew bookstore staffs welcomed her. Without a doubt they always offered her a comfortable seat along with a regiment of brand new pens lined up next to a perfectly piled stack of her newest book. All their polite gestures would seduce an indulgent smile from Milagros as she listened to her adoring fans whisper requests that she inscribe the inside cover of the tome they pressed so closely to their chests moments before they offered it to her.

But now it seemed my fantasies regarding Milagros' writer-as-celebrity routine were not really happening. As far as I could determine, in recent months she hadn't made any promotional appearances at all. She hadn't shared her thoughts about writing with any of the online interviewers whose programs I listened to regularly. She hadn't fluttered her wings on any of the social networks I habitually visited. She hadn't responded to any of the LGBT book clubs that must have requested question and answer sessions.

Someone, perhaps Milagros herself, had taken down her website as well as her author's page on Facebook. Her Twitter voice no longer tweeted and she wasn't LinkedIn to anyone.

When I typed her name and asked Google to search for her, I saw nothing but links to past news articles. When I sent emails to her publisher and agent, they responded curtly and claimed they weren't able to contact her either.

"If your efforts to correspond with Ms. Farrow prove successful, please urge her to contact us," her publisher's representative wrote.

I already had enough contributions from other writers, but I didn't want to exclude Milagros because her work was important. Her stories were as unique as her name. Hers was a singularly different voice in the chorus of African-American lesbian writers. It was one to which I especially related, and I knew the anthology wouldn't be complete without something from her vast imagination.

The second task I hadn't accomplished yesterday was to sit down and confront the first chapter of a novel that hovered at the borders of my mind. I'd let another day go by without typing a single word or jotting notes about characters or a story arc. Once again, I'd found myself at the beginning of a new week with nothing more than a vague notion of needing to commit words to the computer screen. Phrases spun around, a character's profile and name appeared out of nowhere, fragments of dialogue zigged and zagged endlessly through my mind, but I lacked the discipline to get started. My imaginary characters were little more than a closely guarded secret, and so far they'd shown little inclination of leading me to their story.

My first and second books had flown out of my head with little effort, perhaps because after years of keeping my thoughts to myself, I'd opened up and had a lot to say. More likely, it was the encouragement I cajoled from Paula and the academic environment that surrounded me in those days that helped me write with ease.

The university provided the perfect backdrop for the long hours of solitude I needed for my writing. Books, lectures, the exchange of questions and answers with students and other faculty members cocooned me in a comfortable ecosystem that nurtured my creativity. My writing flowed smoothly during those five years when I had a secure contract with the university. Paula wore my teaching and writing success with the pride of a race horse posing in the winner's circle, festooned with floral leis.

"We're not worried about the publish or perish game. With two books already written, London's working on earning her tenure and then a full professorship," Paula frequently boasted to friends and strangers alike.

When my contract with the university expired however, my failure to earn a tenure-track position became a financial and emotional liability that assumed the ugly guise of writer's block. The following two years found me teaching at a community college, glued in place at the rank of underpaid adjunct with neither healthcare benefits nor a retirement fund.

Faced with the prospect of having to pay the lion's share of our bills, Paula convinced me the business world offered more money and prestige than I'd ever find on a college campus.

"You need to get out there and earn some real money. We're supposed to be running this household fifty-fifty. How long do you think I'm going to keep carrying you?" She reminded me more times than I cared to recall.

I left the protective bubble of academia and applied for a position writing promotional materials and placing ads in the media for Whittingham Builders, a construction firm. It seemed to be a job where I could use my writing skills in exchange for a salary commensurate with Paula's plans.

Soon after I was hired, the housing boom hit the industry and Clive Whittingham, the company's owner, decided to expand his sales force. He suggested I divide my time between writing ad copy and assisting various sales people. Some days I did little else than observe how one particular salesperson steered customers through the process of selecting their house's flooring materials and fixtures for the kitchen, bathrooms, and laundry room. Other days I watched salespeople help customers choose the lots their homes would be built on. It seemed to be all about listening to the clients and then matching their preferences to Whittingham Builders' products.

Hours spent observing the other employees morphed into months. While I continued to create ads, I studied for and earned my realtor's license. Despite that achievement, Clive Whittingham didn't change my job description. I remained a rather well dressed listener with ever expanding knowledge regarding real estate sales, but scant experience actually selling houses. I'd spent my money and a lot of my free time studying for a real estate license. When would I start to sell houses and earn sales commissions?

Instead of complaining about my situation, I nudged myself into leaving Whittingham Builders, Pennsylvania's most successful minority owned construction company.

"But Clive Whittingham's been honored by the Human Rights Campaign. He's more than a successful black businessman. He's a successful gay man of color who gives a lot of money and other resources to the gay community," Paula said.

"I know that. But what's he given to this gay woman of color in terms of a job promotion or a salary increase?" I flew my résumé across the desks of a few other construction companies and hoped to hell I wasn't making a mistake. In short order, Kensington Builders, a non-minority non-gay owned firm hired me.

"I wonder why they've taken you on," Paula said. "Why would they hire an inexperienced sales person?"

Paula's lack of confidence in my employability sent me tumbling down a hill of self-doubt. Had Clive Whittingham not promoted me to his sales force because he saw some deficit in my skills? Had I been too impatient with him? If I'd allowed Clive more time, would he have given me a chance to produce home sales as well as ad materials? I had questions that were never answered.

I've worked for Kensington Builders for ten years now, and during that time the economy has had its ups and downs. These last three years, my work has become more challenging. When the number of new housing starts plummeted, Kensington Builders' sales force shrank and I had to master the art of the hard sell. My job evolved from selling homes to folks eager to spend their money on superfluous upgrades to convincing prospective buyers they'd be able to sell their present house, easily capture a mortgage for the new one, and walk away from the settlement table with enough money to keep their new stainless steel appliances gleaming.

The head of the company, Roger Kensington, began to meet regularly with his sales team. He was quick to offer us salary bonuses if we could invent promotional ploys that resulted in increased sales contracts.

"If we can't get customers through the models' front doors, we won't have any damn sales," Roger said.

Some of my colleagues grabbed his offer and ran with it, like cats chasing mice through a maze.

"Let's have an open house each holiday." One guy suggested.

"Here's the line-up," he continued, "We'll have a Valentine's Day get-your-sweetheart-a-free-sunroom event, Easter and Passover flooring upgrades, springtime kitchen cabinet specials, and a Fourth-of-July-free-fireplace-in-the-great-room offer."

"Consider it done." Roger smacked the top of the conference table.

I pictured the ads I'd be expected to produce. A sunroom in the middle of a Valentine's heart, a Seder spread out over a Brazilian Koa wood floor, the Easter bunny leaving baskets of foil covered chocolate eggs atop the stain proof plush carpet, a happy family dressed in red, white, and blue and sweating to death in front of their roaring fireplace.

I liked my job from the day I was hired, despite or perhaps because I had to master a steep learning curve. Anything that echoed learning was comfortable for me. I was busy twenty-four-seven, but it was a good busy. I was learning a new skill set and accomplishing something concrete. I felt proud of myself, renewed, and happier than I'd been in ages.

Paula seemed pleased also. She'd stopped hovering above my head in anticipation of filling in my gaps or spackling any cracks she perceived in my behaviors.

I'd become so busy and happy with my job, so content with Paula's demeanor, that the reason for her good mood never occurred to me until the night she declared she'd fallen in love with someone else and wanted to end our relationship.

"I don't understand. Why?"

"You're just not enough for me, London."

"Enough of what?"

"You're not genuine, not real enough for me."

I crossed my arms in front of my chest and gently squeezed my left elbow. The bony protuberance and the flesh that surrounded it felt real to me.

"What do you mean?"

"You don't seem sure about your blackness."

"What are you talking about? I know I'm black."

"Do you? You could have fooled me. Most of your friends aren't black. You don't talk like a black person. You couldn't even keep working for a black-owned construction company."

"My friends are all different colors. I speak the way I was taught to speak, and I left Clive Whittingham's firm because I wasn't climbing the ladder there, not because I didn't want to work for a black man's company."

Although I stood my ground, I'd defended myself in vain. My ethnic credentials didn't make Paula's cut. She and I settled our financial arrangements, and she left. I grieved her loss and became morosely introspective about my identity. I was black, wasn't I? Who endowed Paula with the authority to define race and ethnicity?

As I relearned how to live alone and be single, I clung to my father's wise counsel.

"It must be uncomfortable trying to make a life with someone who doesn't accept you for who you are. You're a precious being, London, and you deserve to be with someone more worthy of you than Paula was."

I wrapped his words around me like a homemade quilt. Then I vowed to stay busy with work and writing and not spend time simply waiting for the worthy one to arrive. I knew certain kinds of women could still stop me in my tracks. A particularly deep-throated female laugh could set my imagination in motion. But my hormones no longer commanded me to share my bed on a regular basis with beauties who were graced with round breasts and smooth hips, especially if those body parts weren't accompanied by an intelligent brain, a kind heart, and the maturity to understand life didn't always flow seamlessly and without ripples.

In time I became a more patient person. I no longer expected every date to turn into a relationship bound with dual Powers of Attorney.

The change in my expectations made my life less complicated, less painful.

A few of my job experiences taught me how much I didn't know about marketing and selling new construction. My supervisor, Sandra Linton, tutored me. Despite my not looking for romance behind every door, in the two minutes it took for Sandra to explain the difference between truss and joist systems, I developed a school-girl crush on her. Just as quickly, she let me know she was flattered, but spoken for, and my attraction to her dissipated as fast as a drop of rain turns to vapor after it crashes on the sidewalk in mid-July.

I appreciated Sandra's honest response. More importantly, I recognized my sudden ardor hadn't been fueled by any genuine desire to be with her, but by all the dents in my ego as it struggled to regain its original shape.

Like deeply embedded splinters, Paula's accusations stung long after she'd left me. Her fascination with a woman whose blackness she found more bona fide than mine caused me to blur the lines that defined me. It took a long while for me to redraw those lines clearly. It took even longer for me to see who I was as I searched for myself through a lens I needed to clear of regret and uncertainty.

All of that pain seemed to have happened so long ago, certainly more than within the last decade. Occasionally, when some random event, sound, or scene catapulted me toward the memory of Paula's departure, I've tasted a trace of bitterness and then I've reminded myself she wasn't the arbiter of my identity.

Chapter Four

London At Work

THE SECOND I opened the front door and bent down to scoop up the newspaper, the morning's heavy air convinced me someone had dropped a damp wool blanket over my head.

Crap. No wonder that hummingbird didn't stick around. The humidity must have threatened to saturate his little wings.

I stuffed the paper into my work bag, locked the front door behind me, and trudged to the carport. For the past five months, I've had a short commute. Most days I've driven directly to Oak Hill Estates, Kensington Builder's foray into the—fifty-five and better—housing market. I've become adept at selling new homes and creating promotional materials, sometimes simultaneously.

I've shared the sales duties with Susan Rafferty and a third member of the crew, Mark Jacobson, who comes in each weekend to relieve Susan or me. Neither Susan nor I work both Saturday and Sunday. Since yesterday was my day off, I was responsible for opening the model this morning. Susan wouldn't arrive until noon.

If we were in a more active housing market, typically we'd see a few of the weekend shoppers return on Monday to take a second look. We'd watch them carry a notebook in one hand and a tape measure in the other and walk through the model planning where they'd put the sofa and the flat screen TV.

Lately though, the stop and start economy has forced the shoppers to return home where they've splashed the cold water of reality on their faces. They've taken a second look at their current abodes and reappraised their plans to move. The active adults Roger hoped to attract to his new houses no doubt have decided to stay where they are. They've concluded the best way to remain active after age fifty-five is to continue mowing the grass, shoveling the snow, and climbing the stairs to their second floor master bedrooms.

With their 401K's still in recovery after the injuries they sustained a few years ago, these folks have figured they'll be okay living in a house without the Americans With Disabilities Act's mandates for extra wide doorways and strategically positioned light switches.

The Oak Hill Estate houses were not selling at record speed and Roger had become a role model for testy behavior.

"If I read—Don't buy new. Age in place—one more time, I'm going to spit," Roger said during a recent staff meeting.

I started the car and thanked the gods for air conditioning as I drove the short route from my neighborhood to the development. The summer's heat combined with the season's sparse rainfall had transformed the thick green sod at the entrance to the new community into rectangular mats of straw. The landscape contractor had failed to stay on top of this project. The patches of lawn that had been verdant now looked more like ill-fitting pieces of dry yellow fabric. I knew this poor welcome to Oak Hill could be corrected with one e-mail to Sandra.

All Kensington employees had to park their cars in a gravel-filled area riddled with ruts. The smoothly paved surface adjacent to the models was reserved for prospective home buyers. My tedious trek to the models seemed even more so today because of the heat. An air force of gnats strafed my head and face as I made my way over the jagged stones.

It was July and the sticky humidity we usually suffer through had crept in to replace the dry heat we'd had for the past few weeks. Although there was nothing extraordinary about today's weather, the story-starved news media had reported the predicted temperature with the same incredulity they would have mustered had they been relaying a duet sung live by Tupac Shakur and Elvis Presley.

Finally, I reached the model's front door and pressed the four buttons that controlled the lock box's combination. I heard the metallic clicks as the contraption recognized the code and unlocked the door. I stepped into the foyer and began my morning ritual, a routine that had become a favorite part of my work day.

Surrounded by absolute silence, I leaned against the closed front door and breathed deeply. The omnipresent aroma of new construction teased my nose. The fragrance of lumber was more persistent than the odor of the model home's fresh paint, of its recently applied floor mastic, or its newly laid carpet in the great room. Wood was the most basic of all the materials used in the newly built structure and I loved how it smelled. I couldn't explain why its pungent sweetness comforted me. Framing lumber played no part in any of my childhood memories. And although I preferred to have an explanation for most things in my life, it was okay that I didn't understand why something simple like the odor of recently hammered wood could deliver to me such an all-encompassing feeling of calm.

I entered the kitchen and walked toward the open door at the end of the run of counter space. There, I stepped down into a room that would eventually become a garage when we no longer needed a sales office. A desk, over-loaded with clerical supplies, sat in one corner. Across the room from the desk, spanning the length of one wall, was a massive rectangular table topped by Oak Hill Estates' thirty-five acre plot plan. Here and there, color coded push pins stood at attention and interrupted the plan's smooth surface. A blue pin signaled a lot was under an agreement of sale. A red one meant the lot had already gone to settlement, and a green pin showed us a buyer had placed a deposit on a lot and reserved it for seven days while he or she decided whether or not to go ahead with the purchase.

I pushed aside a box of business forms and leaned over my desk to look at the telephone console. The pulsing light on its answering machine assured me there were messages. They would have to remain unattended until I made a pot of coffee and took my morning tour of the house.

I grabbed my clipboard and a pen and set out to do my daily inspection. It was imperative that Susan or I take a careful look at every room before customers arrived. We never knew what we might find. Sometimes we'd spot a minor imperfection we'd correct on our own, like a bedspread in disarray, furniture out of place, or pieces of artificial fruit scattered all over the kitchen floor instead of strategically arranged in the basket atop the table.

The powder-room door was closed.

"That's strange," I muttered.

I opened it and gasped for air as a putrid odor filled my nostrils.

"What the hell?"

Not daring to take another breath, I squinted at the sight of the toilet lid, ripped off the commode and propped against the wall, next to the set of bolts that were meant to attach it to the rim of the fixture.

I approached what remained of the toilet. Without its cover, the bowl gaped open like the mouth of a dental patient in the midst of a root canal. I peered into the porcelain cavity and shook my head in disbelief.

"Shit!"

Exactly.

A huge blob of human excrement stared back at me.

"I can't believe this."

I knew the plumbing and sewer systems hadn't been connected yet, so there was no way to flush the putrefying mound out of existence. I liked to think I could solve problems independently, but this was one time I had to relent and call for help.

I pulled my cell phone from my pocket and punched memorized numbers. "John, it's London Phillips at Oak Hill. I need you to send someone to do a cleanup and repair."

"What kind of repair, Ms. Phillips?"

"A toilet."

"I hate to ask this, but what kind of clean-up?"

"The worst kind, John. I'm sorry to start your day with such a crappy task, but we have to get this done quickly, before we have visitors."

"No problem, Ms. Phillips," John said. "Now let's see. Which one of my guys has been a pain in the ass recently?" John chuckled. "I'll get somebody over there ASAP."

"Thanks. I appreciate it."

I pocketed my phone and backed out of the bathroom.

"Damn." I'd slogged through muddy home sites and slalomed with aplomb and grace through all sorts of construction trash. But I drew the line at literally cleaning up someone's crap.

I continued this morning's tour in the dining room where I adjusted the light from the chandelier. If it was too bright, the sharp glare bounced off the table's hard finish. Too muted, its dullness lent the room a lackluster atmosphere sure to kill the liveliest dinnertime conversation and blunt the heartiest appetite. Somewhere in the middle of the light spectrum was a hue that suggested the room was as perfect for an intimate dinner for two as it was for a festive gathering of twelve.

On my way to the staircase, I stopped at the coat closet, opened the door, and saw the same paint cans I'd seen for weeks stacked in the middle of the floor. Annoyed, I jotted—paint/closet/O'Neal—on the clipboard's pad of paper. We wanted clients to look into a totally empty white closet and imagine their coats and jackets nestled in with space to spare. To encourage this illusion of extra space, the carpenter installed only half the ventilated shelves each closet could accommodate and the stager hung only a few pastel colored garments in the bedroom closets. I guess we were counting on selling to buyers who owned monochromatic wardrobes.

With my circuit of the house almost complete, I returned to the first floor and approached the master bedroom. I strode through the room's double doors and noticed a wide swath of sunshine wash over the large space and make its gray walls whisper violet. I stood just inside the entrance and took in every detail, the heavy oak furniture, the lush duvet cover, the magazines fanned artistically on top of one of the night tables, the leather framed photos atop the chest of drawers, and the sparkling glass doors closed in front of the fireplace. This was a scene right out of a home design magazine. Who in their fifty-five years old or better mind could resist buying this house?

Satisfied everything was in order, I returned to the office area. Now I was ready to listen to the phone messages.

Susan's was the first voice I heard. "Good morning, London. A prospective buyer, Rand Carson, is supposed to come back at nine o'clock Monday morning. She arrived shortly before closing yesterday. I would have stayed late, but I promised my son I'd be home in time for his special birthday dinner. Anyway, this Ms. Carson seemed real eager to buy. She's interested in the Cambridge, and she said something about a cash deal. Just wanted to give you a heads up. See you around noon."

A cash deal? This was a promising way to start the day, especially since it followed two consecutive weeks without so much as a single deposit on a home site. Earning a salary partially based on sales commissions worked best when I actually sold a few houses. I'd be on the lookout for Rand Carson.

"Good morning. Anybody here?"

A man's voice startled me. I left my desk in the garage-office and walked into the kitchen. There, standing near the refrigerator, was a barrel-chested guy with wisps of gray hair combed over his mostly bald pate.

"Good morning. Welcome to Oak Hill Estates. I'm a sales associate, London Phillips."

"We saw your ad in yesterday's paper, so we thought we'd drive out here and take a look," the man said.

Before I could ask who "we" was, he continued.

"My wife's outside, still looking at the flowers and shrubs. That kind of thing is important to her."

I approached the kitchen's island, retrieved one of the development's information portfolios, and opened it to the first page.

"We have four different models here, the Devon, the Shropshire, the Lancaster, and the Cambridge. We're standing in the Devon." I pointed to the architect's rendering of the house's floor plan.

"Here's the list of standard features."

The man turned around slowly and took in the panorama of the room. He waved his hand through the air, as if it were a magic wand.

"I bet you got a lot of extras and upgrades in here, right?"

I smiled. "A few."

"Hello?"

A woman's birdlike voice chirped from the front of the house.

"We're out here, hon." The man took a couple of steps toward the voice.

"Oh, what a pretty kitchen." The chirper entered the room. "I like this, George."

"Yeah, I figured you would."

"Good morning. I was just telling your husband about our four models."

"We're in the kitchen of the Devon," the husband said.

"And it's lovely."

"Would you mind filling out our visitors' form?" I asked.

"Not at all, dear."

The petite warbler picked up one of the Kensington Builders pens and began to write.

"Is there a golf course in this community?" The husband asked.

"No, but there are two public courses and a private country club within a short drive from here."

He nodded his approval.

"How about a community center? I think I remember reading about one in your ad." The wife handed me the completed form.

"Yes, the community center is almost finished. There's still work to be done on the theater and the indoor swimming pool, but we opened the outdoor pool three weeks ago, just in time for the summer."

I visualized the view I'd seen an hour ago as I drove by the flower beds that were now filled with fading red, white and purple petunias. I imagined the ground crew would need to replace the plants as well as replant the sod.

I cast a quick look at the names listed on the document the woman had given me.

"Please take your time looking at all four models, Mr. and Mrs. Hanson. If you have any questions, I'll be more than happy to answer them."

Mr. Hanson gazed at his wife. "Okay, hon. Let's get started."

They began their earnest examination of the kitchen and morning room and I made a beeline to answer the telephone.

"Good morning. Oak Hill, London Phillips speaking."

"Happy Monday, London. It's Sandra. How are you today?"

"I'm well, Sandra."

"Good. Listen, Roger wants to meet with each project's lead salesperson today at one o'clock."

"I'll be there."

"See you then. And if you have any new promo ideas, bring them with you."

The change in today's agenda didn't surprise me. While sales still lagged, the number of new home starts in May had exceeded April's figures, and June's stats were due by the end of the week. No doubt Roger had dreamed up some new incentive packages and he wanted us to market them right away.

I checked yesterday's visitors' log and saw Susan had been busy. There were sixteen names listed and hallelujah, two new green push pins protruded from the plot map. One of the pins was associated with Rand Carson, I assumed. Susan's phone message lead me to believe Ms. Carson would cross our threshold promptly at nine o'clock, but it was now ten and the hot-to-trot home buyer hadn't arrived.

I shrugged a minor ache from my shoulders and started to examine the paperwork Susan and Mark had filled out for the other prospective buyer. It was premature for me to do so, but I faxed that person's financial disclosure sheet to our business office. I had difficulty being idle at work and wasting precious time.

Eager to accomplish more, I referred to the visitors' list and contacted the first person who'd included his phone number. I invited him to come take a second look, and asked if we could send him notices about future events at Oak Hill. I wished him a good day, hung up, and jotted my coded version of his response next to his name. During the next sixty minutes I either spoke to or left messages for yesterday's other visitors who'd left us their contact information.

"Hi, there. You look busy." Susan walked into our office as I reached the last phone number on the list.

Startled, I looked up.

"Good morning, or rather, good afternoon. You're early."

"Nope, I'm late. It's five past noon." Susan pointed to the clock above the development's map. "Are you working on Ms. Carson's forms?"

"I'm afraid not."

"Didn't she come in and leave a deposit?"

"No, she never showed up."

"Damn it. I thought for sure she'd be back here this morning."

"Did she hand over a check yesterday?"

"No, but she wanted to. I could tell."

"And you could tell how?" I felt the birth of a frown.

"She had this decisive way about her, like a woman on a mission. The only thing that stood in her way was not having enough time to select a lot."

"I trust we'll have enough time to accomplish that today."

Susan and I turned and looked in the direction of the third voice in the room. We saw a deeply suntanned woman near the office's entrance. She smiled at Susan and strode toward her, her hand outstretched.

"I expected to be here earlier, but better late than never, right?" she said.

"Oh hello, Ms. Carson. My sales partner and I were just talking about you." Susan gestured in my direction.

"Oh?"

The woman bent down slightly to shake my hand as I arose from my chair.

"I'm London Phillips."

"Nice to meet you."

"Susan told me you visited us yesterday."

The woman nodded and smiled.

I noticed little lines at play on either side of her mouth, like a set of commas.

"I did, and I was very impressed with your models, especially the Cambridge."

Somehow I wasn't surprised to hear this woman was attracted to our most expensive home. Ms. Carson's formal demeanor, combined with her understated tailored slacks and jacket, suggested she was used to purchasing the best she could afford. I'd learned to quickly evaluate a customer's spending potential, just as I'd learned to describe seemingly insignificant details about my fictional characters, details that revealed characters' personality and behavior traits.

"Wonderful. Why don't we look at the available lots and select a couple that interest you?" Susan gestured for them to move closer to the table with the development's plot plan. "Then we'll go out and actually take a close look."

Mindful that Ms. Carson was Susan's customer, not mine, and I needed to leave soon to get to the one o'clock meeting, I busied myself with a different chore.

"Can the Cambridge be built on any of the unclaimed lots?" Ms.

Carson asked.

"Certainly," Susan answered. "We have some standard lots that haven't been sold as well as several premium lots."

I watched Ms. Carson study the multi-colored map.

"I don't necessarily need a premium space, although I would prefer to have one with privacy. Maybe that one?"

I saw her rest one of her slender tanned fingers on a large irregularly configured lot. Although I was seated across the room from her, I had a clear view of the section she'd chosen.

"Excuse me, but you'll notice that particular lot is close to the community's swale," I said.

"London's right, Ms. Carson. Once in a while the swale holds standing water. You won't want to deal with mosquitoes in the summertime."

"Oh, you're right. Thank you." Ms. Carson nodded my way.

I watched her massage her left shoulder and look down at the map once again.

"How about this one?"

I followed the trajectory of her finger and noticed she'd selected a space that backed to a wooded area instead of a row of backyards. I flashed a smile of approval, but said nothing.

Susan waved her hand over the virtual trees in the back of the property. "This area will give you more privacy."

My cell phone beeped an incoming text message. I glanced at its small screen and read a reminder about the meeting with Roger. If I left now, I could get to the corporate office with five minutes to spare. As I gathered my belongings I heard Ms. Carson utter her decision about buying a house.

"I'd like to put down a deposit," she said. "Shall we fill out the paperwork?"

That was the quickest no-selling sale I'd ever witnessed.

"Oh, oh of course," Susan stammered.

The two women walked across the room and sat in the chairs near Susan's desk.

Ms. Carson reached for her shoulder, kneaded it, and looked off into space.

"Susan, I've been summoned to a meeting with Sandra and Roger. If it doesn't consume the rest of the afternoon, I'll come back here when it's over."

"Okay, London. See you later."

I turned to our newest home buyer and spoke as warmly as I could.

"Thanks again for coming back today, Ms. Carson."

"You're quite welcome, Ms. Phillips." She smiled and seemed to appraise my sincerity.

I returned her steady gaze.

"We'll do everything we can to make sure you have a good

experience with Kensington Builders."

"Thanks," she said. "I'm fairly certain we'll see each other again."

When I left the office and navigated my way over the uneven terrain between the row of model homes and my car, I thought about Rand Carson and wondered why she was sure we'd see each other again. She was Susan's client, so she'd confer primarily with her during her home purchase process. I'd review her paperwork, of course. But we wouldn't need to meet with each other. And because I was on the cusp of a vacation, it wasn't likely I'd run into her any time soon.

I got into my car and cursed the leather seats for singeing my rear end. With the windows fully open while the air conditioner operated at full blast, I pulled away slowly from the parking spot. I drove past the row of model homes and saw Ms. Carson and Susan in front of the Cambridge. Ms. Carson was pointing at the building's roof. I wondered if our new customer had seen something amiss or if she was merely asking Susan a question. Whatever the case, Susan would take care of the answer. And if not, she'd run it by me when I returned from the meeting.

Chapter Five

Lenah Miller

"DAMN, I CAN'T believe this."

Lenah Miller felt the droplets of sweat spread across her forehead as she walked from the back door of her house to the driveway. A morning this hot had to be mythical, she thought. Nothing short of one bell-ringer of a storm with winds so fierce they'd blow down traffic lights, uproot garden sheds, and rip children from the shelter of their parents' embrace could end this oppressive humidity.

Lenah slid into her car and looked to her left and right, as if she were searching for something big and ominous at either end of the street. She didn't notice anything out of the ordinary, so she turned the key in the ignition and gave life to the engine and simultaneously the car's radio. Lenah scowled at the latter and turned the volume control counterclockwise to muffle the announcer's perky voice just as he promised his listeners the day's temperature was going to break a record before noon arrived. She was glad today's shift was a vacation fill-in that required her to work only four hours. She'd be back at home before the thermometer threatened to burst.

"You're not going to like today's weather, Candace. Not one moment of it."

Lenah frequently uttered her thoughts aloud, even though Candace hadn't been present to hear Lenah's utterances for some time now.

"Now what?" Lenah concentrated more on the sound coming from under the vehicle's hood than the music flowing from the car radio's speaker. "Is it the heat and humidity that's causing you to sound heavier than usual."

The motor lumbered as it struggled to chug from one red light to the next.

Lenah swore all six cylinders heaved a grateful — thank you — when she steered the car into a slot in the employees' parking lot.

She felt an arc of moisture at the top of her forehead as she covered the distance between her parking spot and the large tan and brick building and swabbed it away seconds before she reached the entrance.

Twin doors whooshed open to reveal a small rectangular lobby. Beyond the lobby was the registration area for Madison Hospital's Emergency Department.

Lenah walked toward the end of the registration counter. She went behind it and focused on the employees' time clock that was mounted on the wall. She swiped her identification card through its slit of a mouth and then, without really looking at her, she greeted a co-worker.

"Good morning, Sally. Thank God for the twentieth century's two best inventions, penicillin and air conditioning."

"You got that right," Sally said.

Lenah turned to face Sally. Then she inclined her head in the direction of the Emergency Department's waiting room.

"How's it looking this morning? Do we have a full house?"

"Far from it," Sally said. "It's a run of the mill Monday."

Contrary to many working people who wished they could avoid Monday mornings and the slightly off-center feeling that day brought with it, Lenah looked forward to the beginning of the week. Monday's slow pace gave her a chance to straighten the disorder that was usually left in the wake of the weekend's emergencies.

When she'd first begun working at the hospital, Lenah's shifts included some nights and every other weekend. In no time at all she'd experienced the downside of working in a hospital's Emergency Department on Friday and Saturday evenings. It puzzled her why so many people got drunk and then convinced themselves they could drive as skillfully as they did when they were sober. Then, there were the other folks who chose to accessorize their date night ensembles with a weapon they felt compelled to use to act out the anger they felt toward so and so about first one thing and then another. Lenah hadn't been naïve about the seamier side of urban life, but she hadn't bargained on seeing that much of it during her first year working at the hospital. She'd labeled her newbie twelve months her "year of blood and guts."

That freshman year Lenah spent in the Emergency Department supplied Candace with plenty of tickets for the worry train.

"What if somebody swaggers into the registration area and just starts shooting?" Candace asked more than once.

"What about HIV? Do you touch people when they're bleeding? Do you wear gloves or what? Do you wash your hands frequently? You're going to take a shower before you get into bed, aren't you?"

For the sake of survival, and because she needed the job, Lenah learned to deal with each crisis as it arrived in front of her at the registration counter. But Candace's litany of questions and worries had been persistent and Lenah struggled to respond to her lover's expressions of fear and dread. The unrelenting weight of Candace's daily harangues hung from Lenah's shoulders like sacks filled with cement.

After a while, Lenah began to question why Candace was so worried. Were Candace's warnings and admonitions more about her fear of being left behind in the event Lenah became ill, than feelings of genuine concern for Lenah's well-being? She suspected Candace's alarm regarding some random shooter in the emergency room, or an HIV-AIDS patient purposely spreading contagion to all with whom s/he came in contact, were for her own safety, not for Lenah's.

For a year and a half Lenah stood by patiently while Candace spouted her near hysteria.

She was willing to give Candace the time she needed to believe she could handle her job just fine. As Candace's warnings about the dangers that lurked within every encounter with a sick person became less frequent, Lenah's hopes about the health of their relationship soared. But, when Candace replaced the warnings with lectures about Lenah's failure to seek a promotion at the hospital, Lenah threw down her hopes like so much dirty laundry. The day she finally convinced Candace she was satisfied with her job and wasn't planning to leave her Emergency Department post for a safer, more prestigious one, Lenah felt Candace begin to pull away from her. The tension and distance between them grew from a muffled yawn to a jaw-gapingly huge one. Determined to keep working in the ED, Lenah dug in her heels. She never noticed that Candace had begun to sublimate her frustration with achieving her own ambitious goals.

"You might want to stay harnessed to a dead end job, but I'm moving forward," Candace said one Sunday afternoon. "Tomorrow I'm giving notice at work that next month I'm leaving. I've accepted a new position with Continental Assurance Company."

"In Philadelphia?" Lenah asked.

"Exactly. And I want to live near my job, so I'm buying a condo unit in Olde City. My settlement is scheduled two weeks from today. I'll move out of here the next day."

Lenah stared at her lover, in search of a glimpse of a Candace-less existence. She inhaled once, deeply.

"Okay. If I'm at work the day you move, just leave your key on the kitchen table."

Disturbed far less by Candace's defection than she was by most of the accident victims who arrived regularly in the ED, Lenah knew she was much wiser and far luckier than she'd been when she'd first started dating Candace.

Lenah turned her gaze from Sally and looked at the short pile of computer generated paperwork resting on the table to her right.

"Who's here?"

"We've got a man being treated for burns," Sally said. "He was trying to repair his air conditioner and forgot he wasn't an electrician. And we have another man who came in bent over in two with severe back pains."

"Is anybody waiting for them?"

Sally nodded.

"The woman out there in the waiting room is with the do-it-yourself air conditioner repairman, and the young man sitting on the opposite side of the room is with the backache guy."

"Got it."

Without looking down at her hand, Lenah unfastened her wristwatch, laid the timepiece on the counter, and rubbed the dampened skin where the watch's large round face had been.

"I know. It's so hot outside, you started sweating under your watch. Right?"

Sally asked.

Lenah blew a puff of air through her lips.

"This heat is amazing, Sally. And it's not yet noon." She retrieved the timepiece and dried its back against her sleeve before she refastened it on her wrist. Candace had given her the watch for Christmas the first year she worked at the hospital. As Lenah brushed away an imaginary atom of lint from its face she thought she heard Candace's voice.

"I picked this one because the numbers are big and you won't have to squint when you're logging the patients' arrival time," she'd said as she handed Lenah the rectangular box wrapped in shiny gold paper.

Now Lenah glanced at the watch long enough to notice the tiny scratch etched near the Roman numeral eleven. Usually she simply noted what time it was, but once in a while, her eyes zeroed in on the crystal's flaw. She knew sooner or later she'd need to have the glass replaced, and she'd already decided if the repair was too expensive, she was more than willing to trash the watch and get a new one.

"With the triple digit temperatures they're forecasting today, we're gonna see a lot of heat strokes and dehydrated people, don't you think?" Sally asked.

Lenah grinned. "You wanna bet how many show up between now and three o'clock?"

"You're on. I'll bet you a large cup of coffee we see a half dozen."

"I say we'll see more, ten or twelve; some of the laborers from the crew working on the new office building four blocks away," Lenah said. "How about a cinnamon bun to go with that coffee?"

"You got it."

Lenah smiled in anticipation of tasting the pastry's gooey topping and feeling the coffee's liquid heat kiss her lips.

Sally pointed at the wire bin atop the counter.

"Looks like they were busy this weekend. Almost all the intake forms are gone."

Lenah frowned and then ambled to the supply cabinet, opened a drawer, and withdrew a stack of papers. She set the stapled pages in the bin and tapped them, as if they were a deck of newly shuffled pinochle cards.

"The weekend staff never leaves this place as neat and orderly as we do every Friday afternoon."

"You got that right," Sally said. "How about you? Did you have a neat and orderly weekend?"

Lenah thought about the past Saturday evening and the two boring hours she'd spent keeping a barstool warm while she sipped a couple of beers. She hadn't even enjoyed the music from the bar's sound system.

Who likes that crap, she'd asked herself. You can't understand a word of the never-ending stream of nonsensical rap songs. And the twangy-voiced country and western singers all sound like they're singing out of their noses.

She grimaced as she recalled the different women who'd arrived and occupied the barstools on either side of her. Lenah had felt grateful that other than nodding at their awareness of her presence, they'd reserved their conversation for their partners. She realized there hadn't been a single person at that bar who'd interested her, not the dour looking woman who threw down vodka shots as quickly as some people played the one-arm bandits at the casinos, not the life-of-the-party type who'd tried to include Lenah in her comedy routine. Not even the henna- haired young thing whose lame attempts to stare provocatively at Lenah had fallen flat.

"Sally, this past weekend I stayed as busy as a corpse."

"Oh, that bad, huh?"

"I would have had a better time doing a double shift here."

Both Lenah and Sally felt a sudden rush of air as the Emergency Department's doors swept open. They looked toward the entrance and saw two women framed by the doorway. They watched the shorter woman hesitate and then glance over her left shoulder at the other woman.

"This way, hon," she said. The shorter one reached back and touched her companion's arm, urging her forward.

Lenah took in all the details she needed before she picked up the phone and tapped four of its keys. Then she looked past the shorter woman who remained in the lead, and concentrated on the taller one's appearance.

"You're going to be okay, hon," the shorter one said.

The other woman stood in silence, yards away.

Lenah noticed the woman's feet were stuffed into unlaced sneakers and her watchband cut into the flesh above and below it. The woman's distended eyelids made a mockery of what had been normal facial features. She seemed to be too distressed to be able to verbalize her predicament.

"My cousin's been stung by bees and I think she's allergic to them."

Lenah pointed to a door not far from the counter while she spoke into the phone.

"Triage One... Good morning... I'm sending a patient to you...possible bee venom allergy."

The women walked slowly in the direction Lenah pointed to. When they reached the door labeled T-1, the shorter one turned to the stricken one.

"It's just a little further now. You'll be feeling better soon."

Lenah supervised their stop-and-go pace and watched them disappear as the door closed behind them.

"Good call," Sally said. "That's got to be the twelfth bee allergy we've seen this summer, and it's only July."

Lenah attached three papers to a clipboard.

"I'll give them time to get her vitals and get the epi line going before I bug them for her details."

Lenah glanced at her watch and decided to wait for ten minutes and then go into the triage room to record the bee sting victim's information. She was sure the shorter of the two women would be able to supply all of the other woman's identity and insurance details she'd need for the hospital's forms, because she was certain the two women were not cousins. Lenah didn't need anyone to verify that they were related by love, not by blood. The tenderness she'd heard in the shorter woman's voice revealed their truth. Over the years, Lenah had crafted a variety of methods to let patients know their reality was safe with her. Her stockpile of covert communications had grown broad and large. Sometimes she'd emphasize the word *everyone*, when she assured patients and their loved one that they'd receive good care. Other times she'd say pointedly, "I'll be sure to keep you informed about so-and-so's progress." Without fail, Lenah would receive a familiar smile of recognition from the patient and the patient's companion.

"Family always knows family," she'd explained to Candace.

As Lenah accumulated more experiences with all sorts of people, she'd discovered sometimes she needed to speak less subtlety to gay, white patients and their partners, especially when the white patients treated her as a functionary, nothing more. They spoke to her dismissively, as if she were merely their first step in the process of receiving the medical help they deserved and would no doubt receive. Since Lenah wasn't wearing scrubs embroidered with the name Dr. So-and-So, what could she possibly know? How could she possibly help, other than register them and summon someone else who really counted?

Lenah often wondered if she'd be more visible to those who quickly wrote her off if she wore a rainbow tattoo stamped across her forehead. More than once she'd needed to trot out her—we all deserve to be treated equally—speech before she could coax a knowing smile from a white gay or lesbian couple. She was always tempted to reward their—aha—moment by yelling, "Bingo! I've been right in front of you all along!"

Lenah checked to make sure the computer and small printer were securely attached to the portable cart and then she made her way to the first of the ED's triage rooms. Within ten minutes she'd entered the patient's information, assured the shorter woman she could stay with her partner in the treatment room while they waited to speak to the doctor, and returned with the completed registration forms. She retrieved a new file folder, peeled off a small rectangle of paper with the patient's name printed on it, and smoothed the label across the top of the folder.

"No heat victims yet, my dear," Sally teased. "You might not win your cup of coffee."

"We've got time. And as the afternoon passes, it's only going to get hotter out there."

On cue, the swoosh of the doors announced a new arrival, an elderly woman who'd been gently deposited in one of the wheel chairs that was perpetually stationed near the Emergency Department's entrance. A middle-aged man dressed in a gray business suit steered the chair toward the registration counter.

"Can I help you?" Lenah asked.

"Yes, please. My mother phoned me this morning. She was complaining of dizziness, and she wasn't making much sense. She kept saying she needed to pack her suitcase. I couldn't leave work right away, but I went to get her as soon as I could."

Lenah inched the sign-in sheet forward.

"Could you write your mother's name here, please? And the time?"

"Oh, sure."

While the man obeyed Lenah's request, Lenah watched the elderly woman's jaw tremble.

The involuntary movements emphasized the looseness of the skin covering the woman's high cheekbones. Wrinkles, some faint and on the surface, others carved deeply, sprawled out over every bit of her small olive-tone face.

Lenah tried to imagine how the woman looked thirty years earlier. Eyes that were now colorless and opaque had most likely been gray or perhaps hazel. Here and there, rolling crimps of wispy white hair suggested that loose waves had no doubt covered her head and fallen to her shoulders once upon a time. The elderly woman's imperious bearing, narrow beaklike nose, and thin lips had probably imbued her with power and social privileges she'd learned to take for granted.

Lenah picked up the phone and dialed the number for Triage Two.

"We have a patient who needs to be seen. Thank you."

She engaged the son's attention.

"You can push your mother toward Triage Two, over there to the right."

He nodded.

"Thanks."

The woman snapped to attention. Her watery eyes locked onto Lenah's. Before her son could put his muscle to the wheelchair, she spoke with even steady tones that proved to be a dramatic contrast to the quiver of her jaw.

"Why are you smiling at my son that way? Are you flirting with him, girl? You come from the ghetto, don't you?"

"Mother, that's rude."

The man looked at Lenah.

"I'm sorry. See what I mean? She's not making any sense."

"Jesus," Sally gasped.

"Don't worry about it," Lenah said. "The doctor will see her soon."

Lenah watched the man steer his mother toward the appropriate door. She turned to Sally and winked.

"I'll bet that old woman is speaking her kind of sense, the kind she's spoken her whole life."

"What do you mean?"

Lenah's thoughts flashed to Candace's mother and the framed photograph of her that Candace used to keep on her desk. The portrait exhibited the same overbearing expression this elderly woman wore. More than a few times, Lenah had seen a similar look cross Candace's face, a look Candace had erased quickly, but not before Lenah heard her own mother's voice and the warning she'd intoned often.

"Don't ever trust those light-brights. They'll turn on you in a second 'cause you're browner than a paper bag."

Lenah gazed at Sally.

"All I mean is when you get old, you become an exaggeration of who you've always been."

"Yeah, I've heard that," Sally said. "So who's that old woman always been?"

"A person who wouldn't have wanted her son to be interested in someone like me, that's for damn sure."

"Why do you say that, Lenah?"

Lenah sighed. "Maybe one day I'll explain it to you."

"I won't hold my breath," Sally said.

"Well, it looks like we've checked in today's first dehydrated patient," Lenah said.

"Yup. And maybe she's got a urinary tract infection also. That would explain why she's talking nonsense."

Sally pointed to the entrance.

"While you were busy with the old lady I gave the fix-it-yourself air conditioner mechanic his discharge papers. He just left."

"That's one down and two to go," Lenah said.

"Yeah, Mr. Back Pain's still in there. The kid who came in with him has been sitting in the waiting room for a couple of hours now."

Lenah picked up the sign-in sheet and read the first name. Based on Sally's description of Harry Lawnton's pain and posture, Lenah suspected she knew what had caused him to lean over the counter when he arrived.

"Sally, are you up for a second bet?"

"Uh-oh, another bet. That must mean I'm on the verge of winning the first one."

"Not necessarily. There's still plenty of time for more dehydrates to arrive."

"So what's the wager?"

"I bet I know Mr. Back Pain's diagnosis. How about it? Double or nothing."

Sally grimaced. "I always fall for your schemes, Lenah. Good thing we place bets for coffee and buns and not for a lot of money."

"What do you say? What's his diagnosis?" Lenah asked.

"I say it's his gall bladder. They're probably prepping him for the O.R. as we speak."

"Nope. It's a kidney stone," Lenah said in a matter-of-fact voice. "They've had him in there for two or three hours, pumping fluids intravenously, trying to force the stone out. Right about now, they're writing him a script for pain meds, giving him a list of urologists' names, and handing him a strainer to pee in."

Sally tweaked Lenah's shoulder as she passed behind her.

"I'll go find out, Nurse Know-It-All."

"It's Dr. Know-It-All, if you don't mind."

Moments later, Sally sauntered back to their cramped quarters. She stood beside Lenah, her hands on her hips and bottom lip jutting to the right.

"You're twisting your mouth the way you always do when I've won."

"You're right again, damn it. Mr. Lawnton is signing his discharge instruction papers." She slapped two dollars onto the desk. "Here. Go buy your own damn cups of coffee, Smart-Ass."

"Excellent. Fastest two bucks I've ever earned."

Lenah grinned, scooped up the bills, and pushed them into her slacks pocket. She shifted her attention to the patient information forms stacked to the right of the computer. The top sheet fluttered ever so slightly as the air currents shifted. Instinctively, she glanced through the glass doors and saw leaden clouds where the sun had been an hour ago. The sky's gray backdrop outlined the silhouette of a woman headed straight toward Lenah and the registration area. She walked quickly and as she got closer, Lenah could see the woman's eyes were focused straight ahead, like twin laser beams. When she was three feet away from the registration counter, the woman spoke.

"Good afternoon. I believe I'm having a heart attack," she said. "My left arm's ached since early this morning, and an hour ago I began sweating for no reason."

She thrust her right hand toward Lenah.

"Here's my insurance card and my driver's license."

Lenah took the cards and checked to see if the names typed on both of the ID's were identical. She tapped four keys on the telephone, the numbers that alerted the Triage team to prepare to treat a patient having a stroke or a cardiac event.

"Hold on to this." Lenah returned the woman's insurance card. "We'll get your information later. Do you have any allergies?"

"Not that I'm aware of."

Lenah read the data on the driver's license, turned to face the computer, and then typed the patient's name and address. A second later, the printer sprung to life and belched a paper onto the table beneath it. Lenah reached for the paper and peeled off an inch wide strip.

"Let me put this on your wrist."

As the woman lifted her right arm, Lenah snapped the light blue ID bracelet in place.

The doors to the ED's interior opened and a man dressed in loose-fitting green pants and a green shirt approached. He pushed a wheelchair.

"Hi," he said gently. "Would you like me to help you get into the chair?"

"I'd rather walk," the woman answered.

"If you don't mind, I'd like you to ride in the chair."

"Oh, all right."

"My name is Herb and I'm a Physician's Assistant. Come on with me, and we'll see what's going on with you today."

Lenah watched the woman and the P.A. disappear behind the doors. She turned toward Sally.

"She's not having a heart attack."

"You can't tell just by looking at her. Women have different symptoms from men, you know." Sally hooked her thumb toward the closed doors. "That's why they're the doctors and we're not. They'll find out if there's anything wrong with her ticker."

"I'm sure she's not having a heart attack. She's too composed to be having one."

Sally rolled her eyes at Lenah. "I suppose you wanna place another bet?"

"Nope. Two bets a day is enough for me, and besides, I'll probably be out of here before I can find out if I've won. Today's my short shift, remember?"

"Hmm. Sounds to me like you're not as certain about this one as you were about the kidney stone."

Lenah grinned. "Oh, I'm certain all right. I just feel sorry for you and I don't want you to have to buy me coffee for the next week."

"Overconfidence is not attractive, my dear."

Lenah laughed at Sally's feeble attempt to upbraid her. She tilted her head toward the triage area.

"I have enough time to do the paperwork for our calm-as-a-cucumber heart attack."

She put the woman's driver's license next to the computer and looked at the name, address, and photo.

Why did she come to the ED alone if she thought her heart was attacking her? she wondered.

The printer hummed and one by one, issued a series of papers onto its tray. Lenah scooped up the forms and slid them under the jagged metal clip affixed to an orange plastic clipboard. She picked it up and strode the short distance between the registration area and the treatment cubicles.

As she passed the first of several treatment rooms, Lenah heard an authoritative voice from the other side of a door that had been left ajar.

"You're not having a heart attack, Ms. Carson. Your enzymes aren't elevated and your EKG results are well within the normal range."

"What else is new?" Lenah mumbled to herself and kept moving.

"Hey, how's it going out there?"

One of the nurses asked from her roost behind a desk.

"Typical Monday. It's pretty calm so far."

"Well, it won't be for too much longer. I heard we're in for a bad storm."

Lenah recalled seeing heavy rain-sodden clouds the last time she'd looked beyond the Emergency Department's doors.

"Maybe a good heavy rain will break up this heat," she said.

"That would be a good thing," Herb, the P.A. who'd escorted the possible heart attack patient to the treatment area, chimed in.

"Here's the paperwork for Ms. Carson."

Lenah handed the sheaf of papers to the nurse.

"Thanks."

Lenah turned and retraced the path she'd walked. Seconds before she crossed the threshold to return to the registration area, she stared at the cubicle from which she'd heard a doctor's voice moments ago. Her feet betrayed her professionalism as they slowed their pace and softened what little noise they customarily made.

"I'd like you to make an appointment for an echocardiogram and a stress test so we can rule out any problems."

"What kinds of problems?"

Lenah heard fear wrapped around the woman's question.

"Blockages, irregular heartbeat. We'll take it one step at a time. If we find a problem, we can treat it and you'll be fine."

"How do you treat an irregular heartbeat?"

"We've got a couple of different tricks up our sleeves. But I don't want you to get ahead of yourself. Let's wait until you've had your echo and stress tests before we select a treatment."

Lenah listened for the woman's response. There was none. Then, she chided herself for having spied on a private conversation. Never before had she eavesdropped while a physician spoke with a patient. But, she reasoned, never before had she registered a patient who'd stated so calmly that she was having a heart attack. The woman hadn't clutched her chest, arm, or shoulder. She hadn't even touched them. She wasn't pale nor did she complain of nausea. She'd simply self-diagnosed with no trace of alarm in her voice. All of those elements piqued Lenah's curiosity as she returned to the counter in the ED.

If it weren't so slow today, I'd have more to do than wonder about the woman with the pseudo heart attack, Lenah thought.

Sally looked sideways at Lenah.

"You feeling bored?"

"How'd you know?"

"We've been working together long enough for me to be able to read your body language."

"Well, read my back as I walk toward the elevator. I'm going upstairs to the cafeteria. Do you want anything?"

Sally shook her head.

"Don't be gone too long. What if we get an influx of heat stroke victims?"

Lenah's shoulders moved up and down with amusement as she listened to the sarcasm spill from Sally's voice.

"Don't worry. I'll be back soon."

"I'm counting on that."

Lenah turned and grinned.

"You do know me, don't you?"

Fifteen minutes later, when she returned to the registration area, Lenah saw right away that it wasn't the same space she'd left. There were people everywhere. They congregated in duos and trios, some holding another one erect, a few using a wall to prop themselves on their feet.

"Jesus, what happened?" she asked as she took a head count of the people clumped near the counter.

"It's the heat," Sally said. "Those workers a few blocks from here are falling over like bowling pins, and the rain that's just started hasn't helped one little bit."

"Okay, who's next?" Lenah asked. She took her post behind the counter and hunched her shoulders in concentration as she began gathering information about a middle-aged man who could barely stand.

For the next couple of hours Lenah worked steadily. Instead of being overwhelmed by the procession of incoming patients, she seemed to find satisfaction in staying busy. When the registration area was finally cleared of people, she looked at her watch.

"Hey, it's almost time for me to be out of here."

"Lucky you," Sally said. "Your workday's over and done with."

"I love these vacation coverages, Sally. They make me think I should be a part timer."

"Don't forget you need full time benefits, my dear," Sally said.

Lenah freed her employee identification card from its hinged clip attached to her waistband. She grasped the card between her thumb and forefinger, and swiped it through the opening on the time clock.

"Yup, that's a wrap."

"Okay, Lenah. I'll keep the home fires burning for a bit longer. Then I'm out of here as well."

Suddenly, the printer's buzzing and clicking drew Sally close. She retrieved the first of four sheets of paper before the machine could spit it onto the floor. While she awaited the next three pages, Sally scrutinized the one she'd caught.

"You did it again, Lenah," she said. "The woman in Triage Two? No indication of an infarction. How come you're always so accurate?"

"I know people, Sally. And it's a gift, a real gift."

"Or more like some weird talent."

Lenah grinned.

"Every time you guess right, you look so happy. It seems to give you such joy."

"Remind me to tell you about my joy one of these days," Lenah said.

"I'll look forward to that, just like I look forward to all the little things you've promised to tell me one day. But here's my question. When is that day going to arrive?"

"I'm sure it'll be soon, Sally."

"I hope so. We should go out for lunch or dinner some time. Do you know why?"

"Because we'd have a good time?" Lenah asked.

"Yeah, and because I really like you."

"That's a nice thing for you to say. I like you too, Sally."

Lenah bent forward slightly and peered through the Emergency Department's doors. She tugged on her shirt's collar and persuaded it to shelter her neck as she prepared to confront the rain storm.

"See you tomorrow," she said.

Sally took a turn looking through the glass doors.

"It's really coming down out there. Stay safe."

"Will do." Lenah walked away from the registration desk.

"And check your calendar for a time when we can go out for a meal and you can keep your promises to tell me all about the little things you've mentioned."

Lenah held up one hand and waved. When she reached the entrance to the hospital, she paused next to the gaggle of wheelchairs lined up to the right of the doors. She touched the front of her shirt, near her throat and made sure the top button was fastened before she exited the building. The double doors opened and Lenah half-ran, inclining her head against the assault of the pelting rain. While still yards away from her car, she pushed the spot on its security fob that unlocked the vehicle and disarmed its security system. Then she glided into the driver's seat and gunned the engine.

As if on cue, the car's radio awoke and began to play a song whose tempo matched the rhythmic repetition of the windshield wipers as they swept back and forth across Lenah's field of vision. The sounds were hypnotic and they would have lulled Lenah into a trance had her attention not been galvanized by stop signs shuddering against the wind and overhead traffic lights swinging violently above the intersections along her route home. When she looked up and gazed through her car's moon roof, Lenah saw the asphalt colored sky staring back at her.

From a short distance away, the blare of an emergency vehicle's siren invaded the car. The high pitched alarm screamed louder as it traveled closer. Lenah looked in her rearview mirror but didn't see the reflection of flashing lights. She peered through the hazy windshield. There, coming toward her, was an ambulance. Lenah slowed the car's speed and steered to the side of the road, away from the emergency vehicle's approach. She knew Sally might not see this particular ED visitor, but some of the doctors and nurses she'd just left would meet the person.

Moments later, Lenah parked her car in the narrow driveway between her house and her neighbor's. As she sat in the driver's seat and waited for the rain to abate, she watched the water rush out of the end of the downspout and gush over the gray flagstone that signaled the end of the path from her front door and the beginning of the paved parking area. The minor flood covered branches and leaves that the wind had ripped from their rightful places.

What would Candace say about all this crap covering the walkway? She'd say I'd have to clean up this mess, she thought.

Lenah thrust her key into the lock and opened the front door. The day's mail lay at her feet. She bent down and scooped up a pile of envelopes.

"Not much today," she said aloud.

"One for the junk pile, one for the bill hill. A circular for the junk pile. A second one for the bill hill. And of course, one for Candace."

Lenah picked up the two candidates for the junk pile and tore them in half. Then she propped the bills against the base of the little lamp on the table and picked up the piece of mail addressed to Candace. She passed her fingers across the embossed return address, "Superior Styles."

Candace's favorite magazine, she thought. It's probably time to renew her subscription, and during the thirteen months she's been out of here, she never filled out a change of address form.

When the misaddressed mail first started to arrive, Lenah hadn't minded reposting it. Doing so had been a way for her to maintain contact with Candace, albeit a connection without sight or sound. By now though, redirecting the mail had become an unpleasant task, one that reminded Lenah of past hurts. The stamped rectangles bearing Candace's name angered Lenah.

She smacked the unopened envelope against the palm of her hand. Then she strode to the living room and approached the large weathered wicker basket next to the hearth. Lenah tossed today's piece of mail into the basket, where it would rest with all the other envelopes destined to become kindling for next fall's first blaze.

Lenah frowned as she remembered the times Candace sought to extinguish the pride and satisfaction she felt about her job at the hospital. She'd absorbed Candace's endless verbal blows filled with accusations of laziness and lack of ambition.

"What do you want me to do, become a freakin' doctor?" Lenah once screamed.

"That would be nice," Candace answered, "unrealistic, but nice. You could at least get a Master's Degree. If you'd started that a few years ago, you would have earned it by now."

"And that would make you happy?"

"Happier than I am now, with a girlfriend who registers dead weights without health insurance to the Emergency Department."

Lenah's frustration grew like mushrooms in warm damp soil. She'd felt ensnared in a tug-of-war. Half of her grew stone deaf to Candace's arguments while her other half began to believe Candace was right. Perhaps she did need to light a fire under her goals.

Now, as Lenah stared at the basket's ever growing pile of misdirected envelopes, her frown smoothed itself. She walked toward the other side of the room and sat in an armchair. She gazed at her laptop computer at rest on the table beside her. The machine beckoned and she reached over and picked it up. She pressed the power button, clicked on her documents and moved the cursor to highlight, "My One Sentence Journal." Plunged into thought, Lenah stared at the fireplace and let her fingertips tap dance against her left cheek before she began to type.

"Now it's my turn to be the fire starter, but not the kind Candace has imagined."

Chapter Six

Roberta Baker: That Was Then

ROBERTA PEEKED OUT from where she was waiting, between the privet hedge and the porch's wooden foundation boards. She heard the familiar creak of rebellious old springs as someone pushed open the ancient screen door.

"Come on outta there before you get all scratched up by them bushes."

Roberta obeyed. She stepped away from the shrubs and onto the narrow dirt path that connected the road to the porch. When she straightened her posture, she saw she was standing in the abundant shadow of Miz Myjoy Henderson, the local healer woman.

"You spyin' on me again?" Miz Myjoy asked.

"No, I just wondered if you had any patients visiting you this morning." Roberta stared up at Miz Myjoy with all the self-possessed confidence of an adult.

Miz Myjoy chuckled. "You just wondered, did you?"

"So have you had any patients yet today?" Roberta asked.

"Just one, my regular malingerer, Frankie Sparks."

Roberta nodded. She knew she could count on Frankie Sparks' visit with Miz Myjoy as surely as the number five followed four.

"He's always tryin' to get out of going to work, right Miz Myjoy?"

"Right."

"You'd think someone named Sparks would always be rarin' and ready to go to work." Roberta said.

Miz Myjoy cocked her head to one side.

"You know what?" she said. "I never thought about that. How'd you get to be so smart?"

Roberta beamed the smile of someone supremely pleased with herself. She moved out of Miz Myjoy's shadow and climbed the steps to join her on the porch.

"I guess I was just born smart." Roberta squinted. "Miz Myjoy, how'd you get to be a healer woman?"

Miz Myjoy stared straight ahead.

"It just came to me naturally. You see, some folks are sick a lot of the time and some are perpetually well. Other people are put on this earth to help the ones who seem to stay sick."

"I was born to be mostly well," Roberta said.

"I hope that's so, baby. I hope that's the truth."

"Maybe one day I might be able to help the ones born sick, just like you do, Miz Myjoy."

"Maybe so."

"That is, if I don't do something else."

"What else do you want to do with your little skinny self?"

"I wanna help little kids who have mean parents," Roberta said quicker than she could blink.

Miz Myjoy rested her hand on Roberta's thin shoulder.

"Do you know any kids who have mean parents?"

Roberta nodded. "Some, where I used to live."

"Do you have mean parents, Roberta?"

Roberta gazed upward into the healer woman's eyes.

"My father used to be mean to me and my mother. That's why we moved down here. I think that's why I try to be good for her. I used to talk back a lot, but I don't do that anymore, even when I have a lot to say."

Miz Myjoy patted Roberta's back.

"You're wise beyond your years. I believe you've been here before, honey."

"Nope, this is my first time living here. I think I'd remember if I'd been here before."

Miz Myjoy laughed and Roberta kept talking.

"Do you make a living from all the ones who get sick in this town, Miz Myjoy?"

"I get by," she said. "Some people pay me with the vegetables and fruits they grow in their gardens. Or they come by and offer to fix things that get broke in my house. A few even pay me in dribs and drabs when they get paid at their jobs."

Roberta soaked in everything Miz Myjoy told her.

"I think I'd rather get a regular paycheck like the ones who give you money in dribs and drabs," she said.

"There's nothin' wrong with that, honey, especially if you can get a job helping the kids who have mean parents. Something tells me there's a lot of those kids around."

"Around here, Miz Myjoy?" Roberta scanned the little bit of the horizon she could see from where she stood.

"Yeah, even around here." Miz Myjoy moved closer to Roberta and lowered her voice.

"You know anyone around here who needs help because they got mean parents or mean relatives?"

"Nope. Not really."

"You sure?"

"I'm sure." Roberta took a step away from Miz Myjoy and raised her thumb to gesture toward the house's interior.

"If you don't have any more patients in there, I can come back later."

"That's fine. You can come back any time you want."

Roberta descended the steps. When she reached the bottom, she looked back at Miz Myjoy.

"When school starts next week, I won't be able to stop by every day."

"Oh, I know. You'll have your schoolwork to attend to."

"Plus all my chores."

"You helpin' your mama and your auntie?"

"Yup."

"What about your uncle Leroy?" Miz Myjoy asked as Roberta retreated toward the road.

Roberta stopped walking, turned around, and glared at Miz Myjoy.

"He doesn't need any help."

"No, I 'spect you're right about that. He's good at helping hisself, isn't he?"

Roberta didn't answer. She was already past the fringe of grass that delineated Miz Myjoy Henderson's front yard from her neighbor's small plot.

Chapter Seven

London at the Sales Team Meeting

I SLOWED THE car and spoke the words posted on the gold and burgundy sign, "Kensington Builders," before making a left turn into the company's parking lot. I steered into a space between Sandra Linton's late model white German import and an ostentatiously large red SUV, the show-off machine one of the other salesmen, Ken, leased for the purpose of impressing his clients and supporting a foreign oil cartel. With ten minutes to spare before the sales team meeting was scheduled to begin, I sat in my modest-sized gray Japanese sedan and rewarded myself with a few moments of reflection. I turned to my right and then my left and concluded I'd parked between quietly understated and loud and raucous.

These days I seemed to be living with so many "betweens." My hair color was between its former dark brown and its present brown-mixed-with-white strands. My July complexion was between its winter coffee with cream and its mid-summer deeper brown. My slacks and shirt didn't fit me as neatly as I wanted because I was between two different clothing sizes. Every morning found me engaged in a civil war between the melt-in-my-mouth croissants I favored and the more sensible bowl of whole grain cereal my body needed. Twenty-four seven I was stuck between the success of my first two novels and my doubt filled fears that I'd be able to pen a third one.

Everywhere I turned I found myself between something or another. I drifted between the memories of my father as he was before cancer arrived at his door, and the father I came to know after the treatments robbed him of hope. I was twelve when a car crash stole my mother from us. I'd been old enough to possess significant memories of her, yet I was unable to recall her tenderness. I had to rely upon my father to reassure me she'd had her soft moments, moments that had been free of reproach regarding my appearance, my expressions of my childish dreams, or my attempts at diplomacy whenever her disapproval hovered above my spiritedness, tamping it down if not obliterating it completely.

With Paula's self-exile from my life, I was between relationships. Or was I? Would there be another woman on the other side of this particular state of between? If not, I was prepared to accept the situation, because I'd noticed the pool of available candidates was perilously close to dry. Someone must have blown the whistle and warned all the single lesbians my age to abandon the water. Those who caught my eye had already climbed out of the pool to join someone else, and those who sought my attention were either aggressive swimmers poised to pull me under the water's surface, or they were weak willed non-swimmers going under for the third time. For the present, I was satisfied to sit by the side of the water, periodically wade in up to my waist, and paddle around on my own.

I took one last look at my watch and then hurried to the office building's entrance. When I arrived at the conference room, I expected to see the other members of the sales staff already gathered there, but the room was empty. My co-workers' absence made the space appear larger and more sterile than it was in reality. I approached the large oval table and chose a seat that faced a wide window and afforded me a view of the outside. I gazed at a broad expanse of manicured lawn, bordered by King Crimson maple trees whose plum colored leaves curled defensively against the summer's heat.

What they need is a soaking rain, I thought.

I looked up at the darkening sky. A deep gray cloud cover lent everything an eerie glow.

And it appears we're in for a hell of a storm.

"Hey, London. How are you?"

I'd been so absorbed in the scene on the other side of the window that I hadn't heard Sandra Linton enter the room.

"I'm fine, Sandra. And you?"

"Up to my ears in work, as usual."

We turned toward the sound of another voice.

"How's everybody?" Ken Green's booming alto preceded his entrance. "Are we selling houses or what?"

"We're trying," I murmured.

"Trying isn't good enough, London. Economic slowdown or not, we have to sell our asses off," Ken countered.

As I watched Ken pull out a chair and maneuver himself into it, I tried to not look at his posterior. I failed. Ken's rear end was as big as his bulging belly, so it was obvious he wasn't following his own instructions to sell our asses off.

Jocelyn Vega and Mary Barnett, two other project sales managers, arrived unobtrusively and seated themselves. In unison they set their notebook computers on the table, opened them and began reading their screens.

I figured their concentration on all their electronic gear, coupled with their reluctance to make chit chat with the rest of us suggested their recent sales numbers were either spectacularly high or distressingly low. Both women were competitive. Jocelyn captained the sales team at a new town house community, and Mary headed Kensington's latest estate home project.

"So, Mary, how's it going at your mega-mansion development?" Ken asked.

Mary barely looked at him.

"About the same way it's going in your development, I imagine," she said.

"Then it's not too bad. We're seventy-five percent sold." Ken sat back in his chair and smirked.

"That would make you just about golden, wouldn't it?" Mary said.

Ken was oblivious to Mary's sarcasm. He continued his survey.

"How about you, London? Are you fifty percent done yet?"

"She and her staff have sold sixty percent, Ken. How about that?" Roger Kensington answered Ken's query before I could.

I'd been so preoccupied listening to Ken's bombast that I hadn't noticed Roger's arrival.

"London's dealing with a challenging demographic at a most difficult time. Some of her potential buyers lost a bundle in '08, and they're far from willing to put their current house on the market while they're still undervalued."

Roger paused and looked directly at me.

"I can't say too strongly how pleased I am about the number of homes you and your associates have under contract so far, London. I appreciate all of your diligent work as well as your leadership at Oak Hill, and I plan to reward you for it."

I nodded and hoped the reward Roger mentioned would be the promotion to Director of Residential Development, a position I'd not only handle well, but one which I coveted.

"Thanks, Roger. We're all working hard," I said.

"And I'm eager for you and everyone else to get back to work this afternoon, so this meeting will be brief."

I took my notepad and a pen out of my work bag. Unlike Jocelyn and Mary who typed every meeting's details on their computers, I preferred writing notes in longhand. I'd noticed during previous meetings, Ken neither typed nor wrote any notes. No doubt he had the ability to commit every item on the agenda to memory.

"As of now, we intend to keep each of our projects moving along as scheduled. I know you're all working hard, even when the buyers don't seem to be there." Roger paused long enough to look at each of us.

"The latest report I read said new home starts have increased. The stats have grown for a couple of months now," Ken said.

"That's correct, Ken. The situation looks more promising than it has in a while. Accordingly, we're planning a new promotional activity. The second weekend of September we're going to stage a mega sales gala right here at headquarters. We'll have mock ups of each of the developments along with fully detailed presentations about each one. Of course, we'll have refreshments and plenty of personnel here to assist and serve our guests. In addition, we'll have multi-passenger vans available to transport people to each of the projects."

"That's a great idea, Roger. I was thinking you should do something like that," Ken said.

"Really, Ken? Feel free to make suggestions whenever you have a brainstorm," Roger replied.

Roger's reaction to Ken's having reached the tipping point of his obsequiousness amused me.

Sandra must have felt amused also, if her barely suppressed grin was any indication.

"When the guests arrive at your developments, your sales staffs will welcome them with brochures, invitations to tour the models, and chats with residents who've volunteered to answer any of their questions. The vans will keep shuttling back and forth between your projects and our headquarters here."

Clearly excited about his plans, Roger paused for air before continuing.

"London, I'll send you a memo with all the details. Please prepare the ad copy as soon as possible. I want to get this posted in all the usual places."

"Of course," I said.

Crap. There goes tonight's work with the anthology, I thought.

"Will you want us to be here that day, or at our sales sites?" Mary's eyes shifted from her computer screen to Roger long enough to wait for his response.

"I haven't decided that detail, Mary. Sandra and I need to sort that out."

I didn't care where Roger and Sandra would want us. This was July, and September seemed far away. Wherever I'd be, I hoped the weather would be more comfortable than it was now. I caught a glimpse of the ever darkening sky and thought I heard the low rolling growl of thunder.

"Excuse me, Roger."

Timothy Belton, one of Kensington Builders' home stagers, stood at the room's entrance, his back braced against the open door and his arms burdened under the weight of four boxes.

"Sorry to break in like this, but I didn't want Jocelyn and London to leave before I could give them some items for their models."

"No problem at all, Tim. Our meeting is almost finished."

Roger fixed his gaze on us.

"There's one more promo detail I need to mention. The same weekend we have our open house tours, Kensington Builders will start offering to list and sell our buyers' existing homes."

Roger waited for one or more of us to say something. When no one responded, he continued.

"We're going to provide our customers top notch realtors who'll sell their homes commission-free. The customers won't have to pay us a penny to advertise, show, get a sales deal, and host their settlements."

"That's an incredible incentive," Ken said.

"Above and beyond that, I'm willing to sign our agreements of sale with a contingency clause. If the customer's existing house isn't sold, he can back out of the agreement to buy one of ours without any penalty whatsoever," Roger said.

Ken whistled softly. Jocelyn and Mary folded their hands prayerfully, and Sandra offered us a kind smile.

"London," Roger said. "I'll get all this information to you later today, because I want you to include it in the ad."

"Okay. I'll look for it," I said.

Roger nodded at all of us. "Okay, team, meeting's over. Ken, if you could stay back for a bit, I have a few issues we need to discuss."

I closed my notebook and saw Tim approach Jocelyn and me.

"Looks like you have an arm full of goodies for us," I said.

"You're right about that, London."

Tim navigated his way to the conference table and carefully set down the boxes. He picked up the smallest one and handed it to me.

"Hmm, a sealed box. Must be top secret."

"You might want to wait 'til you get into your car before you open it." Tim pointed at the window. "It's raining buckets out there and I wouldn't want the contents to get wet."

The thunder I'd heard moments earlier had been the precursor to rain so abundant it looked like a series of liquid walls stood between the building we were in and the trees beyond it.

Tim tapped the box.

"This is the final detail for the child's room in your Devon model. You know, the one with the military theme. Just put this item atop the dresser, or on one of the pillows on the bed."

"Whatever this is, it's gender neutral, right, just like the room is?"

I enjoyed teasing Tim about his gender free décor schemes. He refused to stage children's bedrooms with the regalia of male-centered sports teams or girls' ballet costumes. Pink and blue paint or wallpaper were anathema to him.

"Of course it is, love. You know my opinions about that. Girls can be soldiers and boys can play with dolls." Tim winked at me.

I tucked the small box under my arm and left the conference room. I wondered if I'd need to protect the box by concealing it under my shirt. But when I arrived at the building's entrance, I saw the rain had slackened. Steam as thick as you'd find in any sauna wafted from the surface of the parking lot.

I opened the door to my car and gently placed the box on the passenger's seat. Before I turned on the ignition, I stole a glance at the cardboard cube. Tim hadn't given me the slightest clue about its contents, so I decided to give in to my curiosity. I peeled off the tape that secured it shut, and pulled open the top. Inside I saw a receipt bearing the words *Army-Navy Store* tucked in the upturned brim of a starched white sailor's cap.

Tim was right. The hat was the perfect addition to the bedroom's décor. I fingered its brim and plumped the inside of its crown with my fist.

"Perfect," I said. "You're ready for a little head, be it sailor-boy's or a sailor-girl's."

I put Tim's prop back in its box and then pressed the ignition button to start the car.

The windshield wipers swished away the rivulets of rain as I remembered I still had a few hours of work to do today. I backed out of my parking spot and cautiously steered the car around a large puddle.

The rain had ceased and left the air slightly cooler. Certainly it wasn't as cool as I would have liked, but the sudden mildness reminded me how much I enjoyed writing when the weather was clear and breathable. I longed for a story that wanted to be written, although longing wasn't enough. I knew stories had to simmer their way to freedom, regardless of the summer's heat or winter's cold. My writing never depended upon the weather. It showed no deference to the season or the time or the place. When the words and characters decided it was time for them to arrive, they wouldn't be stopped. If I tried to hurry or postpone their arrival, I'd do so at my own peril.

I understood this process well. That's why I couldn't fathom Milagros Farrow's disappearance from the world of stories. What had forced her to abandon her career just as it was in full bloom? Oh well. Hers was a mystery I had no way of solving, especially on a day when I had more work to do at Oak Hill Estates.

I drove from the parking lot onto the main road and joined a procession of cars moving cautiously through deep puddles and around tree limbs scattered here and there. Ahead of us a traffic light turned red. I braked and sighed. At this rate it would take me twice the amount of time it usually took to get back to the development. I reached over to the passenger seat and pulled my over-stuffed workbag closer. My hand routed through the bag until it found its goal, that morning's newspaper. I pulled it out of the bag, unfurled it, and stole a glance at the headlines.

LID BLOWN OFF LGBT ORGANIZATION'S FINANCIAL FAILURE.
An investigative report by Francis Monahan and Rand Carson.

Whoa! Was this the same Rand Carson I'd met at Oak Hill Estates this morning? Was this reporter Susan's new customer?

"How about that," I said. "It's a small world."

I squinted at the traffic light which was now green and followed the cars in front of me. As we inched our way toward the intersection, my phone rang. It was then that I learned all hell had broken loose.

"London. Where are you?" Roger Kensington screamed.

"I'm in my car, about ten minutes away from Oak Hill."

"Susan just called. The storm blew through the development and left a lot of damage. I'm leaving the office now. I'll meet you there."

"Was anyone hurt?"

It seemed like an entire minute before Roger spoke again.

"Two of the landscaper's guys. One's in pretty bad shape."

"Okay. I'll get there as quickly as I can."

"Be careful. Susan said it's a royal mess. There's crap everywhere."

I gazed through the moon roof and saw a clear blue sky looking back at me. How was it possible that moments ago the same sky had emptied itself? How could the slight breeze that now did nothing more than ruffle leaves slightly have been a wind so furious half an hour ago that it sheared limbs off trees and left them scattered across the road, blocking my route back to the housing development?

I drove impatiently, fueled by Roger's phone call and a sense of urgency and dread.

As I approached Oak Hill Estates, I wondered if Roger's alert had been a cruel prank, because everything near the entrance looked as it had when I'd left a few hours ago. When I turned onto the street leading to the models, I jammed my foot on the brakes. The road was littered with pieces of shattered signs. Their disconnected words were jigsaw puzzles of the names of faraway places. I steered my car around the pile of Shrop-caster-Cam-von, and felt the first hint of bewilderment that would soon overtake me. I got as close to the cluster of models as I could without puncturing my tires with the remains of nail-studded two-by-fours and parked the car right where I stopped, in the middle of the street.

Mesmerized by what remained of the third and fourth model houses, I moved ahead like a sleepwalker and entered our sales model.

"Susan? Are you here?"

"London? I'm back here."

I walked through the unscathed kitchen and then to our office space.

Susan stood next to her desk. She held the phone in mid-air.

"He died, London. They couldn't save him."

"Who died?"

"Oh my God. I don't even know his last name."

"Who? Who died?"

"Efraim, one of the landscaper's crewmen."

Susan began to cry.

"What happened?"

"The wind blew out one of the Lancaster's side windows, and a big shard of glass flew right into his neck. They tried to stop the bleeding, but they couldn't. I guess he'd lost too much blood before the ambulance got here. It was just too late to save him."

Susan and I stared at each other. I watched her tears fall silently to the carpeted floor and felt absolutely helpless.

"London? Susan?"

Roger's voice boomed from the front of the house.

"We're in the office," I answered.

We listened in silence as he walked closer to us.

"You two all right?"

"Yes," I said for both of us. "Susan just learned that Efraim, the landscaper's guy, died."

I saw Susan brush a tear from her cheek.

"Yes, I know. I'm going to the hospital right now. There's a second guy who was injured, but he's not too bad off." Roger leveled his gaze at us. "I called Artie Castor, the property adjuster, and asked him to come over here to assess the damage. He and Sandra should be here shortly."

"I think there's a lot of destruction, Mr. Kensington," Susan whispered.

"That's why I want them to take a look. And I've called the insurance company. They'll send someone here as soon as possible to take pictures and then run the numbers."

"What would you like us to do?" I asked.

"Give a hand to Sandra and Artie. But what's most important is that you two stay by the telephone. As soon as word gets out, the buyers we have under contract are going to call us to get information about their properties. They'll want to know how all of this will impact their deals."

"What would you like us to tell them?" Susan asked.

"That unless they're buying one of the two models on the end of this cluster, they don't have a thing to worry about. We're going to stay on schedule and deliver each house by the date we promised."

I'd have no trouble following my boss' directives because I knew he was correct. He'd pay his construction workers overtime to complete the terms of his sales contracts, if that were necessary. I wondered what we should tell the customers who would phone us and want to cancel because they didn't want to purchase a home in a development where a worker had lost his life. I knew for sure they'd call us, but I didn't know what we should say to them.

"Under the circumstances, I'm asking both of you to work later than usual today."

"No problem," I said.

"I can do that." Susan nodded slowly.

"All right, then. I'm going to the hospital."

We listened to the sounds of Roger's retreating footsteps and then the sound of the Devon's front door as it closed behind him.

"He's all about business, isn't he?" Susan asked.

"I guess that's what makes him successful."

"He didn't even blink when you said Ephraim had died."

"Yeah, I noticed that."

I had seen it and mentally filed it under—the real Roger Kensington.

"I sure hope the customer I signed this morning doesn't call."

"Ms. Carson?" I asked.

"Yes. I'll have to figure out what to tell her."

"Follow Roger's directions and say her project will be delivered on schedule."

"But she wants to buy the Cambridge model." Susan's voice dropped near the end of her sentence. "It's one of the damaged ones."

"I thought she was interested in the larger lot, the secluded one."

Susan shook her head.

"She changed her mind. When I told her we wouldn't be selling the models for at least a year, she said waiting a year before she took possession of the house fit her plans perfectly, and maybe she'd be able to get a bargain on all the model's upgrades."

I frowned.

"Well, that's shrewd of her. Did you check her financials?"

"Yes. She's qualified. Maybe she had a change of heart and didn't want to sink all that cash into a house."

"Maybe."

I recalled how decisive Ms. Carson sounded when she chose her house and her lot and I wondered what had changed in the few moments between her making her selection and then signing the construction agreement.

Susan looked at me apologetically. "I was going to talk to you about this when you got back from your meeting. Then the storm happened."

"I'll run it by Sandra, but perhaps not today. Right now Ms. Carson's deal is just a small blip on our huge radar screen."

I didn't want Susan to think she'd made a mistake when she agreed to sell her customer one of the models, but I knew the final decision to do so was out of my hands. I felt at loose ends and shifted my weight from one foot to the other.

"I'm going to walk by all the models and take a look at what the wind left us."

"Okay. I'll stay here in case anyone calls." Susan gazed at me forlornly. She hesitated, and then asked, "London, are you upset about Efraim?"

"Yes I am."

I looked down at the floor and sighed. Shock, sadness and something more I failed to recognize crept under my skin. I understood the shock and accepted my sadness. I wasn't able to name the third feeling that had settled over me until five minutes later when I stood face-to face-with all the damage.

I confronted roof shingles torn off and flung across the driveways, shredded and soaked strips of pink insulation wrapped around spears of framing lumber, planks of vinyl siding crudely snapped apart, broken panes of glass shimmering in the afternoon's sunlight, and that one jagged transparent missile propped against the stub of a torn sign post. That one piece of window that had sheared through a man's jugular vein and now bore his blood like a medal of some perverted victory.

I stared at the red-tinged glass and named my unknown feeling. It was guilt. This morning, if I'd been just a little less conscientious about the dried sod and dying flowers, I wouldn't have asked Sandra to issue a new work order to the landscaper, and Ephraim might still be alive.

I turned around, ready to go back to the shelter of our office. With each carefully chosen step over and around the broken pieces of two houses, I struggled to convince myself I wasn't thinking logically. How could I be held accountable for a man's death? How could I be responsible for one of nature's murderous acts?

I looked at my car parked where our visitors usually stop, and suddenly remembered the box with the little sailor's cap inside of it. I opened the passenger side door and reached in to retrieve it. Then I entered the Devon and climbed the steps to the second floor. The child's bedroom beckoned me. I stood just inside the doorway and surveyed the pieces of furniture. Our stager, Tim, told me to place the cap atop the bed or the dresser. I opted for the more prominent location, the dresser. Then I stood back and admired it. The little cap, the room's silence, and the emptiness of purpose swirled through my head and pulled me into a memory from long ago.

"London, come up to your room for a few minutes."

My mother stood at the top of the stairs and summoned me.

"Your father and I are going to spend Friday and Saturday night in New York City, and you're going to spend that time staying with your Aunt Virginia."

My mother didn't waste a single second as I climbed the steps to the second floor. She opened the door to the hall closet, reached in, and extracted my suitcase from the top shelf.

"Pick out the clothes you'd like to take."

"Okay," I said obediently.

I followed her into my bedroom, where she'd put the open suitcase on my bed, and I began selecting shorts and tops and pajamas from the chest of drawers.

"Don't forget your underpants and socks," she said. "And you'll need to take your slippers."

"Can I pack my blue jeans?"

My mother had just bought me a new pair of blue jeans and I couldn't imagine going anywhere without them.

"No, the weather's too hot to wear jeans."

How could it be too hot for blue jeans? Didn't cowboys always wear them, and wasn't it always real hot out West?

"You can wear your shorts on Friday and Saturday but you'll need to pick out a dress and pack your patent leather shoes for Sunday."

I knew better than to question my mother's declarations. In school I'd learned all about declarative sentences. In fact, I'd mastered the concept so well, I'd become the go-to student when it came to walking over to the felt board and placing the big soft dot between the end of one sentence and the beginning of the next one. So whenever my mother's voice took on that authoritative tone, I visualized that huge felt period pressed in place at the end of her sentence. There was absolutely no use in my uttering another word after she pronounced "Sunday."

"Will I be going to church with Aunt Virginia?"

"To church? With Aunt Virginia? I doubt it very seriously."

I wasn't surprised by her answer even though I didn't know much about my great aunt. Whenever my parents talked about her, they lowered their voices and spoke in half sentences without soft dots at the end. The same year I'd mastered using punctuation, I'd learned to avoid run-on sentences and their opposites, fragments. When I heard how my parents talked about Aunt Virginia, I wondered if it was all right to speak in fragments, just not write them. After all, my mother assured me both she and my father spoke the King's English, although she never named the king

I never understood why I needed to pack a dress and my pastel colored patent leather shoes with the cross-over strap as well as my brown everyday saddle shoes if I wasn't going to attend a church service. I wished blue jeans could be considered dressy. I'd wear them at the drop of a hat, along with my imaginary penny loafers, the pair I'd been coveting for years, every time we went to the shoe store.

My ever-active imagination suggested Aunt Virginia might be planning a Sunday party for me and some of the kids who lived on her block. But then I remembered I'd never seen any kids in Aunt Virginia's neighborhood. My aunt's best friend, Jo-Anna, a heavy set Italian woman, had a team of kids. I'd met them once a couple of years ago, but other than recalling the oldest one, Gianna, I couldn't remember any of the others' names.

I barely knew my Aunt Virginia, having seen her fewer times than I had fingers on one hand. In between visits to her over furnished house on Long Island, I had trouble visualizing what she looked like. I did recall she usually wore dull colored dresses whose faded flowers never seemed to match the bright glint in her eyes. I'm sure the totality of my aunt lay somewhere beyond the borders of my consciousness, probably because she was absent from my day-to-day life and she wasn't a member of the cast of adults I was learning to navigate.

My mother closed the lid of my little plaid suitcase and gave it a final tap of approval. She approached me and with both hands at once, firmly pressed down and smoothed my hair from its part in the center to the edge of my braids.

"Aunt Virginia is willing to take care of you for forty-eight hours, as long as it doesn't interfere with her going to work on Friday and playing Pokeno with her friends that evening," my mother said.

I nodded and felt a twitch of adulthood because my parent had confided the plans she'd made for my upcoming custodianship.

"What will I do when she goes to work?"

I felt it only fair that I should know a bit more information about how I'd spend the weekend. I wondered if my aunt expected me to help her at work. I already knew how indignant I'd feel if she did. Right or wrong, I had trouble accepting the truth about my aunt's job.

She was a housekeeper who worked for the Grants, a wealthy Long Island, New York family. I knew what the word "housekeeper" meant. It was a fancy name for a maid who didn't live with the people for whom she worked. What I couldn't, or didn't want to accept was anyone related to me by blood or marriage having to clean and straighten up for white people. I knew for sure I was colored, or Negro. That was the word written in small print to the right of my name in my teacher's roll book at school. But no one in my immediate family nor in my close friends' families had a job cleaning houses for white people.

Every adult I knew went to work in some kind of an office, or for the Post Office, or in a school. If they served people, they served folks who were white and black and maybe, on occasion, yellow, and the service was only temporary and for the greater good. No one I knew or spent time with held a job keeping white people and their property clean. I concluded my aunt's employment must have been an accident, an act of charity, or at worst, a wound on the bark of my family tree.

The next morning, my parents and I left our home in Philadelphia before dawn, and we arrived at Aunt Virginia's in time for all of us to have breakfast together in her kitchen. She called it a continental breakfast. I called it not much of anything. Only juice, coffee for the adults, an untouched glass of milk for me, and rolls with butter and jam.

"It's what they serve for breakfast in Europe," Aunt Virginia explained. "Mrs. Grant always eats this way."

My mother looked at me from the corner of her eye. An expression of worry crossed her face.

"I have a feeling London will be ready for a bigger meal at lunchtime. You're going to have lunch, right?"

"Oh, certainly. There's plenty for us to eat at the Grants. And we can always get a piece a' pie at the train station." Aunt Virginia smiled.

Pie? I blinked and looked frankly at my mother. I expected her to be even more worried. If my aunt and I were going to have another continental meal like the Europeans, I sure hoped they ate more than milk and rolls at noon time.

Less than an hour after my parents' departure for Manhattan, I found myself aboard a train with my aunt, making our way from

Hempstead to Garden City. From there, we climbed onto a bus that deposited us three long, tree shaded blocks from the front door of the biggest house I'd ever entered. The bottom section of the house's exterior was made of brick, dark rectangles the color cherry licorice takes on when it's left out of its wrapper and dries. The top half of the house reminded me of creamy sections of vanilla icing divided by flat wide boards made of bitter sweet chocolate. My aunt took a key from her handbag and opened the front door. I stood in the middle of the foyer and waved my arms in ever widening circles.

"It feels cool in here, Aunt Virginia."

"That's because it's so hot outside, honey. Wait 'til we go upstairs to the second and third floors. It won't be all that cool up there."

I followed my aunt from one area to another, from one floor to the next. There were so many rooms in that house, I lost count of them. I hadn't seen that many chairs, tables, and sofas in one place since I'd gone with my parents to a furniture store to pick out my very own desk and matching dresser and chest.

"Are the Grants cold-natured?" I asked.

"Not particularly. Why?"

"I was wondering why they needed all these fireplaces."

"Probably because in the old days, people used to heat their homes with fireplaces," Aunt Virginia said. "They didn't have radiators like they do today."

"Do the Grants have you and a butler?"

My aunt stared at me for a few seconds before she offered an answer.

"No. Mr. Grant's parents used to have a butler when they lived here, but there isn't any butler working here now."

"Then why do they have a room called a butler's pantry that's bigger than my family's entire kitchen?" I asked.

Aunt Virginia laughed. "Because they're rich, honey. And when you're rich, there are things you have just because you can have them."

"Oh." I tucked away that little gem of knowledge, sure I'd need to reveal it to someone younger than I was at some time or another in the future.

"How did they get rich?"

"Mr. Grant's father and mother as well as his grandparents made their money from the coal mines."

Whenever I'd heard my parents mention someone's winning a contest or stumbling upon a fortune, I'd seen my mother shake her head and say, "The rich get richer."

My father always agreed and added, "If they invest it, the money will grow."

With his words in mind, I continued my questioning.

"How does Mr. Grant keep his money growing?"

"You mean, what does he do for a living?"

I nodded.

"He's a big time lawyer, works in Manhattan in an office near Wall Street."

"Does Mrs. Grant work? Is she a lawyer, too?" My curiosity had no end.

"No, she's not a lawyer. She volunteers and does committee work."

I understood what it meant to work on a committee because last year I'd served on the new student welcoming committee at school.

"What kind of committee?"

"Oh, at the local hospital, and the Let's Keep Garden City Beautiful Committee."

I pictured Mrs. Grant in a starched nurse's uniform while she dug holes and planted flowers in the park we passed on the way here today.

"And remember," Aunt Virginia added, "The Grants have five children, so she has a lot to do just raising them."

My aunt looked off into space, as if she couldn't continue dusting and think about the five Grant children at the same time.

"Mrs. Grant doesn't go out of the house as much as she used to. She's sickly."

Silently, I wondered if having all those kids might be why Mrs. Grant was ailing.

Aunt Virginia went on to explain the whereabouts of each of the Grants' children.

The oldest was in college, but he was living at home during the summer. The other four were somewhere along the continuum of elementary to high school. The youngest two, a boy and a girl, were twins.

Each child had his or her own bedroom. As I followed Aunt Virginia from one bedroom to the next, I didn't know what stunned me the most, that none of the kids had made their bed, or that every one of them had left a God awful mess of clothes, trash, and half-eaten breakfasts scattered on chairs, desks and the floor. Mrs. Grant might have enjoyed eating continental breakfasts, but her kids ate a heck of a lot more in the morning.

Aunt Virginia took it all in stride as she narrated tales about each bedroom's inhabitant. I could tell she felt genuine affection for the Grant kids, although I couldn't understand why. How can you love someone who throws their crap on the floor and expects you to bend down to pick it up?

Aunt Virginia worked quickly. If I'd been looking at a stop-watch, I'm sure it took her only twenty seconds to make a bed and no more than an additional two minutes to hang pajamas in closets, stuff trousers, shirts, blouses, skirts and underwear into huge laundry bags, and pick up plates filled with crusts of toast and glasses cloudy with the remains of milk or fruit juice. I didn't know how she accomplished all of that with only two hands and two arms.

Finally, we went into the last of the bedrooms, the one that belonged to Alton, Alice's twin brother and the Grants' youngest son. Hands full, Aunt Virginia used her foot to ease open the closet door.

"You see up there?" she asked me.

I tilted my head and looked at the closet's two upper shelves. "Uh huh."

"Do you like that sailor's cap?"

"Yes."

What tomboy didn't like military accessories? Suddenly I worried that my aunt had discovered my best kept secret.

She walked to the bed and put down one handful of used dishes. Then she reached up and plucked the hat from its roost.

"It's yours," she said.

"But, Aunt Virginia. This belongs to Alton."

"He has plenty of hats. He won't miss this one."

She planted the cap on my head and stepped back to admire it.

"That looks cute on you, London. I want you to have it."

"But I'm not allowed —"

"I said it's yours, and I don't want to hear another word about it."

Two hours after she first topped my head with the little white sailor's cap, and before we boarded the Long Island Railway car for the return trip to Hempstead, Aunt Virginia treated me to lunch. From my first bite of a delicacy named pizza pie, I knew my mouth wanted to taste the chewy cheese and tomato concoction again and again. I hoped I'd be able to find pizza pie closer to home, because the trip to Garden City, Long Island was a long one.

As I swayed in tandem with the train's rocking motion, I was aware my mind had more to digest than my stomach did. I thought about the Grants' huge house. My arms recalled the cool air that enveloped us when we first crossed its threshold. My hands remembered the alternately smooth and rough texture of the intricately carved furniture. My nose acclimated quickly to the different odors floating about the different rooms.

The train slowed and I became aware of how heavy my shoulders felt. They sagged each time I thought about the stiff-brimmed sailor's hat perched atop my head. Why had I let Aunt Virginia insist on giving it to me? Did accepting it mean I was a thief, or worse, needy? Suddenly confused by the ambiguity of who I was because a part of me was willing to accept that hat, I wasn't at all comforted by my aunt's reassurance that I wore it well. The facts were the facts. The hat wasn't really mine. I hadn't bought it, nor had I earned it. Alton Grant hadn't relinquished it voluntarily, and probably, if given a chance to do so, he wouldn't have donated it to me, a complete stranger. But worse than that was the possibility that indeed he would have given it to me because I was the little colored niece of their reliable Negro maid, er...

housekeeper, Virginia.

"London, are you upstairs?" Sandra's voice yanked me away from my past.

"Yes, I'll be right down."

Sandra and Artie stood in the foyer, notebooks and pens in hand, ready to survey what the storm had left in its wake. I had to return to the ravaged model houses and help the two of them do their inspection. I knew I'd have to look once more at the scarlet stained window section. I'd have to point to it and explain it was the lethal thing whose edges had delivered a quick death to an innocent laborer. I'd have to stand there and watch Sandra and Artie and try to divine what they were thinking. I'd need to swallow the knot of guilt that blocked my throat, force it down my gullet and into my gut, where it would reside in that same place of shame where I kept the memory of how I came to own Alton Grant's sailor's cap.

Chapter Eight

Candace Dickerson

CANDACE DICKERSON SHOT a cursory look at the Corporate Events Manager placard affixed to the wall next to her office. She closed the door and headed toward the elevators at the end of the carpeted hallway. As she passed the receptionist's desk, she slowed to speak to the woman seated there.

"Nancy, I'm expecting a delivery from the printer. When it arrives, have someone put the boxes in my office, please."

"Certainly, Ms. Dickerson."

Candace nodded her thanks and quickened her pace. She reached her destination and tapped the button summoning the elevator. She was certain her early departure from work would ensure smaller crowds clogging the streets as she walked the blocks between her office building and her condominium flat.

When the elevator cubicle yawned open, Candace stepped in and joined three other passengers. In silence, they descended from the twentieth floor to the ground level, where they all exited and scattered like mice in search of food.

Candace walked quickly and stared straight ahead, like most of the other people who traversed the lobby. Most of Candace's physical movements matched her decision making habits. They were fast. Their speed belied how well thought out and deliberate they were.

As she passed by the lobby's beverage concession, Candace ignored the one voice that emerged clear and sure from the jumbled background noise.

"Coffee, Miss? Latest stock figures?"

Candace kept walking. Her feet barely grazed the marble floor. As she passed by him, she heard the coffee and newspaper vendor utter, "That woman is a pure bitch." It sounded to her like he spoke with the Caribbean sun drained from his customary Jamaican lilt.

Candace paid no attention to him. She hooked her thumb in the scant space between her blouse and the strap of her handbag and accelerated her speed. She remained oblivious to everything and everyone in the lobby. At least three or four times a week, twice a day, she failed to offer the vendor as much as a nod when he spoke to her.

As she left the office building, Candace glanced at the bronze square embedded in the structure's stone façade: Continental Assurance Company, Division of Global Comprehensive Insurers, Founded in 1958.

Continental Assurance paid Candace a good salary to do the tasks she accomplished so skillfully. The day she interviewed for her position, she'd asked the Human Resources Director more questions than she'd had to answer.

"How difficult could it be to organize social events and invite the kind of people who can afford to make a sizable contribution in order to attend?" she'd asked.

"It sounds like you know what you're doing, like you already have your finger on reliable resources," the H.R. Director said.

"I know how to raise money and I'm confident I can do this job."

"Consider yourself hired, Ms. Dickerson."

Candace propelled herself into the throng of pedestrians on Walnut Street. She frowned and gritted her teeth as she took in shallow breaths of the putrid air. It seemed to her that this summer's atmosphere was more malodorous than usual. After walking one block, she made a fist and pressed it to the center of her chest. She coughed twice, as if she were trying to expel the pollution from her body.

No wonder my heart races now and then. She thought. It's trying to beat its way through all of the poison in the air.

Although she was drawn to the excitement of living in the city, Candace detested its urban grime and the rank mixture of gasoline fumes, stale cooking oil from nearby eateries, urine, and human sweat that she frequently smelled when she traveled the streets. Humidity punctuated this afternoon's heat. The combination covered Candace's arms and legs with a thin sheen of moisture.

Suddenly dreading the walk that lay in front of her, she crossed the street and claimed a spot near the curb from which she hailed a taxi.

"Second and Arch," she said as she slid into the cab's back seat.

The driver nodded and punched a button on the vehicle's meter.

"Hot enough for you?" he asked.

"If it weren't, I'd still be walking."

"Better you than me, Miss. I got this air conditioner going at full blast and I'm still sweating."

Candace remained silent. She saw the cabbie looking at her through the rear view mirror.

"Weatherman said we're gonna get storms any time now. Some pretty rough ones. The suburbs are already getting hit."

"Well. There's nothing we can do about the weather, is there?" she said.

"No, Miss. I guess not."

The sluggish pace of the cars preceding them forced the cab to slow down. Candace turned her head and paid attention to the pedestrians who seemed to move more quickly than the vehicular traffic. Usually she was part of this same army of people hurrying to go somewhere. This afternoon as she watched the other commuters, Candace felt separate and somehow superior to the hordes of workers who dutifully traveled to and from work every day.

One thing that differentiated her from them was not being tethered to an office five days in a row. She could work at home a couple of days each week. More frequently than not, she was the one who decided which days she would leave the comforts of her Olde City condo and travel the short distance to her office and which days she would use her home office. Owning the power to make that decision, she believed, was one of the factors that set her apart from all the other sidewalk pounders she witnessed from the back seat of the taxi during this impossibly hot afternoon.

"Yup, we're in for some boomers alright. Some weather changers. It'll be cooler and drier tomorrow." The cab driver prattled on. He might as well have been by himself because Candace offered no response. She'd already contributed her last words to their conversation.

Stuck in a line of cars a block and a half short of their destination, the cabbie inched his vehicle toward the curb.

"Is this okay, Miss? Otherwise it'll be another five minutes before the damn traffic moves."

"Yes, this is fine."

Candace stuffed her fare through the small opening in the Plexiglas screen that separated her from the front of the cab. She clutched her handbag, stepped out of the taxi, and left its driver dangling in mid-sentence.

"Have yourself a..."

...drink and a shower. Candace thought the end of his remark.

She walked to the intersection and while she waited for the traffic light to change from red to green, she glanced through the window of a French bakery. Baguettes crisscrossed each other in a wicker basket. A platter of golden brown croissants stacked like the pyramid outside the Louvre kept company with loaves of brioche.

Just then, a customer flung open the bakery's door and the aroma of fresh bread escaped to the outside. Candace inhaled deeply. She let the fragrance along with the store's old fashioned gold and black lettering dissolve the dank smells of the city and take her back to mornings she'd spent in Paris decades earlier.

There had been mornings dunked in deep bowls of hot milk-infused coffee, when she'd skipped going to a mandatory class and instead, flirted with any of the several men or women who didn't need to rely on scholarships because they could afford to pay their own school fees. They were the mornings when Candace caught the first hints of the power she possessed, the power to ensure better, more comfortable times awaited her.

The traffic light signaled "go." Candace stepped off the curb and left her memories of long ago on the corner behind her. Purposely she walked a block beyond her condominium building and entered the high-ceilinged lobby of a United States Post Office. The lobby's subdued light washed over her as her fingers probed the depths of her handbag. She felt the familiar silver disk and its key chain. She grasped it and approached a wall of mailboxes. She zeroed in on one particular box and guided the key into its slot. Reaching inside the metal rectangle, she extracted two envelopes, a magazine, and a thin cardboard mailer.

She returned to the street and retraced her route toward her building without ever glancing at the pieces of mail she held tightly in her hand. She knew she had the patience to wait until she was inside her condo before she examined the envelopes' contents.

After she entered the building, Candace inhaled the cooler air. She walked past an alcove and headed toward the elevators. As was her daily habit, she gazed at her reflection in the mirror hung on the wall between the two lifts. It didn't matter to her that the image she saw was her reflection at the end of a long hot day instead of the beginning. Candace could always find something to admire about her appearance.

She knew her light brown face with its sparse make-up was as close to perfect as it could be. She had no need to verify the appeal of her narrow but well defined lips, or the softly feathered eyebrows shaped to lessen the severity of her piercing gaze. In defiance of the humidity, every one of her chemically straightened hairs was in place.

Candace felt nothing less than totally secure regarding her looks. Self-assurance was as natural to her as right handedness. It was attached to the double helix of her DNA.

She entered her unit and placed her handbag and the pieces of mail on a narrow table in the foyer. Then she went into the kitchen and removed a bottle of white wine from the refrigerator. She uncorked it and poured some into a glass she'd used the previous night. Candace took two sips of the wine, smiled, picked up the television's remote control, and began to watch the local news.

"Today, a spokesperson for the School District of Philadelphia spoke candidly about its impending fiscal collapse," the newsreader warned.

"What else is new?" Candace asked her wine glass as she turned her back to the television.

Convinced she could delay looking at her mail until after she'd rinsed the day's grime from her face and hands, Candace walked out of her shoes and headed to the master bathroom. There, she turned on the tap and soaked a washcloth in cold water.

She covered her face with the square of fabric, and allowed its soft coolness to prepare her for what she hoped to find when she examined the day's mail. After she dried her hands and massaged lotion into both palms, Candace returned to the kitchen to retrieve her glass of wine.

"The Phillies were in top form last night as they battered the Pirates." A different news reader's voice filled the room.

"Now that is new," she said as she picked up the glass and swirled its contents before tilting it against her lips and drinking all that was left of the liquid. She poured herself a second glassful.

"And now, the mail I've been waiting to open."

She returned to the foyer, pushed aside the magazine and the red, white, and blue cardboard mailer, and grasped the first of two envelopes. Candace slid one of her manicured nails under the seal. She did the same with the second envelope. Although neither one bore a return address, Candace knew the senders' identities. With accuracy she could guess the envelopes' contents as well. She spread each of the envelope's edges apart and watched their stationery protected contents fall to the table. The small rectangles of paper lay there, disheveled and out of order, totally unlike Candace's plans for her future.

Candace's lips grew the kind of smile she reserved for the happiest occasions, a smile that completely obliterated the news chatter that screeched from the television in the kitchen.

"This just in. The city is under a severe storm warning. The damaging wind, rain, and hail that struck parts of Chester and Montgomery Counties are approaching Philadelphia."

Chapter Nine

Lenah Approaches a New Chapter

LENAH KNEW FULL well she still heard Candace's voice echo in her ears the afternoon she first saw the woman. Despite the constant push and pull of that distraction, she'd decided it was time to be receptive to whatever possibilities might come her way.

"I'm not dead, just wiser," she'd told Sally during a rare moment of sharing.

Lenah parked her car after returning from a lunchtime errand. She spied the woman from a distance. She saw her form take shape hazily against the roiling waves of heat that arose from the tar-striped parking lot. Lenah's steady even pace never faltered as she closed the gap between herself and the woman. They would arrive at their common destination at the same moment.

Lenah hoped her stare went undetected behind the shield of her large sunglasses. Still yards away from the stranger, she compared the woman's physical presence to her own. She noticed the unknown woman was shorter than she was. Her skin was a shade or two less brown than hers, and she walked with purpose, but without Lenah's natural athleticism. She wore her precisely clipped hair in its natural state, a style Lenah always associated with a lack of pretense, or at least with self-acceptance. The newcomer carried a handbag slung over her right shoulder and she cradled a large bouquet of summer blooms in the crook of her left arm.

As Lenah and the woman closed in on the Emergency Department's double doors, Lenah willed her smile to hold the woman in its glow. She inclined her head the slightest bit and then spoke.

"Good afternoon."

"Hello."

The woman looked up at Lenah and cautiously returned a smile. After she crossed the hospital's threshold, she seemed to hesitate. She gazed first to the left and then to the right.

"Can I help you find your way?" Lenah offered. With one hand she lifted her sunglasses away from her face. Her other hand brushed against her employee identification badge clipped to the waistband of her slacks. She watched the woman focus quickly on the badge's photo and name.

"Uh, maybe you can," she said. "I'm here to see a patient. Is there a reception area where I can ask about his room number?"

"Sure. I can help you with that. Why don't you come with me?"

"Thanks."

Lenah walked toward the registration counter and the woman followed.

"What's the patient's name?" she asked.

"Richard Biaggio, B-i-a-double g-i-o."

Lenah went behind the counter and stood in front of the computer. She typed the name the woman had spelled. Seconds later she read aloud the information posted on the screen.

"He was admitted yesterday afternoon. He's in room five-oh-four."

Lenah paused and gave herself another opportunity to look at the woman. Satisfied, she continued.

"Just go through those doors over there on the left, and take one of the elevators to the fifth floor."

"Thank you very much."

"Don't mention it."

Lenah pointed to the flowers in the woman's arms.

"Are they for Mr. Biaggio?"

"Yes."

"Then he's a lucky guy." Lenah winked and flirted as effortlessly as a butterfly flutters its wings.

The woman allowed herself a quick smile.

"Actually, Mr. Biaggio isn't lucky at all. He was working at a construction site yesterday during that bad storm we had. He fell from scaffolding and fractured a leg, broke an arm and suffered two bruised ribs. If he were lucky, he would have climbed down from his roost before the storm started."

Lenah smiled. "That sounds about right. But he's lucky today. You're here visiting him with those beautiful flowers."

"I'm here to represent my boss. I've never met Mr. Biaggio. I wouldn't recognize him if I tripped over him."

Lenah cocked her head to one side. "And if you did that, you might have a fractured leg also."

"Oh, perish the thought," the woman said. "And thanks again for helping me."

Lenah reached over the counter and extended her hand.

"No problem. My name's Lenah Miller, by the way."

The woman grasped Lenah's hand.

"I'm London Phillips. Nice to meet you."

"London?" Lenah stared at her new acquaintance. "That's a unique name. I'll bet you get a lot of smart ass remarks about it."

"I used to when I was a child, but not so much now. There are a lot of strange names floating around."

"Yeah. I know what you mean," Lenah said.

She tapped the counter decisively.

"After you visit Mr. Biaggio, why don't you stop back here, London?"

"Stop back...here?" The expression in London's eyes flashed from neutral to surprised.

"Sure. Let me know how he's recuperating."

"Oh. I guess I can do that," London said. "But it depends on what time it is when I leave his room. I have to go from the hospital back to work."

"Understood," Lenah nodded. "I wouldn't want you to be late."

London took a step backward before she turned around. She narrowly missed colliding with Sally who bustled past her.

"Oh, sorry," London mumbled.

"No problem, dear."

Sally watched London retreat toward the bank of elevators.

"She seemed in a hurry. Was she waiting for someone here in the Emergency Department?"

"Nope. She asked about a patient's room number."

Lenah tapped one of the computer's keys and exited from the Patient Location page. She glanced toward the elevators and wondered how awkward she'd sounded when she suggested London return to the Emergency Department after she visited the unlucky Mr. Biaggio.

"Those flowers she was carrying sure were gorgeous," Sally said.

"Yeah, they were, weren't they?"

Lenah shifted her weight from one foot to the other. Suddenly uneasy, she didn't want Sally to suspect she'd found London more than a trifle interesting. In an effort to conceal her restlessness, Lenah made herself busy. She picked up a stack of unused forms, aligned their edges, and tapped them against the counter. Next, she walked to the waiting room and counted the number of people sitting there watching the television screen. Then she returned and stood in front of the department's white board where she tried to match the number of patients being treated in rooms on the other side of the double doors with the people sitting in the waiting room.

With three hours of her workday still stretched out before her, Lenah wished several more sick and ailing folks would arrive in the Emergency Department and rescue her from thinking about the woman she'd just met, the woman who shared her name with the capital city of England.

She looks like any other business woman. Most likely she's always in a hurry, with no more than clipped consonants to share with us menial workers, Lenah thought. I feel like I already know everything about her, like I've traveled to where she lives, and I don't plan to make a second trip.

Minutes passed by slowly. With no new arrivals in the ED to divert her thoughts from London Phillips, Lenah remained idle. She pictured London standing in front of her, beautifully framing the armful of flowers. Lenah compared the blooms to the fragrant roses and southern born camellias of her own past. She remembered the times she'd buried her nose into lush bouquets and inhaled the summer-soaked blossoms.

She conjured up the aroma of sweet honeysuckle and the taste of fresh picked blackberries, their juice and seeds skating across her tongue.

With absolutely no one new to seek her attention, Lenah's only recourse was to think about the woman she'd just met, breathe deeply, and then give in to the memories of scents that accompanied the warm breezes long ago. She recalled also the odors that clung to the icy winds of the past.

Chapter Ten

What's New is Really Old

"ONE OF THESE days you're going to find yourself on the wrong side of trouble, London. When that day comes, don't say I didn't warn you."

For years now, my friend Theresa has predicted a sorry fate for me. Frequently she's chided me for taking risks at work as well as in my social life. When I mentioned I planned to meet a new acquaintance for drinks and conversation, she launched into her oft repeated augury.

"I think I know what I'm doing, Theresa. After all, we're meeting in a public place." I spoke firmly and silently chanted a short prayer for Theresa to be as wrong about this as she'd been about other things in the past.

I pictured Lenah Miller and mentally ran through the short list of facts I'd learned about her. She appeared to be intelligent, gainfully employed, and close to my age, qualities that mattered to me when it came to sharing a couple of hours socializing with someone.

The day I visited Richard Biaggio in the hospital, I'd pretended I wasn't aware of Lenah's presence as we both approached the hospital's entrance. Truthfully, I found her intriguing, even from a distance. It was easier for me to label her intriguing rather than attractive because I could deal with intrigue. It was a mental concept, something about which I could think. Physical attraction always made me feel uncomfortable. I never knew what to do about it. Smile and say hello or avert my gaze? Flirt brazenly or state my business and be gone?

Unfortunately, the moment Lenah and I spoke to each other, I noticed two physical characteristics, her skin and her voice. The former was warm, brown. Its texture invited me to experience its touch. Her voice was just the opposite. When Lenah talked, she sounded coolly detached, even as she suggested I return to the Emergency Department after I visited Mr. Biaggio.

I was curious about her ambivalence, and even more curious about how it pushed me away even as it pulled me toward her. I wasn't sure Lenah was gay, but that brand of uncertainty was not new to me. In the absence of blatant clues, I haven't always been able to read the sexuality of other women of color. Perhaps there have been women who haven't been able to decode mine either. For the sake of survival we've worn so many masks, we've hidden ourselves from each other.

That afternoon, surreptitiously I'd examined Lenah's stance along with the frank way she'd stared at me, and I'd decided she was telegraphing who she was. I decided also that Lenah was probably bold enough not to care whether or not I was a lesbian. I believed that in the time it took her to take one breath, she'd decided I was a woman she wanted to know. The second she made that decision, I became fair game.

That day I saw her eyes sweep over me, blink slowly, and then narrow as they focused on mine. I watched her step away from the computer and prop herself against the edge of the counter. I noticed how the veins in her arms and hands stood in relief against her smooth skin, and I imagined how my fingertips might feel if they dared to land gently on those arms and hands and trace the path her veins made.

My curiosity about Lenah grew stronger as I watched her lips form the words, "Let me know how Mr. Biaggio is recuperating." When I heard the unexpected chill in her voice that surrounded, "I wouldn't want you to be late," my fantasy of touching her dissipated. I reminded myself that Lenah was a stranger, albeit a stranger whose invitation I'd felt oddly compelled to accept.

Five minutes after I'd left Mr. Biaggio's room, I stood on the other side of the Emergency Department's registration counter and waited motionlessly for Lenah to finish gathering insurance information from a new arrival's next of kin. Then, like an unplugged fire hydrant spouting gallons of water per minute, I'd proceeded to tell her all about Richard Biaggio's pain, his wife's frowns of worry, and their just-hired attorney's questions about the accessibility of Kensington Builders' certificates of liability. For the life of me I couldn't understand why I'd shared all that news with her before I phoned my boss to let him know what was going on. Nor was I sure why I'd agreed to meet Lenah for coffee or drinks soon after our first encounter.

Maybe we'd exchanged phone numbers because neither of us had anything more entertaining to do, or because we both hoped we'd have enough in common to sustain a conversation while we sipped a cocktail or two. Perhaps it was the warmth that emanated from Lenah's skin that had me jotting down her contact information as I gave her mine. Maybe it was my need for connection with a woman whose presence subtly suggested familiarity.

I quickly forgot something I'd known for a long time, that inaccurate memories tend to bloom like weeds in the fertile soil of neediness. I suppose that's why I didn't pay attention to the detachment in Lenah's voice. Not only did that detail lose its importance, it completely disappeared from my memory. By the time Lenah phoned me at home two days later, I'd buried even the vaguest recollection of her tepid enthusiasm deep under the ground.

The evening we met for drinks, I arrived early. When I entered the center city lounge and restaurant, I spotted Lenah right away. She was seated at a small table near the middle of the room.

"No flowers?" she asked.

I smiled broadly. "Not unless you're sick or injured and this is the hospital."

The chair's legs glided noiselessly across the wood floor as I eased the seat away from the table and sat down.

Lenah looked at me. A semi-smile played at the corners of her mouth. "So, London, you know where I work and what I do. How about you?"

"I work in real estate. I sell new houses."

Lenah nodded as if she'd been anticipating my answer. "You work mostly indoors in an office, right?"

"Yes." I blinked and thought about all the time I'd spent outdoors recently, consulting with the siding and landscaping contractors who were still putting things right after last week's storm.

"Why?"

Lenah pointed to my arm.

"Because I can see you don't get outside much."

I stared at the back of my hand and then at my forearm. A flush of warmth crept from my neck up to my face and I felt the slightest urge to apologize for my color, or rather, for the lack of it.

"You should be a detective," I said.

Lenah's smile had disappeared.

"So, do you work for a real estate company?"

"Right now I'm working for Kensington Builders."

"Right now? Where did you work before?"

"For a different firm, Whittingham Builders."

"I've heard of them. The CEO is a black guy, right?"

I nodded.

"Yeah, he's very successful. And he's gay." Lenah sat back in her chair. She tilted her head. "Why did you leave a construction company owned by a black, gay guy to go work for a white owned firm?"

"What would you ladies like to drink?" A young man with a rail thin waist and hair as stiff and spiky as a startled porcupine's quills stood at our table.

Lenah spoke first. "I'd like a frozen margarita."

"A vodka and grapefruit juice for me, please."

"You got it."

I watched the waiter's whippet slender body take off and head toward the bar. Eager to divert the direction of our conversation, I said, "I'd kill for his measurements."

Lenah turned to look at him. She frowned.

"Nah, he doesn't have any meat on his bones. You're good just as you are."

The flush of warmth I'd felt moments earlier changed from self-consciousness about my skin color to appreciation for Lenah's compliment about the rest of me.

"I'm still curious," Lenah said. "Why did you leave Whittingham to work for a white company?"

The need to defend myself filled my throat. I swallowed the feeling whole before it could choke my answer.

"I left Whittingham because they weren't giving me an opportunity to sell real estate. I saw more possibilities for advancement at Kensington."

"You think you're going to get more opportunities from a white boss than you'd get from a black one?"

I stared at her, struck wordless that she would skewer my answer with another question.

She didn't give me a chance to respond.

"I seriously doubt you'll get more opportunities there," she said. "Giving you a step up in the world would violate the rules."

"What rules?" I asked.

Lenah laughed. "Seriously? Were you born yesterday?"

"Do I look like I was born yesterday?"

"What kinds of opportunities are you looking for?"

I convinced myself to ignore the tone of Lenah's questions as well as the preposition with which she'd just ended her sentence.

"I hope to become one of Kensington Builders general managers."

"What's your position now?" she asked.

"I'm a project sales manager."

"What does that mean?"

"It means I manage the sales at one particular new housing development."

"And you're still looking for advancement?" Lenah's eyes narrowed. "Isn't that job important enough for you?"

"I guess it isn't." I felt my smile vanish and my right eyebrow rise a quarter of an inch. Whenever either of my eyebrows moved out of alignment, it meant things weren't going well.

Lenah made a noise akin to a guffaw. She shook her head.

"Why does that amuse you?" I asked.

"It must be my karma. I keep meeting women who aren't satisfied with their jobs, even when their jobs are damn good ones."

"There's nothing wrong with being ambitious, you know."

"Yeah, so I've been told."

I wondered if Lenah had been involved with someone more wedded to her profession than to their relationship. A few seconds of awkward silence parked themselves between us before the waiter reappeared and placed our drinks on the table.

"Can I get anything else for you ladies?"

"No," Lenah said. "We're good."

As I took the first few sips, my mouth and throat welcomed the cool liquid. I watched Lenah sample her drink. Before she could put her glass down on the table, I spoke.

"How about you? Are you happy with your job at the hospital?"

"Very happy. I have terrific benefits, I like most of my co-workers, and I meet all kinds of interesting people. You, for example."

"Me? What makes you think I'm interesting?"

"For one thing, you walk with attitude and purpose. I noticed that right away the day I saw you in the hospital's parking lot. You looked straight ahead, walked deliberately, and held your head high."

"That's a habit leftover from my childhood," I said. "My mother used to tap me on the shoulder and say leaders keep their backs straight and their heads held high."

Lenah drew a long sip of her margarita before she responded. "My mother used to tell me to keep my eyes open and avoid being led by anyone but myself."

"It sounds like your mother was very wise."

"She was wise enough to leave my father."

Lenah spoke without emotion.

"But that's enough talk about mothers and their wisdom," she said. "Tell me what you do when you're not selling houses, London."

I liked hearing Lenah pronounce my name. Her voice dropped into a pool of gravitas and she uttered those two syllables as if they were of consequence.

"I write."

"You do? What kinds of things do you write?"

"Fiction."

"Do you write under a pen name?"

"No. I use my real name."

"That sounds about right."

"Why do you say that?"

Lenah took another protracted sip of her drink.

"You seem like an honest, up front kind of person, someone who wouldn't hide behind a fake name."

Lenah stared into my eyes and I felt unmasked. With one comment she'd stripped away the first level of my armor.

"I guess I'm proud of my work and I want to receive credit for it."

"See? That's what I mean. You're so honest you don't even try to pretend there's a nobler reason to use your real name. You've done the work and you want to get the credit. That makes all the sense in the world to me."

I frowned.

"Also, I'm too lazy to go to all the trouble of creating some other persona. What if Oprah selected one of my books for her book club and wanted to interview me?"

Lenah laughed and I realized it was the first time I'd heard that sound. It jumped out of her throat, free and unfettered.

"Any chance that's going to happen?" she asked.

"Not any time soon. I've written a couple of novels, but they weren't best sellers. They didn't top any of the LGBT readers' lists, nor any book lists to be honest with you," I said. "Not like my role model, Milagros Farrow. She's earned a lot of success with her work."

Lenah nodded. "I've heard of her. Is she a writer you admire?"

"Greatly."

"Do you know her?"

"We've never met, but we've exchanged e-mails a couple of times. In fact, for the past few months I've been waiting for her to get in touch with me. I'm putting together an anthology of short stories and I wanted to be able to include one of hers."

"So what happened? Is she igging you?"

"That's what I thought at first," I said. "but I heard she hasn't been in contact with anyone recently. She's vanished into thin air."

Lenah reached over and lightly brushed the back of my hand with her fingers. She grinned.

"I'm glad you didn't vanish before we were able to see each other again."

I'd neither expected nor invited Lenah's touch. The surprise I felt as I watched her hand travel to mine was exceeded only by my struggle to say something coherent once I realized she'd made skin to skin contact.

"I'm glad also, and I'll take that as a compliment," I mumbled.

Lenah winked. "So what else do you enjoy, Miss London?"

"I like listening to music and going to concerts."

"What kind of music?"

"Jazz mostly."

"But I bet you have classical music piped into your sales office and your model homes, right?" Lenah said. "Jazz would be a bit too ethnic for the home-buying public."

"Most of the time I'm too busy to notice if there's music playing in the background,"

I lied. We always had monotonous generic tunes streaming from the models' intercom systems. The familiar melodies were comfortable. They were the kinds of upbeat songs that encouraged people to ooh and ah at the homes and then open their checkbooks and sign on the dotted line.

It wasn't until I slid into my car at the end of each workday that I had a chance to hear the music I enjoyed. Sometimes I'd let old R and B songs take me to places I'd been years ago, like Motown Review shows at the theater in the rough part of the city, or parties in low lit basements and rented social halls where someone spiked the fruit punch with liquor hijacked from their unsuspecting parents' rec room bar. The boys' sweaty faces all smelled of English Leather as they pressed themselves against the girls' Dixie Peach infused tresses.

So often the music I played when I wasn't at work returned me to places I'd understood, places where I'd been understood, places Lenah Miller just might understand.

The waiter materialized next to our table. "How about another drink, ladies?"

"Not for me, thanks," I said.

Common sense told me one drink this evening was enough. If I had a second one, I might forget to tally all the questions Lenah had asked me along with the few answers she'd yielded about herself.

"Nothing else for me either," she said.

The waiter placed our bill in neutral territory near the middle of the table.

"Take your time," he said.

I put my hand on top of the flat leather envelope that sheltered the bill and pulled it toward me. "My treat."

Lenah glared in mock anger. "I'll let you get away with paying this time, but next time it's on me."

"That's a deal," I said.

I slipped some money inside the bill holder and wondered if I wanted there to be a next time.

"So, where are you from, London?"

"I grew up right outside of Philly."

"A suburban girl. That doesn't surprise me."

"Why is that?"

"Your edges are soft. You were too polite to the waiter."

"How can someone be too polite?"

"He's supposed to be the one who says thanks. You don't need to thank him."

"I disagree with you. I was raised to express thanks to anyone who helps me."

"Well, that's one of the differences between being raised in the burbs versus growing up in the city. While you're busy thanking one person, another one's putting his or her hand in your pocket and taking advantage of your kindness."

I measured Lenah's words and decided I was perfectly fine with having a deficit of urban-honed rudeness.

"So when will I have a turn to treat you to a drink?" she asked.

"Sometime soon."

I was noncommittal. I wasn't one hundred percent sure I wanted Lenah to treat me to a drink, especially if the drink was seasoned with judgments about where I'd grown up or why I'd left one employer for a different one.

"How about next week?" she asked.

I visualized my calendar.

"Next week won't work for me. I'll be out of town attending a writers' workshop."

"Good for you. A writers' workshop sounds interesting."

Lenah's words held enthusiasm, but her voice sounded flat with disinterest.

As I arose from the table, I sensed the same chilly aloofness I'd felt days ago at the hospital when Lenah dismissed me to perform my duty visit to Mr. Biaggio. The coolness threatened to settle atop my skin, but I shrugged it off now just as I'd written it off previously.

"It was good seeing you again, Lenah. "

"Thanks for buying me a drink, London."

I headed to the door and wondered if the chair I'd just vacated would be occupied by another invitee before I could walk the short distance between the lounge and the parking lot where I'd left my car. The possibility of that happening amused and annoyed me at the same time. It was bothersome because I didn't relish being just another part rolling by on an industrial production line. I was amused because I suspected Lenah personified the kind of lesbian who had a production line of females waiting to be invited out for a drink. I was puzzled about her figuring that I'd be willing to occupy a spot on the conveyor belt.

It occurred to me that during the hour and a half we'd spent chatting over drinks, Lenah had plied me with questions, but I'd been a poor interviewer. She'd reminded me she worked at the hospital, but I'd already known that. She'd claimed she wasn't fond of ambitious women, but I hadn't learned why.

Lenah had asked and found out where I worked and where I used to work. She'd learned I aspired to have a position with additional responsibilities and more importance than Project Sales Manager. And she knew I was a part time writer who adored Milagros Farrow, another author.

Lenah seemed to know I was basically honest. Maybe she'd intuited the discomfort I'd felt when I left a construction company owned by a gay, black man in order to work for a different concern owned by someone completely different. Perhaps she'd guessed I'd experienced a tornado of emotional twists and turns when I said farewell to Whittingham Builders. In all likelihood she didn't know how much I'd struggled to convince myself I wasn't a traitor to my own kind, or how hard I'd wrestled with the perception that I'd abandoned a brother in order to work for the other.

Although I hadn't asked Lenah many questions about herself, somehow I knew a few things that had remained unspoken. I knew, for example, that she had some rough edges she tried unsuccessfully to banish from her voice. I knew her laughter didn't come easily, or at least not until she'd had time to judge if the recipient was worthy of hearing it. I knew she would make assumptions about my life rather than ask me all of the—who, when, and why—questions. And I knew she might not be willing to try to understand my answers. I knew all of that because I'd met other women like Lenah, women whose mannerisms were smoother than freshly churned ice cream, who talked glibly but said very little, women who tried to hide their fears and insecurities behind defensive bastions heaped high with bricks of criticism. Their lack of candor and their unwillingness to disclose their truths always convinced me to move far away, not toward them.

Despite all the things I was sure I knew about Lenah, what was it that lodged in my mind and made me want to spend the time to know her better? What was it that pried my fingers away from the safety of common sense and convinced me to approach her warm skin and cool demeanor?

Chapter Eleven

Rand Visits the Island

RAND CARSON SPENT the first half of the ferry ride from Woods Hole, Massachusetts to Martha's Vineyard pondering different ways to commit suicide. She leaned on the outside railing, examined her surroundings, and thought about the many times she'd been on this particular ship or on its sister craft. Today, as she watched the mainland grow more distant, she contemplated how and where a person could kill herself aboard this boat.

What could she say to her journalism workshop students to help them learn how to describe someone's abrupt death in a compelling way? Would she coach them to write dispassionately and stick to the naked facts, or would she advise them to describe the victim's motives empathically? Certainly it had to be the former course of action if her student-journalists were writing for a newspaper. If they were composing a longer story for another kind of publication, they'd be freer to speculate about why the victim had done herself in.

Rand pictured the ferry's lower deck where a forlorn desperate soul might park her car. With the vehicle's front and rear bumpers nestled against those of the cars in front and in back of it, the victim would lock the doors and slide down low in the passenger's seat, hidden from view. Silently she'd guide a razor blade across both wrists and wonder, as she faded into unconsciousness, from which arm her life drained faster. This suicide would be a quiet, secret one.

If a person wanted to attract more attention, she'd seek a more populated area of the boat. She'd whisper a farewell to all those who'd never acknowledged her worth. As she consigned her body to the churning depths of Cape Cod Bay, she'd hear the desperate scream of a witness.

Other passengers would gasp and turn away from the unpleasantness that had interrupted their sojourn. More than one onlooker would stare dispassionately and dryly speculate how to retrieve the body. They wouldn't feel the impact of the stranger's suicide until days later, when some unrelated event reminded them of what they'd seen. They'd realize, with a mixture of surprise and shock, that life really does have an end and no one has ever returned and testified that there was anything more to look forward to.

During her journalism career, Rand had reported several suicides. The first couple of stories flew from the keys of her word processor with clinical speed. She felt removed from the reports, totally objective. The later stories left her wondering about the victims' final thoughts. Why had they resorted to such a permanent solution to their problems? Recently, during her darker moments, Rand felt she'd become acquainted with the kind of desperation that could lead a person to her final act.

Having imagined the modus operandi of two ferry-based suicides, Rand moved toward the front of the boat where she spied a vacant seat. She sat down and gazed at the water ahead. Full of thought, she spent the second half of her short ride to Martha's Vineyard pondering the whereabouts of some of the women who had loved her thus far. One of them, Willa, represented Rand's longest relationship.

She and Willa were together for eleven years. It was Willa with whom she'd spent so many days and nights on Martha's Vineyard. When she was completely honest with herself, Rand admitted what she'd really loved about her relationship with Willa was the education she'd gleaned from her.

Her union with Willa had been Rand's first experience knowing a black person intimately, and their most obvious difference became their springboard for a series of lessons. Rand never intended to be the student to Willa's teacher. They both thought acting out those roles brought the wrong elements to their romantic relationship. It added tension where ease should exist.

Whenever she and Willa were in the company of others, black or white, Rand noticed the averted eyes, the dampened spirits, the lips spread in smirks instead of smiles, the stares that never really saw them as individuals, and the body language and barely concealed frowns that were intended to reduce their worth.

Rand demanded to understand why. Willa, her guide, explained, sometimes patiently, other times not. Rand wouldn't allow the slights to go unchallenged and Willa soon grew tired of hosting confrontations where once, had she not been with Rand, passive acceptance used to live.

When the passage of time added the tedium of daily routines to the reality of changed bodies, faces, and dreams, Rand became restless. She traded her union with Willa for superficial dalliances with other women, some of color, who satisfied her ego and curiosity. She skipped away from Willa and spread out her justifications for doing so the same way a poker player fans a deck of cards atop a table. She danced away from the most honest explanation, that of boredom, and accused Willa of being too cautious and afraid to take chances in life.

Try as she did, Willa couldn't make Rand understand that simply being herself in a world where there were so few "Willas" was not at all cautious. It was the apex of bravery.

"I take risks every day," Willa said. "I've forgotten more risks than you'll ever know."

Rand remained unconvinced. She found Willa's unwillingness to jeopardize her stability, comfort, and security unbearable. Her disappointment with Willa leaked all over their conversations and spilled onto their bed. The disenchantment arrived dressed in criticism and petty arguments. Toward the end of their relationship, Rand spoke to Willa in single word sentences, and Willa acted out her silent responses by pressing her fingers into the fleshy parts of her hands with such force that her nails' imprints left indentations.

Neither woman thought it a good use of time and energy to beg the other for a simple gesture of affection or a gentle word.

They parted and after several years, Rand found herself thinking less and less about Willa. She wished her no harm. She had no wishes for her at all. The space in Rand's heart where Willa used to exist filled quickly with other women, with writing assignments, and with local fame. The space in Rand's mind where Willa used to live filled with the realization that she'd never loved Willa completely. She loved being different and Willa had been the visual part of that difference.

Rand felt a soft mist kiss her face as the ferry turned slightly. She gazed straight ahead and watched the shore come closer. When she was able to decipher the words, "Ferry Terminal: Oak Bluffs," spelled across the side of a long rectangular building, she arose from her front row seat in the boat's open-air section and joined the line of passengers already headed toward the stairwell.

The parade of people dragging suitcases or burdened with backpacks, reminded Rand of ants obediently following their leader along the seam where the wall meets the floor. The orderly line of passengers arrived at the bottom of the stairs. A few scattered to claim seats near the boat's exit. Most planted their feet right where they stood and remained motionless while they waited for the ferry to dock.

Rand remained near the starboard side of the boat. She shifted her weight from one foot to the other as she heard the low rumbling of the boat's engines. She smelled the acrid odor of marine fuel. Aware that a fellow passenger stood next to her, Rand turned her head to better look at him.

"Beautiful day, isn't it?"

"Spectacular," he answered. His eyes brightened and he smiled at her. "Day tripper or do you live on the island?"

Rand hesitated before she answered.

"I'm just here for the afternoon."

"I thought so." He pointed to the handbag slung over her shoulder. "You're traveling light. Business or pleasure?"

"A little of both," Rand said.

"Well, you've picked yourself a splendid day to be here. Enjoy."

"Thanks."

As the wide ship eased into its berth and came to a stop, the knot of passengers involuntarily moved forward a full step and then backward. The dock steward stepped up to a console and pressed two buttons. The portable ramp swung into place. Another steward shouted a coded message into his hand held radio. The sound of metal slapping cement meant cars would soon stream out of the ferry's gaping mouth and be free once again to navigate their way on the land.

"Okay, folks. Step off carefully." The uniformed Steamship Authority worker waved his gnarled hand.

Rand joined the surge of island visitors and made her way down the steeply inclined walkway. Setting foot on the wide path at the end of the ramp, she focused straight ahead.

Across the street from the boat terminal lay the wide expanse of manicured green lawn that was Ocean Park, in Oak Bluffs, Martha's Vineyard. Multi-storied pink, yellow, gray, mauve and light blue houses, their Victorian styled exteriors seasoned with turned railings and corbels of all kinds, bordered one side of the turf. A squad of buses stood in line on the street while the ocean, gleaming under the late morning sun, edged the other side of the walkway.

The houses of Ocean Park are beautiful, but I wouldn't want the responsibility of keeping one painted, Rand thought. Give me a small cottage, like the one Willa's family owned, or better yet, a Cape Cod bungalow like the one I want to buy at Oak Hill Estates.

Rand crossed the car clogged intersection. She navigated her way around a procession of little bobbing heads, waving arms, and chattering voices, children, with their parents in tow, all headed to the ornate wooden building that sheltered the Flying Horses. One of the town's claims to fame, the painted merry-go-round's equines were up and running until the end of the summer season.

After putting another block behind her, Rand turned left onto Circuit Avenue. Just short of her destination, she took a deep breath. A thin line of sweat edged her hairline as she threaded her way along the bustling commercial strip. Although it was crowded to the gills with cars parked on the diagonal and slow paced pedestrians who threatened to spill over the sidewalk and onto the street, this area represented only a small section of the town Rand had learned to see through Willa's eyes.

Home to an African American population for three centuries, Oak Bluffs, more than its neighboring villages, had a long history of ethnic diversity. To this day Rand thanked Willa for exposing her to a part of black America most other Americans never knew existed. She felt enriched by her exposure to people who'd been absent from her own upbringing. She thought her knowledge was tantamount to membership in a secret society, one to which she had only limited entrée, but enough for her to understand that the privileges of bloodline weren't all positive. Those privileges could be divisive. They could bring with them bias against one's own kind and all the hurt, pain and anger that comes with that discrimination.

Rand continued walking. She passed by an endless row of small store fronts peddling tee-shirts, candy, kites, toys, maps of the island, postcards, and house wares. At the end of the block was a neat brick building trimmed with wood painted white. Its federal architecture suggested similar rows of shops in the adjacent village, Edgartown, more so than here in the midst of Circuit Avenue's paean to Victoriana. The shop's neatly lettered name, Martin and Sarah's Book Store, beckoned Rand.

She entered and heard the hushed chords of taped piano music in the background. Immediately she felt her forehead dry as cool conditioned air replaced the outside turgid atmosphere. She saw a young woman facing a bookcase and touching the entire row of books with her index finger, as if she were scanning each one's title. Rand looked to the right toward the checkout counter.

An older man stood there, his back to her and his head inclined. He appeared to be writing something. Rand approached him.

"Jonathan?"

The man turned around, a grin already spread across his face.

"My dear, Rand." His outstretched arms pulled her into a delicate hug. He touched her cheek with his.

"Well, I'm not surprised to see you here," Jonathan pointed to an eight-by-twelve inch poster tacked to the bulletin board to his left. "I knew you'd be on the Cape for the workshop."

Rand glanced quickly at the poster and then back to her friend.

"I came up a day early just so I could see you."

Jonathan smiled broadly.

"I'm flattered, and I'd love to believe you, but I suspect it's your curiosity about my e-mail and not your eagerness to see me that's brought you here."

Rand hung her head in mock shame.

"Okay, guilty as charged," she said. "Is this a good time to talk, or should I come back a little later?"

Jonathan turned slightly and focused his gaze on a young man who was arranging books on a display table.

"Your timing is great. Let me ask Tom to take care of business for a few minutes while we go across the street for coffee. We can talk there."

"Fine."

Rand watched Jonathan summon his assistant and explain where he'd be for the next half hour.

"It's so good to see you, my dear. What's it been now, three...four years since you've been on the island?" Jonathan touched Rand's elbow and guided her as they stepped off the sidewalk.

Rand squinted in response to the bright sun and silently calculated how long she'd been absent from the place she'd come to enjoy so much.

"I was here three years ago, but just for the day," she said. "We didn't see each other."

"Well, not much has changed. Life goes on."

Jonathan advanced a half step in front of Rand and then opened the door to the café. They perused the vacant tables and selected one near the back of the small eatery. Rand plucked one of the laminated menus from the jaws of its metal holder.

"The Top Sail looks just as I remember it, but I see they've expanded the offerings."

"Yes," Jonathan said. "They have to keep up with the whims of the caffeinated public. See anything you like?"

"I think I'll try the Secret Service Sipper." Rand chuckled. "The menu says it's designed to keep you awake and alert on the hottest days, extra strong iced tea laced with limeade and a splash of lemon soda."

"That's one of the beverages they added when the Obamas vacationed here the first time." Jonathan said.

"I bet that was exciting."

"It was kind of surreal. Here in Oak Bluffs we felt proud, really proud."

Rand reached across the table and patted Jonathan's hand.

"I imagine you were."

"Oh yeah. The Obamas are our kind of people."

"I know."

"Let me get you that drink." Jonathan got up and walked to the counter where he spoke to one of the waitpersons.

Rand gazed at the room. The walls were the color of rainbow sherbet. The polished wood floor wore scars here and there. Rand thought she could see slight depressions near the doorway and at the end of the counter where customers stopped to pay their bills.

Jonathan returned to their table. He looked less like a bookseller and more like a waiter carrying a tall glass of milky iced coffee and a tulip shaped vessel with the light colored iced tea mixture.

"My treat," he said.

"Thanks, Jonathan. I'm parched and these drinks look good."

"As do you, Rand. You look spectacular."

"Let's not exaggerate."

"I'm not exaggerating," he said. "Is everything going well for you?"

"For the most part." Rand's jaw tightened perceptibly. "How about you, Jonathan? Is business brisk?"

"So far I'm keeping my head above water, but the e-reader revolution is nipping at my heels."

"Even now during high season?"

"Especially now. Think about it. Who wants to buy a bunch of books while they're on vacation and then pack them to get them home?" Jonathan sighed. He looked away and then back at Rand. "All I want is to turn a profit for the next two years. Even if it's a small one, I'll be content. After that, I'll be ready to entertain any and all offers from anyone who wants to buy my building."

"If you sell the bookstore, what will you do?"

"I'll retire, my dear. It'll be time, don't you think?"

Rand took note of Jonathan's look of resignation. She figured he'd arrived at his decision after much thought.

"Maybe then you'll write that novel that's been churning inside your head for years." Her eyes sparkled.

"Oh, undoubtedly." Jonathan smiled broadly. "And how's your writing going?"

"I have a couple of projects started, but right now the newspaper gig and the magazine articles are paying the bills. And I'm thinking seriously about buying a house."

"No kidding?"

Rand nodded.

"I'm close to signing an agreement of sale for a house in one of those age qualified developments."

"Only close? You didn't sign it?"

"I'm still interested in buying there, but I might have to scale back my dream house wishes."

"Well, you've got a good head on your shoulders. You'll make the right decision." He smiled gently, then leaned forward.

"You're probably eager to hear the details of that e-mail I sent you."

"Yes, I am."

He lowered his voice. "A few weeks ago, a young woman came into the shop two days in a row. Both days she went immediately to the LGBT fiction section. The first day she was there, she bought two of your books. One of them was the last autographed copy we had. When she approached the checkout counter, she asked me if I knew if the signature in the book was genuine."

Jonathan sat back and pursed his lips before continuing his recitation. "I asked her why in the world she would think I'd affix an — autographed copy — label on the book if the signature were bogus. I was pleasant to her, but I was really pissed. What kind of question is that?" Jonathan's voice rose as he recalled his indignation.

"The second day she came in, she browsed for a bit and then walked over to me at the counter. I could tell she wanted to strike up a conversation. She complimented the bookstore and said how homey it felt. She was practically fawning."

Rand smiled. "Maybe she was flirting with you."

"Not at all. Anyway, I was sure she was family from day one. I wasn't my usual charming self because I remembered her grilling me about your signature the day before."

Rand sipped her drink.

Jonathan wiped a tear of condensation from his glass. "Here's where the story gets interesting. The woman had a boat load of questions to ask, and most of them were about you."

"What kinds of questions?"

"She said she'd heard you spend a lot of time in Oak Bluffs in the summer and she wondered if I knew where you stayed. She asked if you did a lot of your writing on the Vineyard, and if you stayed here by yourself or with someone."

"What did you say?"

"I told her I'd heard you visited the Vineyard from time to time, but I knew nothing more than that."

"Thanks, Jonathan. I'm sorry you had to stretch the truth."

"I didn't owe her any information. Frankly, there was something about the woman that made me uncomfortable. She wanted to know too many details about you. It wouldn't have surprised me if she'd asked what brand toilet paper you use."

Rand grinned.

"Her curiosity went far beyond that of a fan. You'd think she was doing research for your biography." Jonathan sounded exasperated.

"Do you remember what she looked like?"

Jonathan looked up at the coffee shop's painted tin ceiling.

"Not really. Had she been a man, I assure you I'd remember far more."

"I'm sure," Rand said. "But you must remember if she was young, middle aged, or old, short, tall, blonde or dark-haired."

Jonathan squinted.

"I'd guess she was fortyish. Her hair was tinted, or at least highlighted. You know, predominantly brown with red streaks here and there. She was dressed conservatively, linen slacks and a tailored blouse. Carried a designer handbag. I'd say she was a Philadelphian, or maybe from North Jersey. Definitely not a D.C. type. She wasn't gracious enough. And not New York. She wasn't sufficiently dismissive when I claimed I didn't know anything about you."

"Not bad, Jonathan. You do recall a few of her details."

"Uh huh. And by the way, she was black. I know you're not in the habit of asking that particular question. Bless your heart."

"Nope. Never have been. Is that stupid of me or simply naïve?"

"Neither. It's just rare."

Rand tapped the rim of her glass. She looked off for a second before refocusing on Jonathan.

"Are they on the island now?"

"Who?" Jonathan asked.

"Willa and her family."

"The James family has been here for generations, honey. You know that."

Rand frowned.

"Yes, Jonathan. I do know that. I meant...is Willa up here for the season?"

"I believe I've seen her once or twice in the last month. Why do you ask?"

"I was just wondering, that's all."

Jonathan's gaze softened.

"I don't think Willa would hop on the ferry, go to the mainland, and interrupt your writers' event. She's a class act."

"I know she wouldn't," Rand said. "Is she up here with a partner?"

Jonathan shrugged. "Who knows? The Cottagers hold on to their secrets. By the time they show up with this one's cousin and that one's best friend since childhood, you can't tell who's sleeping with whom. I gave up the annual game of trying to figure it out long ago."

Jonathan turned his head and looked through the café's picture window in time to see two adults with three children enter his bookstore.

"I'd better get back to the shop. Tom just started working for me a month ago, and he's not exactly an expert yet."

"I understand."

Slowly, Jonathan rose from the table. Rand looked up at him and extended her hand. Her slender pale fingers disappeared within his large brown hands.

"Thanks for giving me a heads up about Ms. Curiosity."

"Well, I wanted you to know about her. Her questions may mean nothing at all, but I noticed she never explained why she was asking them. When I sent you the e-mail, it didn't occur to me you'd come all the way up here to see me about it."

"The timing fit my schedule."

"Well, it was good seeing you, Rand, if only for these few minutes. Please take care of yourself."

"I will, Jonathan. Good seeing you also."

"And watch out for curious black women with dyed hair and tons of personal questions," he added.

Jonathan released Rand's hand. His fingers fluttered a wave as he retreated to the café's door.

Rand finished her drink and decided to stroll to the ferry terminal. This time of year, when the ships sailed back and forth frequently between Martha's Vineyard and Massachusetts's mainland, she knew she wouldn't have to wait long before she'd board the next boat and return to the Steamship Authority's public parking lot in Woods Hole.

Energized but somewhat troubled, Rand thought about Jonathan's admonishment to be on the lookout for curious black females armed with probing questions.

"His warning is two months too late," she muttered as she felt the familiar stress induced pain coursing through her left shoulder.

Chapter Twelve

The Price of a Cup of Coffee

"SHIT." CANDACE CRUMPLED the tersely worded memo and threw it into the trash basket.

Due to budgetary constraints, her request was denied. Continental Assurance did not plan to hire an administrative assistant to work with the Corporate Event Planner. In addition to that, she needed to remember the Event Planner's annual review and progress report was due one month from today.

Candace glared at the phone and then punched a few of its keys.

"Marilyn? It's Candace."

"Hey, Candace. How are you?"

"Fine, and you?"

"Just fine, thanks."

"Good. Listen, are any of your summer interns floating around without enough assignments to keep them busy?"

"I do have one young man without a steady assignment. I've been using him as a per diem sub wherever we're short-staffed."

"Great. Could you send him up to my office?"

"Only for today?"

"Every day for the foreseeable future, if you can spare him."

"Sure. I think I can do that. It'll be great to have every intern attached to a department."

"Terrific. Thanks. Talk to you soon."

Candace hung up the phone.

"Budgetary constraints, huh? I've hired my own damn administrative assistant."

She donated three additional seconds to feeling smug before she picked up a pair of scissors and stepped toward an unopened box perched on a table at the far end of her office. She spread the scissors' blades and used the broader one to slash an incision through the box's binding. She tugged on the cardboard, reached inside and extracted the box's list of contents. "Okay, Mr. Intern. This will be your first job."

Four rapid fire knocks on the office door answered Candace.

"Come in."

Candace watched the knob turn quickly. The door opened and a mustachioed young man entered the room.

"Ms. Dickerson?" he asked.

"Yes, that's right."

The young man stepped forward into Candace's work space. His outstretched hand assumed the lead and he smiled confidently as he introduced himself.

"I'm Ted Williamson, the intern. Nice to meet you."

"I'm the Corporate Event Planner, Candace Dickerson."

"I'm glad I've finally gotten a permanent assignment. It's rough bouncing from one office to another."

Candace withheld her smile. She pumped the young man's hand twice and then pulled her hand away from his.

"Don't get too comfortable, Mr. Williamson. This assignment will last as long as I have tasks for you to do. It's not permanent by any means."

"Oh, sure," Ted said. "I understand." He gazed at his surroundings. "You have a nice office here."

"Thanks. Right now it's filled with work that needs to be done."

"I'm ready to roll up my sleeves. Just point me in the right direction."

Candace ignored his small talk.

"Do you see that box?" She pointed to the newly opened package. "It's filled with thank you letters that have to be mailed to people who attended our last big charity event. There's a printer over there." She gestured to the business equipment. "You're going to count out two hundred sixty of those letters and load them into the printer. I'll send you the data you need and, one by one, the printer will affix each guest's name and address to a letter. Then, you'll print the address labels, fold the letters, put each one in the appropriate envelope, and deliver everything to the mail room."

Ted listened. His smile broadened to a grin. "I think I can do that." He moved closer to the table where the box of paperwork was stacked.

Candace strode to the computer stand which was placed at a right angle to her desk. She hovered above it and pressed a few keys. As she waited for Ted to finish counting the requisite number of letters before putting them in the printer's tray, she examined his appearance.

Well, she thought, he's certainly dressed for business with his polished shoes, crisp pale blue shirt, striped necktie, and khaki trousers with seams as sharp as a blade of saw grass. He's preppy. Princeton, Yale, or maybe someplace more local, like Penn.

"Okay, I've got two hundred sixty counted out and loaded. You can send me the names and addresses," Ted said.

"Add five or six more letters, in case the printer eats two at a time by mistake," Candace said.

Ted turned to look at her. "I'm on top of it. You can send the data."

Candace tapped the keyboard and then sat down at her desk.

The printer clicked to life. Its mechanical hum played a steady counterpoint to the higher pitched swish as each sheet of paper exited the tray and deposited itself on top of the one before. Ted shifted his weight from his left foot to his right as he waited for all the letters to go through their lock-step procedure.

Candace split her attention between her computer screen and her appraisal of her new assistant. She noticed his height and build, his clean shaven face, its hue three values lighter than the color of his slacks, and his hair which was clipped closely on the sides and longer on the top where it lay in wavy rivulets.

As she assessed Ted, one detail at a time, Candace clamped her jaw tightly against the involuntary frisson of discomfort she felt. A distasteful reminder of the way life's ordinary events tend to transpire between folks of color who look like Ted and others who don't catapulted through her thoughts. She chided herself for reacting so negatively to the young man. After all, he was no more than her temporary assistant. She was the supervisor here. She had no reason to assume Ted had signed on to the practice of adhering to a generations old color based hierarchy followed by so many for so many years. This was a different time and social habits had changed. Here, in Candace's office, Ted was in her world, not his.

"Okay. The first part of the job is done," Ted said.

He removed the stack of letters from the printer and then loaded the machine with a ream of blank address labels.

"There's no need to rush. I want the job done correctly," Candace said. She looked at Ted's profile.

"This isn't brain surgery, Ms. Dickerson. I think I can handle it."

The only sound that cut through the heavy tarp of tension was the printer's unobtrusive hum.

"Do you mind if I move the chair over to the work table and sit down while I fold the letters and stuff the envelopes?"

"That's fine."

They worked in silence for the next few moments. Then Ted interrupted their detente.

"I see a mistake you need to correct, Ms. Dickerson."

"A mistake?" she asked.

"You've got the wrong address for Baker Williamson."

"Baker Williamson?"

"Yes, the Honorable Baker Williamson and his wife, Helen. They're my parents. They moved a year ago."

Candace watched a smug smile make itself at home across Ted's lips. She felt the muscles near her shoulders contract. She clicked the computer's mouse several times and sucked air between her teeth. Her eyes narrowed and glared like twin laser beams boring an imaginary hole through her computer screen.

"All right, I've deleted the incorrect information," she said. "Please dictate the new address."

"Fifteen Wanamaker Drive, Philadelphia, 19119."

"Thanks. Now you'll have to generate another letter and a new address label."

"No problem. How often do you update your databases?" he asked.

"Why?"

Ted picked up the stack of filled envelopes and waved them at Candace. A sneer overtook his smile. "I wonder how many other errors there are in here."

Candace summoned her haughtiest expression to use against his false victory. She knew why his impeccable ensemble lacked a jacket. It would have been redundant. He already wore a perfectly tailored coat of arrogance.

"Hopefully there aren't any other mistakes in the address database," she said. "But if there are errors and the Post Office returns those letters, you can research the corrections and we'll mail them again." Candace paused to make sure Ted was paying attention. "If you're still working here, that is."

The young intern's sneer vanished. His cheeks were awash in a rosy colored heat.

In a most feral way, Candace sensed she'd regained command of the situation. She looked dispassionately at Ted and spoke calmly. "We're not off to a very good start, are we Ted? Why is that?"

"I don't have a clue," he said.

"Why don't you take a short break? Go get a cup of coffee."

"Good idea," Ted stood, smiled halfheartedly, and took a step forward. "You know, I wasn't surprised when I walked in here and saw you."

"Oh?"

"I assumed they'd find somebody like you to mentor me."

"Like me?"

"Yeah. Someone of color."

"Why did you make that assumption?"

Ted folded his arms across his chest.

"It's obvious, isn't it?"

"Not to me, Ted." Candace regarded him carefully. "Why don't you take your coffee break? There's a vendor in the lobby."

Ted righted the knot in his tie and left the office.

Candace took a series of deep breaths. She glanced at the door to assure herself it was closed and then reached into her work bag and extracted her tablet computer. After she tapped a few keys, she lowered the machine's volume, sat forward in her chair, and concentrated on the small screen. She picked up a pen and rolled it between her fingers as she waited for an image to appear. Finally, the picture she'd anticipated came into view.

Candace noted the image's date and time printed near the bottom of the screen. She listened attentively to the podcast's muted introduction.

"There you are," she said aloud. "Exactly where I figured you'd be."

A hard-knuckled knock on the door ripped Candace's attention away from her mini computer's screen. Before she could say "Come in," the door swung inward.

Ted swaggered into the office. He lifted his cardboard cup as if he were offering a toast.

"This is good stuff. Sure you don't want one, Ms. Dickerson?"

"No thanks. I've already had my one cup of caffeine for the day."

"At home, right? You never buy a cup in the lobby, do you?"

Stealthily, Candace tapped her computer and exited the podcast she'd been watching. She girded herself for another skirmish with her young intern.

"And how would you know I don't buy coffee in the lobby?"

"From the guy who runs the concession down there. Do you know who I'm talking about?"

"I'm aware there's a little booth down there manned by a loud, black man who sells newspapers and coffee."

"He's aware of you, also. He told me he speaks to you every time he sees you, but you don't even nod in his direction."

"And?" Candace asked.

"He knows most of the bigwigs here."

"Is that so?"

"I bet you didn't know he's a valuable source of information."

"You're correct. I didn't know that." Candace kept her voice neutral.

"He knows I'm a summer intern, and he asked me who I was working for. When I mentioned your name, he threw his head back and laughed."

Candace remained silent.

"He told me you think you're too good to speak to a lowly coffee seller." Ted paused. "When I didn't say anything, he must have thought you were treating me well. He got real serious."

Candace raised one eyebrow.

"He looked me in the eye and said one of these days you were going to cross the wrong goddamn person who'd sooner slap you than try to coax a good morning or good evening out of your evil self."

Candace heard the sound of her fingers as they drummed against the edge of her desk. She thought she felt her heart thump a triple beat and then skip one or two turns. She touched the side of her throat and relaxed when she felt her pulse.

"Are you all right, Ms. Dickerson? For a split second you looked alarmed."

Candace dropped her hand to her lap. "I'm fine," she said. "And I assume you know you can't believe everything you hear."

"Oh, I know that."

"Have you finished stuffing all the letters in their envelopes?"

"Yes."

"That's all the work I have for you today."

"Should I report here tomorrow morning?"

"No. Report to Marilyn Green. She'll let you know if I've requested you."

Candace focused on a stack of papers piled on her desk. She sensed Ted stood nearby, shifting his weight from one foot to the other.

"When Ms. Green assigned me to your office this morning, I was really happy. Corporate Events Planner, I said to myself. I knew I'd learn a lot from you, like how to come up with an event that would draw a lot of participation. Or how to persuade the dollars right out of the money makers' wallets." Ted's mouth stopped moving, but the excited expression in his eyes suggested he had more to say.

"Why is it I have the feeling you've mastered those skills already, Ted?"

He smiled slyly. "You may be right, Ms. Dickerson. I have a feeling you can see right through people." Once again he raised his coffee container. "Here's to my future in corporate America."

Candace dismissed Ted with one long withering glance. She watched him exit the office and then she reopened her personal computer and summoned the podcast she'd started watching during Ted's coffee break. When the program ended twenty minutes later, Candace picked up the phone.

"Hey, it's me," she said. "No, no problems. Everything is going as planned."

"I appreciate the present you gave me," the liquid voice on the phone poured sweetness into Candace's ear.

"I figured you would," Candace said. "I'll be in touch again real soon."

"Can I count on the word — touch — or will you just call?"

"The latter," Candace said.

"I'm disappointed."

"You shouldn't be. We've got a business relationship, nothing more."

All of the liquid in the woman's voice evaporated. "I'll be here, Candace."

"Good. Talk to you soon."

Candace put down the phone. "And I'll be right here for a little while longer, but not forever."

She lifted an imaginary glass and offered a toast to the far wall of her office.

"Here's to my future in a place that's far removed from corporate America. A place where no one who resembles the Honorable Baker Williamson or any of his progeny will ever again attempt to make me feel lesser than they are."

Candace pursed her lips. After a few seconds passed she tapped some keys on her computer, squinted at the screen, and then jotted a note on a piece of paper.

"Who knows? If what I suspect about our slick intern is true, I might need this address sometime soon. "

Chapter Thirteen

London's Second Encounter

"I HATE YOU for making me do this, Tee."

I disliked riding in little airplanes more than I disliked being on small boats. If the former didn't have flight attendants on board and the latter lacked stabilizers and at least two sittings for dinner, I preferred to take some other form of transportation.

"You have to admit we saved time by flying here instead of picking up a car at Logan Airport. If we'd done that, we'd still be slow-poking our way along Route Six."

I felt my stomach hurdle to my throat as the puddle jumper of a plane bounced twice on landing.

"Where did the pilot learn how to take-off and land, at Sears?"

"Shhh. He can hear you," Theresa chided.

"No doubt he can. I'm sitting so close to him, all I have to do is lean forward to touch him."

I swore I could count the hairs on the pilot's neck, and that would be after he'd had a haircut.

"You can breathe now, London." Theresa pointed to the little window. "There's the 'Welcome to Provincetown' banner."

Minutes later we stood beside our suitcases in the car rental agency's parking area outside the Provincetown Municipal Airport's terminal. I circled the compact model that I was about to rent.

With clipboard in hand, the rental agent shadowed me as I pointed to every ding and scratch I could see on the car's surface.

"Well, I think we've gotten everything. Just sign here, ma'am, and you'll be on your way. You've got a beautiful day for your arrival here on the Cape."

Theresa rested her hand atop the car's roof. She inhaled deeply. "Do you smell that sea air, London? We're really here."

"Uh-huh." I pulled my suitcase toward the rear of the car.

"And imagine, that boss of yours, Mr. Deep pockets, asked you to postpone your vacation week."

Roger hadn't asked me to postpone my vacation. He'd ordered me to change my plans. When I learned he hadn't issued the same edict to my fellow project manager, Ken Green, I told him my travel fees were nonrefundable and the workshop for which I'd registered wouldn't be offered at any other time. Maybe it was my—don't-try-to-screw-with-me—tone that persuaded Roger to be more conciliatory. I'd been able to keep my plans intact and, as far as I knew, I still had a job.

Theresa lifted her luggage and shoved it into the trunk. "Why did he ask you to cancel your week off anyway?"

"The mortgage rate hit an all-time low and all of a sudden we experienced a heck of a lot more traffic through the development. He wanted all hands on deck."

"Money. It's always about the money, isn't it London?"

"Always, Theresa." I closed the trunk and we loaded ourselves into the front seat.

"Now wasn't this a good idea? We both get a quick getaway and we've kept each other company for the trip."

I knew the expression on Theresa's face meant she was pleased with how smoothly everything had gone so far.

"You can drop me off at my bed and breakfast, and then head out to Wellfleet to your workshop."

I looked at my watch.

"With any luck, I'll get there in time for the early afternoon sessions."

I maneuvered the car out of its parking space and onto the two lane road that would take us away from the airport.

"Look at this scenery. I never get tired of seeing it."

Theresa was right. The undulating ribbon of road traveled past dunes whose windswept sand spilled onto the path in defiance of the asphalt borders. The light beige backdrop gave way to sun dappled green as the dunes ceded to the scrub pines of the beach forest. Rosa rugosa shrubs showed off their deep pinks and reds to the bike riders who peddled past them. Occasionally a walking trail that ran parallel to the road crossed over it. Sometimes, the trail hid itself from view.

Theresa and I rode along in silence around the gentle curves and over the route's gradual ups and downs. After a couple miles more, the road flattened. Ahead, a traffic light blinked and invited us to proceed toward sun bleached houses interspersed with commercial buildings of all sorts, a boat builder's yard, a liquor store, a kite and water sports' emporium.

"You're sure you won't need the car, Tee?"

"Not at all. I can walk everywhere. And if I want to go out to the beach, I'll take the P-town jitney." Theresa tapped my shoulder affectionately. "Don't worry. I'll be fine without a car. Besides, we're only up here for four days."

I turned left onto Bradford Street. "I'll call to let you know when I'm coming into town for dinner."

"I imagine that would be every day. How can you be so close to gay and lesbian heaven without spending time here?"

I laughed. "You have a point."

Most of the conferences and workshops I'd attended in the past were geared toward LGBT writers. This one wasn't, but I'd decided that was okay. Since most writing issues cut across all sorts of boundaries, the gender, race or sexuality of the workshop participants didn't matter.

It was content I was after and I planned to absorb every bit of knowledge I could, regardless of who disseminated it.

"Here we are, London. Can you park over there?"

Theresa pointed to a no stopping zone just beyond the entrance to the women-owned bed and breakfast where she had a reservation. I steered the car into the cobble-stone niche and she got out. She pulled her luggage from the car's trunk.

"Be careful. You know these Massachusetts drivers are crazy. And call me when you get settled in Wellfleet." Theresa blew me a kiss.

"Will do. I'll probably see you tomorrow night for dinner."

I watched Theresa and her suitcase approach the lodging's doorway. Satisfied she'd be fine, I gradually exited the illegal parking space and continued driving east on Bradford. Although I was eager to make my way to Wellfleet, I drove at a slug's pace. I'd driven and walked along this street many times before. I knew its slopes and its steepest incline, its absence of sidewalk on one side, its rainbow flag festooned inns, its under equipped playground for the children of overwhelmed parents, and its weathered grocery store full of promised lunch rations for day-long sojourns to the beach.

I was acquainted in the most general sense with the people of Provincetown, especially the visitors. I knew the happiness they exuded along with the freedom they'd feel for as long as they were in the little town. I knew what it meant to appreciate simply being here in this pool of acceptance, to be able to gaze unabashedly at your lover and hold hands as you walked along the streets.

Whenever I'd see a man or woman of color bob up and down in this sea of ethnic homogeneity, I always tried to make eye contact, but without staring. Those familiar strangers never stared at me either. We knew each of us were there, even if we didn't acknowledge it. I'd feel something akin to comfort just knowing I wasn't alone nor completely invisible.

Just then my thoughts brought me to Lenah Miller. I wondered if she'd ever ventured here. If she had, I imagined her making plenty of salty comments about the colored folks who'd pass her on the streets and seem to overlook her. Would she realize she wasn't being ignored? Would she decode and abide by the subtle rules at play when there are so few of us among so many of the others? Perhaps if I knew Lenah better I'd be able to guess how she'd react to the presence or lack of presence of gays of color in P-town.

Bradford Street ended in a V-shaped intersection where Route 6A became Commercial Street. With all of Provincetown behind me and Cape Cod Bay glistening to my right, I entered the narrow, populated section of 6A. I drove past the motels with their manicured sea mist moistened lawns, and then past the parade of pastel colored cottages, all named for flowers. As much as I enjoyed the view, I felt eager to get to my destination. So I tapped the accelerator with increased pressure and turned left, away from the water and toward the wider stretch of highway. The reason I'd left home before dawn and risked life and limb in a plane not much larger than a shipping crate with wings, lay a few miles ahead of me.

North Truro became Truro, and the steady traffic flowed toward Wellfleet's town line in no time at all. Soon after I left the highway and crept down a winding road of older weathered houses. I turned into a parking lot whose gray and white sign read, "Wellfleet Artists' Colony." I parked and entered the first building I saw.

"Good morning. Are you here for the Writers' Workshop?" A woman dressed in pedal pushers, a tee-shirt, and eyeglasses greeted me.

"Yes, I am."

"Are you preregistered?"

"Yes. My name's London Phillips."

The woman glanced down at a clipboard and systematically moved her finger from the top of a list of names to just below its midpoint. She picked up a pen and placed a check next to mine.

"Here you are, dear. I see you."

She looked into my face and smiled gently.

"Here's your information packet and here's a map of our facility."

"Thank you."

"I see you've reserved a room across the street at the Captain's Quarters Inn."

"Yes, that's right."

"If you check in right away, you'll have enough time to freshen up and attend all of this afternoon's sessions."

I hurried back to the parking lot. If I hadn't been burdened with a suitcase, I would've left the car where it was. Instead, I drove across the street, parked in an area adjacent to the Captain's Quarters', and claimed my room. After I hung some slacks and a couple of shirts, I decided to make two phone calls.

Although she'd asked me to call her once I'd arrived in Wellfleet, Theresa didn't answer her phone.

"Hey, Tee. I'm here. Hope you're at the beach or in the shops. Talk to you tomorrow."

Next, I checked in with Susan at Oak Hill Estates.

"Hi, it's London. How's it going?"

"Just fine, London. Are you on the Cape?"

"Yup. Have you had much business today?" I asked.

"Only moderate. You're not missing anything out of the ordinary."

"Have you heard anything more regarding Rand Carson's offer on the model?"

"Yes, unfortunately. She sent us an e-mail and followed it with a phone call. She's no longer interested in the model or in any of our houses, for that matter."

"Did she give you a reason? Was it the storm damage?"

"When I spoke to her she was pretty honest. She said she'd miscalculated her resources and she didn't want to be saddled with a huge mortgage at this stage of her life."

I visualized the woman I'd met in our office. She neither looked nor spoke like a person whose financial resources were limited.

"Well, that's disappointing. How about the repairs? Are they almost finished?"

"The roof, siding, and exterior trim are finished. The painter should be done this afternoon, and the new carpeting goes in tomorrow. After that, Corporate will request the inspections."

"Great."

"London, you're supposed to be at a workshop. Soak up the learning and enjoy yourself. Everything's fine on this end."

"If you say so. Good-bye."

I didn't have much time left to get to the first of the afternoon sessions, so I decided to forego freshening up and instead, grab a quick snack at a convenience store I'd noticed two doors away from the Inn. I bought an apple, a pack of cheese crackers, and a large cup of coffee that would fill my stomach and keep me awake.

I'd seen symbols of picnic tables and benches when I examined the map the woman gave me, so I set off in search of them. It didn't take me much time to find a table in the shade of a grove of trees not far from the Wellfleet Artists' Colony's cluster of buildings. Nor did it take a long time before someone sat across from me at that same table."Hello," I mumbled. My mouth had to share the one word greeting with a rather large chunk of apple.

"Hi, there. I'm Allen. Allen Satterwaite."

I extended my hand.

"I'm London Phillips."

"Well, that's better than London Bridges, isn't it? Or London England?"

Based upon that one question, I was certain if Allen Satterwaite were a writer, he had nothing new to express, no novel twists of language, nor inventive turns of character. I stared at him and then took another big bite from my piece of fruit.

"You're right," I said between crunches. "London wouldn't be a good first name for anyone whose surname is Bridges or England, or Ontario for that matter."

The vacant expression in his eyes told me Mr. Satterwaite was not a student of geography. His failure to notice there was a disconnect between the sweetness in my voice and the lack of a smile on my lips told me he hadn't mastered the finer points of reading body language either.

"So far, this has been a terrific workshop, hasn't it?"

"I can't say. I just got here an hour ago."

"Did you sit in on Julie Bradshaw's presentation last night?"

"I haven't had a chance to go to any of the presentations. I've been here only an hour," I said, this time a bit louder and devoid of any apple parts in my mouth.

I successfully fought the impulse to say that I'd sat on Julie Bradshaw's face last night, because I didn't want to alienate Mr. Satterwaite. For all I knew, he might have been the only other black person attending this event. I hoped to hell that wasn't the case, but in case it was, I didn't want to risk his enmity.

I was used to being in workplaces, social events, and writers' conferences where I was the sole person of color and from time to time, I'd felt a particular kind of loneliness. Layers of isolation accumulated silently until I'd reached a breaking point and unconsciously begun to seek the company of someone, anyone in whose eyes I wouldn't appear different. I'd feel free to be who I was, with no explanations necessary.

"Do you write fiction or nonfiction?" Allen asked.

"Mostly fiction. How about you?" I feigned interest in his response.

"I write both. Some poetry also. And I have a weekly blog."

"No kidding."

"Wanna know the blog's name?"

I didn't have it in me to say yes. Instead, I nodded and prayed the last bit of half chewed apple would slide down my throat without choking me.

"Can't Wait for Satterwaite." He slapped the top of the picnic table.

"No kidding."

I figured his ears were so full of his own voice, he hadn't noticed I'd uttered the same monotone answer twice in less than fifteen seconds.

"Right. Right. Can't Wait for Satterwaite," he repeated.

"What a play on words," I offered as I glanced to the left and right and searched for an escape route.

"Oh, Ms. Phillips. I'm glad I found you."

The kind woman who checked my registration information stood next to me. She held a small vinyl rectangle with a lanyard attached to it.

"When you arrived, I forgot to give you your ID badge."

"Thank you."

"But I see you're sitting here and missing the first round of afternoon panels," the woman chided.

I was more thankful than embarrassed that she'd caught me playing hooky. Her interruption was a perfect excuse for me to pick up my cup of coffee and flee.

I turned my wrist so I could see my watch clearly.

"Oh, no. I didn't want to miss anything. I'm off."

I stuffed the pack of crackers in my pocket, scooped up the coffee container, and stood up.

"The panels are in C Building, dear, over there."

I glanced at the sun drenched path she pointed to and hurried away.

"Nice meeting you, London. Maybe we can have dinner together." Allen Satterwaite addressed what was left of my shadow.

My hand shot up in the air and flickered a quick wave as I kept moving. I couldn't imagine a worse plan for dinner.

Building C, a gray three story stone and clapboard structure, stood exactly in the middle of the Artists' Colony's campus. As soon as I entered the foyer, I spotted a large easel propped against one of the walls. I skimmed the text written on it and read the location of the panel I wanted to attend.

"How Can We Tell Their Stories? Journalists Cross Many Lines."

I sped to the room, slipped in through the partially open door, and stood motionlessly in the back. The discussion had started already and at first glance, the room appeared to be filled. A man wearing a multicolored badge stood near the front. He looked my way and signaled there was a chair available. I advanced toward him, quietly and as unobtrusively as possible. It wasn't my habit to arrive anywhere late.

Just as I reached the row with the empty seat, I heard one of the two female panelists exclaim, "But that's the point I've been trying to make. Why aren't there more Latino and African American journalists writing for the major newspapers in this country? Why aren't there more minority journalists writing for the major news magazines? In fact, why aren't there Latino and African American journalists sitting on this panel and attending this writers' workshop?"

I was galvanized in place. I stood stock still and felt the blood abandon my legs, arms and core and rush to my face. My cheeks and forehead burned. I forgot all about the chair I'd been aiming for. I focused straight ahead at no one in particular in the sea of faces surrounding me. Silently I prayed that every soul in that room would stop staring at me and expecting I'd somehow address the panelist's question. I had a response, but the timing of my entrance killed even the remotest possibility I'd deliver it.

Mortified, I imagined my late arrival suggested a congenital problem with punctuality was the answer to the panelist's query.

"They'd get ahead in life if they wouldn't be late for school, late to the opening of doors of opportunity, late to interviews for journalism jobs at newspapers and magazines," the unspoken chorus of onlookers were no doubt thinking.

"She could have been on the panel if she'd gotten here on time," they probably said to themselves.

Just as I recovered my equilibrium, I heard the panelist who had asked the first question fire a second one and utter the words "gay and lesbian."

I sat down and willed my ears to concentrate on what was being said, but concentrating was difficult. How could I concentrate if I could barely breathe? There was no air left in the room. All the oxygen had been sucked out of it the moment the panelist launched her two questions.

I took a long look at the two men and two women seated on the platform. Shocked, I did a double-take when I saw one of the two female panelists, the one who'd unleashed the unanswered questions. Rand Carson, the woman I'd met weeks ago in my sales office, the woman who'd just reneged on buying a new house at Oak Hill Estates, sat there, nodding in agreement with one of the other speakers.

Chapter Fourteen

Rand's Second Encounter

FROM HER PLACE among the panelists seated on the raised platform, Rand had a clear view of everyone and everything in the room. She watched the workshop's official photographer move from one side of the room to the other. She was aware of the placement of the videographer's camera and microphones. From her vantage point, Rand saw London Phillips enter the room, glance quickly at row after row of the occupied seats, and then nod at the workshop's organizer when he summoned her to a vacant chair.

Even as she fired her questions about the dearth of minority journalists and the pitiful lack of black and Latino participants at this conference, Rand concentrated on London's stutter-step, on the whispered "excuse me's" and "thank you's" she saw flutter from London's lips. She barely heard the other panelists' responses to her first query.

When she added, "Not to mention gay and lesbian journalists. Why must that community have its own press, segregated from the mainstream papers?" she was barely aware of the half answers, incomplete phrases, and promises of further inclusion that swirled above the panelists' table.

Rand was surprised when she'd met London at Oak Hill Estates, but she wasn't at all startled to see her enter the room today. Months earlier, long before she met her in the development's sales model, Rand had seen London's name on a list of registered conference participants. As recently as two days ago, during the ferry ride from Martha's Vineyard back to the mainland, she found herself thinking about London when she considered Jonathan's description of the woman who'd visited the Oak Bluffs bookstore and interrogated him.

It couldn't be her, Rand thought. She'd stood against a railing, watching the persistent wake and cast overboard any possibility that Jonathan's inquisitor and the Oak Hill Estates' sales manager were the same person.

Now Rand left her chair and stepped down from the platform. She scanned the fourth row and saw nothing other than empty seats.

"Ms. Carson, I liked your comments about a journalist's personal beliefs interfering with the story they're assigned to write."

Rand heard the young man and she appreciated his polite approach. But she was distracted.

"Thanks."

She glanced at him quickly and then looked toward the back of the room where she spotted the receding figure of the woman whose arrival had reminded her to raise a topic everyone else preferred to ignore.

Rand threaded her way past a collage of faces. When she stepped outside the room, she spotted London's blue shirted form near the display board at the end of the hallway. Slowly she walked toward London.

"Ms. Phillips?"

London turned her head toward the sound of her name.

"Ms. Carson."

Rand offered her outstretched hand.

"It's great to see you here. And please call me Rand."

"Call me London."

"That's a wonderful name," Rand said.

London met Rand's compliment with a look of skepticism.

"I don't hear that kind of comment often."

"Did your parents have a reason for naming you London?"

London gazed steadily at Rand. "Probably so I could be someone other than who I am."

"Wow. That sounds interesting. You must have some intriguing tales to tell."

"Everyone has intriguing tales to tell, don't you think?" London asked.

"Well, I think yours is a great name for a writer or a character."

"You can use it anytime you want," said London. "But you're a journalist. You don't write fiction."

"That's right, I don't," Rand said. "I saw your name listed online in the program booklet, and then when I met you at Oak Hill I figured there couldn't be two women named London Phillips."

"That would be quite a coincidence, wouldn't it?"

"When I spoke to Susan Rafferty recently, she mentioned you'd be out of the office for a week, and that sealed the deal. I knew we'd run into each other up here."

"I spoke to Susan a little while ago and she told me you'd changed your mind about buying one of our homes."

Rand blinked quickly. "Yes, that's true. When I thought carefully about the size of that investment, I decided it wasn't a good idea, at least, not right now."

London nodded.

"There will be other new houses," she said. "Who knows what the future will bring?"

The women remained silent for a few seconds before Rand spoke again.

"I didn't expect to see you at that last discussion. Are you interested in journalism?"

"I'm interested in all kinds of writing," London said.

"Great. Which session are you going to next?"

"I thought I'd sit in on the one about defeating writer's block. How about you?"

"I'm going to my room to have a nap. I had an early start this morning." Rand pointed over her shoulder toward the room they'd left minutes ago. "That was my second stint on a panel today."

"Sounds like you've earned a nap."

Rand shifted her weight from one foot to the other.

"Well, I guess we'll run into one another again. This workshop is comprehensive, but it's not huge."

"You're right. I'll probably see you later."

Rand took a few steps backward as London shifted her attention from their conversation to the information posted on the board in front of her. The women withdrew from each other and headed in different directions.

Chapter Fifteen

Dinner For One

AT THE END of another routine day, Lenah Miller shifted her bag of take-out food from one hand to the other. She opened the front door to her house, stuffed her keys in her pants pocket, and bent down to retrieve the day's mail. There were no incorrectly addressed envelopes for Candace today, no new contributions for the kindling basket.

Lenah walked to the kitchen and put her dinner on the counter. When she turned and used her foot to nudge one of the stools away from its place under the kitchen island's counter, she noticed the answering machine's blinking light. She reached over and pushed the *play* button.

"Lenah, this is London Phillips calling. I hope you're well. I'm up here on Cape Cod, but I'll be back home by the weekend. I wondered if you'd like to meet somewhere for dinner this coming Sunday. Give me a call when you have a chance. Bye."

Lenah pressed *repeat* and listened to the message once again. This time she grinned.

"Dinner next Sunday will be fine," she said aloud.

She pushed *play* once again and listened to a second message, one delivered by a harsh businesslike voice that took Lenah by surprise and stole the smile from her lips.

"Lenah, it's me. I've been expecting to receive an important piece of mail. I phoned the sender and was told they didn't have my present address. They sent the mail to your house. Please bring it to work with you tomorrow. I'll stop by and get it."

Lenah pounded the answering machine's *stop* button.

"Do I look like the fuckin' Post Office?" she asked the empty room.

She picked up the phone and punched ten keys. While she waited for Candace to answer, Lenah paced back and forth from one end of the kitchen to the other.

"Hello?"

"It's me. And yes, I have a piece of your mail."

"Hmm. When were you going to reroute it?"

Lenah didn't answer.

"That's illegal you know," Candace snapped. "I'll come to the hospital and pick it up next Tuesday."

"Fine. You know where to find me."

"I assume you're still behind the same desk in the same place, doing the same job."

"All day long," Lenah said.

She raced to put down her phone before Candace could end their conversation. Then she opened the refrigerator and navigated her hand past the cartons of milk and juice until her fingers made contact with the cold slim neck of a bottle of hard lemonade. Lenah yanked it from its place and spun around to face the lower cabinets. She tugged open the cutlery drawer and extracted an old rusty bottle opener. Deftly she slid it under the serrated edges of the bottle cap. She lifted the ancient tool so quickly that the metal bottle top flew off its mooring, arced into the air, and then came clanging down to the floor.

Lenah left it there, staring up at her. She put the bottle to her lips and took four long gulps of the liquid before she slammed the glass container down on the countertop. She abandoned the drink and strode into the living room where she confronted the wicker basket on the hearth. She bent down to examine the collection of envelopes and circulars she'd left there, her kindling-in-waiting. After a few seconds, she plucked one of the newest arrivals, read the name and address of its sender, and smoothed its slightly worn edges.

"Time to go to your rightful owner, you poor thing."

Lenah moved toward the old sofa and sank into its worn cushions. She tossed the piece of mail onto the coffee table in front of her. Her tongue felt the absence of the hard lemonade's tart sweetness and she remembered she'd left the bottle in the kitchen, still half full. But she lacked the will to go back and retrieve it.

Lenah sat there, completely still. She pictured Candace as she might appear next Tuesday when they'd see each other at the hospital. Her stomach began a roller coaster ride through familiar twists and turns. She could no longer recall any of the excitement and joy that used to be present whenever Candace was near. Instead, there was an ever growing mound of resentment. Lenah realized that during her lifetime, she'd had ample reason to dislike a few people. Never before though, had she felt such anger and hatred toward a woman who seemed determined to bring her unhappiness.

Lenah glared at the envelope on the table.

"Why the hell haven't I just forwarded her mail?"

She picked up the television's remote control, pushed the on button, and then paid no attention to the images on the screen. She reached for a nearby phone and tapped the numbers that might distract her from all her aggravation. After she listened to a pre-recorded message, she left a message of her own.

"Hey, London. Thanks for calling. Sunday dinner sounds like a plan. Give me a call when you get settled in from your trip. Bye."

Calm settled over Lenah's shoulders. Then hunger arrived and reminded her to return to the kitchen and warm her take-out meal. First though, she arose from the sofa, went to her laptop, and made her daily offering to her diary of very few words.

"Weather report: Sunday's predicted clear weather will protect me from Tuesday's acid rain."

Chapter Sixteen

Dinner For Three

DINNERTIME IN PROVINCETOWN starts as soon as the befuddled day trippers stumble along MacMillan Wharf in search of a clam roll or foot long hotdog they can devour before their crowded bus departs for its next stop. It ends at whatever hour the bleary-eyed club goers, who've mixed cheap wine and beer with mozzarella and mushrooms, weave their way out of the Greek owned pizza palace on Commercial Street, and head toward their bed and breakfast lodgings.

In between these two extremes, everyone else has had to find a place to eat. Parents of all sexualities push baby carriages and imitate tow trucks as they haul their tee-ball team eligible tots toward the *children's-platters-available* restaurants. Singles and couples do their best to avoid the four-wheel-drive baby conveyances, especially after six o'clock when parents and kids spill back onto the streets, overfed and in a carbohydrate-laden stupor.

I chose the second day of the workshop to get into my rented car and drive from Wellfleet to P-town. I parked in a municipal lot at the top of a hill and walked down Bradford Street to meet Theresa in front of her inn.

"Hey, London. Did you bring all this humidity with you?"

I looked at the sheen that clung to my arms.

"It followed me from Wellfleet. It was so hot and sticky there I could hardly think."

Theresa grabbed my arm.

"Are you enjoying your conference?"

"I am, Tee. Mostly, I'm learning a lot."

Theresa feigned a headache and massaged her temples.

"Learning a lot? In the summertime? While you're in beautiful Cape Cod? That sounds too painful for words."

I laughed. "Okay, let's change the subject. Where do you want to eat?"

Theresa steered us across an intersection. We walked past Provincetown's City Hall where we watched a cop tuck a parking ticket under a car's windshield wiper blade. Two skateboarders zoomed past us and then slowed their speed in deference to the crowds spilling from the sidewalk on Commercial Street.

"Where do I want to eat? Where else?" Theresa pointed to a restaurant on the right hand side of the street, a block away from where we were.

"I wanted to go there last night, but I thought I'd wait 'til you could join me."

"See, this is why I ate a late lunch, Tee. We're hot, sweaty, and about to ignore half a dozen restaurants with available tables so we can stand in a long line outside The Tourist Pot."

That's the name I'd given to the perpetually crowded restaurant that always attracted Theresa. The place was like an industrial sized magnet and Theresa was a five-foot-four sheet of metal.

We'd walked just short of the restaurant's entrance.

"Look, the line's not that long," Theresa said. "It not even to the front door."

Dutifully I followed my friend through the entryway and we joined the line of hungry customers. I stepped slightly to the left to count the bodies standing between us and a good meal. Fifteen, maybe sixteen people would claim a table before we'd be seated.

"How many?" one of the hosts asked.

"Just two," I answered, hoping the word—just—carried a certain élan that would get us seated before a larger group was accommodated.

"Name?"

"Phillips."

I didn't ask how long we'd have to wait because I didn't want to hear the answer.

"Party of eight!" A different host, a female, summoned a clutch of diners lined up ahead of us.

Theresa turned toward me.

"This won't be too bad," she said. "Not like the last time."

I lowered my head and looked at her from above the rim of my sunglasses. Two summers ago we'd stood in line so long I swore my birthday had come and gone. I'd been so hungry I hallucinated the evening had become the next day and the daily special had changed from fried scrod to broiled halibut.

With the absence of the party of eight, we moved closer to the dining room.

The aroma of cooked seafood hung like a cloud just above our heads. As the fragrance settled over us, it teased our appetites with delicious promises. Because I didn't know how long we'd be held captive by the odors of seafood, chowder and warm bread, I opted to forget I was hungry and concentrate on my conversation with Theresa.

"So how's your mini-vacation going?" I asked.

"Wonderful. I've gone to the beach twice, done some shopping, been to the bar and cut a rug."

"You've packed a lot into a day and a half."

"And I've had the nicest conversations over breakfast with some of the other guests at the B and B."

I winked.

"With anyone in particular?"

"No, no one in particular. Everyone seems to be partnered."

Theresa pouted for a second and then looked beyond my shoulder. She was staring at something or someone.

"Now if I saw her all alone at breakfast, I'd be happy to share my granola," she said.

"Who?"

"A woman standing in line behind us. It looks like she's by herself and she keeps staring and half smiling, like she knows us."

"Should I turn around and look?"

"Most definitely. She's wearing a black shirt and she's got short gray hair. Her glasses are propped atop her head."

I pivoted ever so subtly and gazed where I thought Theresa had spotted her woman of interest. Rand Carson stood yards away from us, smiling. I knew Theresa and her equal opportunity attraction to all women wouldn't mind, so I gestured for Rand to come closer.

"Rand, this is my friend, Theresa. Theresa, this is Rand. She's a journalist and she's one of the presenters at the workshop I'm attending."

"It's a pleasure." Rand shook Theresa's hand.

"Are you waiting for someone?" I asked.

I swear I noticed the quickest spark of amusement light Rand's eyes and then extinguish itself before she answered my question.

"No. I struck out alone tonight. I decided to come here because it's always so crowded, I wouldn't feel like I was eating by myself."

"Well, you're not going to eat by yourself now, Rand."

Theresa could be so charming and hospitable whether I wanted her to be that way or not.

"Phillips!" the hostess shouted.

I raised my hand to signal we were here, and the three of us followed her to a table. Barely able to keep up with her, I yelled at her back.

"We're three now instead of two."

"No problem."

The woman grabbed an extra set of cutlery from a trolley and a chair from a nearby table. She put everything in place in the time it took the three of us to be seated.

"Enjoy your meal."

"Yes, ma'am."

My sarcasm got lost in the woman's wake.

I spied Theresa peering at Rand from above the edge of her menu.

"So you're a journalist? Are you the same Rand Carson who writes for the Inquirer?"

"That would be me."

"Well isn't this grand? I'm about to have dinner with two writers, Rand Carson and London Phillips."

"You'll find we chew our food just like everyone else," Rand said. "But you might see us editing the menu's text."

Theresa smiled tentatively at Rand.

I liked slightly irreverent humor, so if that's what Rand had to offer, we were in for an amusing evening. To be honest, I was glad for the opportunity to get to know her better. The writing student in me constantly sought little wedges of advice about the craft, and my realtor persona was eager to learn why we hadn't been able to negotiate a deal with Rand and sell her a Kensington-built home.

"I was on the lookout for you today, but I didn't see you in any of the sessions I attended," Rand said. An easy smile played at her lips.

"I kept busy. This morning I went to the master class about character development, and I split the afternoon between poetry readings and attending the discussion about editors and what they really want to see in our manuscripts."

Rand nodded.

"I imagine all that activity kept you out of trouble."

"Indeed. And...I arrived promptly for each session."

"You're always on time, London," Theresa said. "I've never known you to be late."

"Thanks, Tee. But I wasn't on time yesterday afternoon when I arrived at one of Rand's panels."

"I saw you walk in. You seemed flustered," Rand said softly.

"I was flustered. I felt like your question focused everyone's attention on me." I turned to Theresa to explain my embarrassment.

"There I was, Tee, walking in late just as Rand asked the panel why there weren't more black and Latino journalists writing for mainstream publications. Before anyone could answer, she raised a similar one about the scarcity of LGBT writers."

"Oh boy." Theresa shook her head.

Reinvigorated by the memory of yesterday's embarrassment, I shifted my gaze from Theresa to Rand.

"Were you planning to ask those questions all along or did my late arrival prime the pump?"

"Your arrival wasn't related to the timing of my questions. It was just a happy coincidence. Really."

"Happy for whom?" My indignation arose in tandem with my distrust of Rand's answer.

"Obviously, it wasn't one of your most comfortable moments," Rand said.

Theresa alternated glancing at Rand and then at me, much like someone engrossed by a tennis match.

"When you're on those panels you get used to people coming in after you've begun, or leaving smack in the middle of the discussion. It happens all the time. People sit and listen for ten minutes, get bored with what they're hearing, and then get up and go to a different presentation that's in progress."

"You may have missed my point," I said.

Theresa's face reflected empathy. She clasped her hands together, almost prayerfully.

"I was embarrassed I was late," I continued. "Your question placed the spotlight directly on me. I felt everyone was staring and pointing their finger at me, if only metaphorically."

"Why did you feel so embarrassed?" Rand asked.

I had neither the words nor the energy to explain to her how history played a role in some of my behaviors. The reasons I'd always followed certain rules were so multi-layered and complex, sometimes it was difficult for me to understand them. All I knew was that my life was easier if I avoided breaking those rules. Questioning their genesis or the rightness of adhering to them could be painful.

"Was it because you think white people still believe the false stereotype about blacks always being late?" Rand asked.

There it was, out in the open. I glared at Rand and tried to decide if I thought she believed the stereotype was true.

"Let's simply agree that you couldn't possibly know how I felt," I said. "Even if you thought you knew, you'd be once removed from the discomfort."

"Agreed," Rand said. She seemed unflappable.

I didn't know whether I admired or resented her composure. At the very least, it threw me off track.

"I'm starved. Is anyone else hungry?" Theresa asked.

I ignored her attempt to bring harmony to our dinner table and continued to skewer Rand.

"Had you planned to raise the gay question also?"

"Absolutely. Did that make you as uncomfortable as the black and Latino topic?"

"I was beyond uncomfortable."

"Why? Are you embarrassed you're gay?" Rand asked.

Just then her words sounded accusatory and her composure looked more like arrogance than equanimity.

"Hardly," I said. "The blurb that's printed in the workshop's program describes my work as lesbian centric."

I knew anger seared the edge of my voice.

"Just because lesbian characters figure prominently in your books doesn't mean you're a lesbian. Fictitious characters don't necessarily define the author's identity."

Theresa sat forward and bestowed a supplicant gaze on both of us. "Have you decided what you're going to order for dinner, other than a debate?" she asked.

"Oh, sorry Tee."

I frowned and then looked directly at Rand.

"You're right of course. But in my case, I've written about what and whom I know."

Rand reached for her glass of water and took several sips.

"I haven't read your work yet, London, but I've read some of the online commentary about it."

"And?"

Why did I suddenly feel like the defensive freshman English student who was seeking an explanation for an undeserved low grade?

"And I wouldn't want any author to limit herself to writing solely about the world she knows."

"Understood."

So it was a professional opinion Rand doled out, not a justification for negative criticism.

"London's like a sponge," Theresa said. "She soaks up everything she hears."

"That's a good thing," Rand answered.

And with those four words from Rand I sensed an end to our contentiousness. The three of us talked about other things, LGBT civil rights, the next presidential election, the summer's annual film festival, and whether either Theresa or I had ever visited Martha's Vineyard.

I didn't learn anything more about Rand's journalism career other than the frustrations she'd experienced with different editors from time to time. The trade-offs for those aggravations had been the satisfaction she's had doing a job that involved her passion for writing, and her ability to earn a decent living from words. I heard her say she suspected she had a novel lurking within her, one which she wasn't eager to bring forth.

"To devote a few years of my life writing fiction demands the kind of self-sacrifice I'm not willing to give right now," she said. "Frankly, London, I don't know how you manage to write and work full time."

Lines crisscrossing her forehead emphasized her skepticism.

"It's not the lack of time that bothers me as much as the obstacles I run into. That's why I was eager to sit in on the presentation about writer's block. A short while ago I found myself in the middle of one of those brain dead periods. It suddenly occurred to me I could stop beating myself about not writing and invite some writers I know, or whom I've read, to submit stories for an anthology."

Of all the topics we touched upon, it was our chat about lesbian fiction that sparked Rand's enthusiasm more than anything else. Her knowledge of black LGBT literature stunned me. It was wide and deep, impressive for someone whose thirsts for reading weren't necessarily quenched by only reading books written by and about queer blacks.

When I mentioned my ardor for Milagros Farrow's work, Rand agreed Farrow was a skillful writer with a wide readership.

"It's a shame she's slipped out of view this past year," I said. "My anthology is going to the printer minus one of her pieces."

"I read somewhere that Milagros is ill, that she has some kind of chronic condition that exhausts her, and she's decided she's not going to publish anything else," Rand said.

"Really?"

How could I have missed seeing that in my online groups and review sites, I wondered. A chronic illness...exhausted...no more books from Milagros Farrow.

Dinner ended and our conversation wound down.

"This has been an unexpected pleasure. Thanks for letting me join you two."

"We enjoyed it also, Rand," Theresa said.

"It's been wonderful meeting you, Theresa. London, maybe I'll see you tomorrow."

The sky wasn't totally dark as we stood just outside the restaurant. The reflection of the red light from the eatery's huge neon lobster shone in our eyes. Rand tapped Theresa's arm. Then she faced me and offered her hand. I accepted it and gazed at our palms and fingers clasped together. It was one of those moments whose recollection you know you'll revisit when you least expect to.

"Are you parked nearby?" Theresa asked.

"Just a block or two from here." Rand waved toward the street. "Would you believe I found a spot on Commercial Street?"

"You must have good parking karma," I said.

Theresa and I watched Rand step away from the sidewalk and onto the street. We set off in the opposite direction, headed first to Tee's bed and breakfast and from there the parking lot where I'd left my car.

"She seems nice, London."

"Yup."

"Her politics are correct."

"Are they?" I asked. "I'm not totally sure about that."

We turned from Commercial Street to the less traveled walkway that ran parallel to Town Hall.

"I wonder why she decided against buying one of your company's new houses."

I didn't fill in an explanation for the failed real estate deal because I needed to protect Rand's privacy.

"If she was planning to buy there, maybe she lives in that general area, not far from where you live."

"Possibly," I said.

"Didn't you check out her address when you reviewed her paperwork?"

"Tee, how am I supposed to remember that information? And anyway, her present address is confidential."

"Oh I know that. And you'd keep her confidence. You're the consummate professional."

We stopped and stood in the driveway outside Theresa's lodging.

"You're not interested in her?" Theresa dangled her question in front of me as if it were a weighted fishing lure.

I looked down at the cobblestones beneath my feet and thought of all the roles Theresa played, matchmaker was my least favorite.

"You know, Tee, it's easier to be in a relationship with a person who already understands how the world treats you without your having to explain it over and over again."

"Granted, but you're not going to receive that understanding from every black woman you date."

Lenah Miller's image raced through my mind. I wondered how well she would understand me.

"No doubt you're right," I said. "But something tells me dating Rand Carson would be too complicated."

"Who knows? She might be worth a complication or two."

I shook my head. "I'm not signing on for any problems."

"Well then, you might as well sign on for being alone." Theresa pressed her lips together.

"Alone isn't synonymous with lonely, Tee."

"I know you want everything to be nice and neat, London. But life's not like that. Just when you think you've got your ducks in a row, one of them steps out of line."

"Yeah, that's been my experience, all right."

"So you've had a couple of losses in your life. Who hasn't? You've got to put all that in the past. You're not planning on being by yourself forever, are you?"

"That's just it, Tee. I'm not planning anything beyond walking up the street to the parking lot, getting in my car, and driving back to Wellfleet."

"What about tomorrow?" Theresa asked. "You'll probably run into her at the workshop."

"Tomorrow will take care of itself. And the day after that, we fly back home."

"You frustrate the hell out of me, London. Don't you need some romance in your life?"

"I need love more than romance, Tee. I need someone who'll accept who I am and cradle my deepest secrets without holding them against me. I want someone who, a few years from now, will embrace my plump aging body, respect that I haven't dipped into the dye pot and disguised my gray hair, and then smile as she recalls all the experiences we've had, the happy ones as well as the difficult ones."

Theresa grew solemn.

"You've thought about this a lot, haven't you?"

"Whenever I've had a free moment between selling houses or writing my stories."

I grinned at Theresa and hugged her before I continued on to the parking lot. As I drove parallel to Cape Cod Bay and past the Shore Route's parade of motels, I replayed pieces of our dinner conversation and tried to figure out if Rand Carson was truly color blind or simply adept at saying the right things.

When I steered the car to the road that leads to Wellfleet, I found myself thinking about the phone message I'd left earlier that day for Lenah. Had I been wise to suggest we see each other again? If Lenah had been at home to answer my call, would her voice have had a chill in it or the warmth of someone whose text messages had overlapped mine with increased frequency and deeper familiarity?

Why did I want to see her again? I didn't know her, not really. I had no idea if we shared enough qualities in common to explore a friendship, much less any other kind of relationship. When I remembered the conversation we'd shared over drinks, I was struck by the notion that I might have more in common with Rand than with Lenah. That notion troubled me, so I exiled it from my mind. I refused to let it tamp down my interest in Lenah.

After all, both Lenah and I were black. Our common ethnicity would bond us. We'd understand the things which go unsaid between sisters of the same skin. We'd speak a common language, comprehend the same subtleties, dance the same dance, hum the same tunes. We wouldn't need to explain things to each other. Or would we? Would we need to bridge the divide that separates the city from the suburbs? Would the harsh edges I sensed in Lenah run roughshod over the softer contours she sensed in me?

In the seconds before I ceded my tired self to a restless sleep, my thoughts turned to Milagros Farrow. Was her fatigue similar to the exhaustion I felt tonight? What kind of illness did she have that would rob her of days filled with words ready to tumble from her head and land across the pages of some new novel? How difficult had it been for her to come to terms with the certainty that there would be no more new stories, no more new books?

Chapter Seventeen

One Unfulfilled Obsession is Better Than None at All

SPENT, AFTER TWO short airplane flights interspersed with long waits in the overcooled air of two different airports, I stuffed my dirty laundry into the washing machine and then sought revival from the other end of the telephone.

"When did you get back?" Lenah asked.

"Thirty minutes ago."

"I'm looking forward to seeing you on Sunday."

"I'm looking forward to that, also."

"You wouldn't happen to be free this evening, would you?"

"I'm totally free," I said.

From the night I'd had dinner with Theresa and Rand in P-Town, until this very second, I'd thought a great deal about Lenah Miller. Numerous text messages and e-mails passed between us each day I was at the workshop and I'd found myself paying more attention to my cell phone and computer than to any of the speakers I'd heard or panels I'd attended.

I imagined sitting down with Lenah, asking her questions about herself, and then blending her answers with pieces of my own history. I created a storyboard in which we confessed and compared our various romances. I wondered if Lenah had known more women than I had. I figured she had. Probably she wasn't the kind of person who would have spent a lot of time and energy building a relationship from its romantic foundation to its multi-storied final product. She was the type of woman who tasted closure the first time she kissed a new lover's mouth...over and over again.

By the time I'd returned home from the Cape, I couldn't wait to see Lenah. I'd be better prepared for our next meeting because I knew going in, that this time I'd be the one asking most of the questions and evaluating the answers.

Once in a while during the past few days I'd let my imagination wander from musing about a platonic friendship with Lenah, to daydreaming about exploring a more intimate relationship with her.

What would happen if I told Lenah I was attracted to her? What if she told me she felt the same way? What if Lenah held me and then moved her lips against my ear and whispered my name? What if I felt I could trust allowing her hands to travel the breadth and length of me? What if I gave her mouth permission to learn the geography of my body?

I became so carried away with my fantasies about Lenah, the things that had mattered the most to me recently became blurred in the background. A new Kensington Builders ad campaign I had to plan, a last minute effort to research Milagros Farrow's whereabouts, and a final pre-print review of the anthology all faded like the images on an ancient photograph found in someone's attic. Even Theresa's intermittent chatter during our return trip was no more than a soundtrack of garbled white noise.

When I stepped into my house, I ignored the stack of mail piled on the floor near the front door. Every envelope remained sealed, every circular and magazine was unread. Phone messages were not retrieved, and the grocery list remained unwritten. I postponed my scheduled phone consultation with Susan Rafferty until some other time.

I was as certain that the mail would be read eventually, the messages answered, the new houses at Oak Hill Estates sold, as I was sure the summer's furious heat and humidity would saunter into fall's russet, gold, and orange. But none of that would happen today while I held on to my obsession with getting to know Lenah Miller.

Tonight I'd block those bits of common sense that stood between the rock solid realistic me and the me that needed connection with someone like Lenah. I'd let myself be seduced by her bold glances and imagined innuendos. I'd act on my infatuation with the possibility that we were mutually attracted to each other.

Tomorrow morning we'd each appraise the other, perhaps comfortably, perhaps warily. Lenah would admit being pleasantly surprised and confess she'd mistaken me for a woman who was not at home in her skin or culture.

I'd mention her surgically precise probe of my thoughts, values, and opinions had failed to cut away the layers of my identity. Instead, the probe reinforced my certainty of who I was. I'd lean in close and brush her lips with mine. Then, I'd pronounce her my miracle of the day.

At least, that's what I envisioned before two phone calls ripped me away from my imagination and restored me to reality.

"London, I have to cancel our plans for tonight. The guy who works the overnight shift just called in sick. I have a chance to do a double shift and I can really use that extra cash."

"Sure," I answered. "I understand. I'll see you on Sunday, like we'd planned."

But I didn't understand how Lenah could trade our encounter for the pittance of the overtime pay she'd receive for working an extra stint in the hospital's Emergency Department.

"You have to trust that everything always happens for the best, London."

My father's oft repeated words draped themselves over my cold disappointment, and I pushed myself into the laundry room to face the sterile metal box that was the clothes dryer. I stood there and mechanically folded piece after piece of the clothing I'd worn during my stay on Cape Cod. I dragged myself up to the second floor, pulled open drawers, and gathered hangars to shelter the still arm shirts, slacks, and underwear.

During one of my robotic trips to the closet, I heard the unrelenting "bing" of the answering machine on my night table. Messages. A queue of them tugged at me with the persistence of a gaggle of children clamoring to jump into a wading pool on a swelteringly hot summer afternoon. I ambled closer and picked up a pen so I could jot down each one of the caller's names.

My supervisor, Sandra Linton, summoned me to a Project Directors' meeting at Kensington Builders' headquarters next Monday morning. Autumn was approaching, and Timothy Belton, our home stager, was scheduled to visit Oak Hill Estates to update his seasonal décor magic in each of the models.

Annoyed, I put down the pen and felt my shoulders sag as I continued to wrestle with my disappointment about the aborted evening with Lenah.

The final message began to play. I listened to it carefully and then replayed it twice more.

"Hello, London. This is Milagros Farrow. So sorry I didn't respond to your invitation to submit a short story to the anthology you're compiling. I'm afraid I don't have anything to submit right now, but I appreciate your asking me. Good luck with your project. I'll look forward to reading it." The voice on the tape paused before it continued. "By the way, I've enjoyed your work. Keep up the excellent writing. It's needed and it's necessary."

I froze. That rich full voice coming from my answering machine truly belonged to Milagros Farrow. I recognized it because during the past few years I'd listened to her online interviews.

She had a habit of drawing out her words and pausing briefly between sentences, as if she needed a chance to preview her next thoughts. Surely, those seconds gave me time to weigh the meaning of what she'd said.

If Milagros didn't have any new fiction to submit right now, would she have a story sometime in the future? If she'd enjoyed reading my novels, could the two of us have a conversation about writing in general or African American lesbian literature specifically?

I played her message a fourth time and concentrated on its last part. I'd make note of Milagros' phone number, but I wouldn't take umbrage and return her call. Instead, I'd feel satisfied. At last she had contacted me. I felt proud that she'd said she liked my work, that it was needed and necessary. Perhaps that meant I was needed and necessary as well.

Chapter Eighteen

The Queen Counts Her Money

CANDACE LEANED ON one elbow and then sat up straight in the darkened room. She pushed aside a pillow, reached forward, and moved the woman's leg from atop her own. She frowned at her own newly exposed limb, now cold and slick with the remnants of the other woman's sweat. Candace knew she hadn't perspired and she didn't appreciate being the recipient of the other woman's salty damp deposit.

It's the middle of October, not July. Why the hell did she sweat so damn much? Candace thought.

Candace used the edge of the tangled sheet to wipe away the moisture. As she swung her legs over the side of the bed and stood, the woman mumbled incoherently. Candace looked down at her to make sure she was more asleep than awake.

I'm in no mood for conversation, she thought.

Candace gathered her clothes from a nearby chair and then walked into the bathroom where she used the toilet, washed her hands, and then splashed water on the face that stared back at her from the medicine cabinet's mirror.

A small clock seated on the back of the toilet ticked away the seconds. Candace turned around to look at it and saw it was eight o'clock, early enough on this mid-week evening for her to go to her own condo unit, eat a small dinner, and relax before she went to bed.

She stepped into her panties and then her slacks. She folded her bra neatly and placed it in one of her pockets before she slipped her arms through the sleeves of her blouse. Careful to remain quiet, she bent over and guided her trouser socks past her toes and up over her ankles. She turned on the water in the basin and waited for the stream to change from tepid to hot. Then she held the woman's comb under the hot water for a half minute. She shook away the excess droplets that clung to the comb before she dragged its teeth through her hair. Candace checked her reflection in the mirror as she used her hand to tamp a few renegade strands into place.

She left the bathroom and silently gave thanks that the bedroom's carpet silenced any noise her footsteps might have created. She tiptoed past the bed and glanced surreptitiously at the woman who lay there. She felt no need to awaken her. Nor did she intend to leave a note on the pillow or taped to the front door. She wouldn't leave any message, nothing that would remind the woman she'd been there.

Candace was faithful to her practiced routine, a drink at the end of the workday followed by an emotionless sexual interaction and then a wordless departure. She anticipated she'd discontinue the routine with this particular woman soon because she'd achieved her objective. She'd absorbed all the useful information this woman had to share with her. Accordingly, the woman served no further purpose.

Candace arrived at the condo's front door. She turned the deadbolt and cringed as the lock's mechanism snapped undone and echoed throughout the quiet rooms. Candace stood stock still. She turned her head toward the bedroom and listened before she pulled the door open.

"Candace, is that you? Are you leaving?"

A voice shrill with the surprise of having awakened suddenly, demanded a response.

"Yes, I'm leaving. I'll phone you later, Willa."

Willa said nothing more.

Silence was Candace's companion after she closed the door behind her and walked quickly to the elevator at the end of the corridor. She entered the conveyance and ascended two floors. As she unlocked and then closed the door to her own condominium, the thoughts keeping her company were familiar ones.

She calculated how much money she'd be able to add to her savings after she deposited the present month's revenues. She'd start with her salary, of course. Then she'd include the additional cash that flowed in regularly now from the self-important Judge Williamson, whose arrogant son had insulted her in her own office when he'd pointed out errors she'd failed to correct and then hid behind the coffee vendor's apron strings to legitimize calling her a bitch.

If he hadn't told me who his father was, I wouldn't have chased down the rumor that our handsome intern was selling himself quite regularly to the moneyed men, many of whom were married to women, who cruised the streets and slowed their cars when they aught sight of him lingering suggestively on one of the gayborhood's corners.

Next, Candace factored in the monthly payment she received from the writer who overestimated her own slickness and underestimated her readership's savviness. She added the additional funds that flowed her way from the writer's gullible surrogate who'd been delusional enough to believe her own game.

Finally, Candace included the money from her former partner, a street smart but emotionally needy woman who'd been so in love with Candace, that she'd trusted her with her life's most important secret.

"You shouldn't ever love anyone that much," Candace recalled she'd whispered in her ex-lover's ear as she claimed ownership of what little extra cash the woman could summon that month.

Candace added all the separate figures and reached a lucrative conclusion. She smiled slyly and calculated how much time would have to pass before she'd be able to tell her bosses at Continental Assurance Company to take her job and stick it up their well insured asses.

Chapter Nineteen

An Open House of Possibilities: Part One

TEN MINUTES BEFORE she left her cottage to begin the forty minute trek to the special real estate sales event, Rand proofread the final sentence of her latest article. She clicked the document into cyberspace, certain it would arrive in the mailbox of the monthly publication's editor who years earlier had labeled Rand's writing "barely adequate but not bad for a person who lacks formal training and no doubt struggles with proper English grammar." This editor was now cloyingly complimentary and never failed to pay homage to Rand's well-earned reputation as a writer of "cogent and clear-headed essays."

"What a hypocrite," Rand muttered at her computer as she turned it off.

She stood and tried to smooth the wrinkles from the front of her shirt before she tucked it into her slacks. She ran her hands through her hair. In a rush, Rand grabbed her worn jacket and ancient handbag from the back of the chair, and headed out the front door. Almost three-quarters of an hour later, she turned down a familiar road and spotted the sign for Oak Hill Estates.

She noticed the red, white, and blue balloons as they swayed back and forth past the Kensington Builders' logo. The message written across a banner was distorted in deference to the gusts of wind that filled the cloth.

"Grand Sales Event" looked more like "Grand Sal ent," or "rand Sales Eve."

Rand grinned at the latter wording as she slowed her car and parked it in an area designated for guests. When she approached Oak Hill Estates' Club House, she cast a glance at the row of model homes nearby. She slowed her pace and took a longer look at one of the models in particular, the one she'd planned to purchase less than six months ago.

A line of regret creased Rand's forehead when she remembered how she'd shared her enthusiasm about the house with Susan Rafferty, the sales associate who'd helped her select a site for the new build. The crease deepened as she relived the disappointment she'd felt the moment she came to terms with the reality of her finances. The difference between the resources she'd come to rely on during the past few years, and those she had left after someone extremely cruel and clever intervened in her career, was catastrophic.

Rand shook off the remnants of her disappointment and spoke a two sentence mantra as she neared the building.

I'm not here to buy a new house. I'm here to connect with London Phillips.

"Hello, Ms. Carson. Welcome back to Oak Hill Estates." Susan Rafferty stepped forward to greet Rand the second she entered the clubhouse.

"Thanks, Ms. Rafferty. It was kind of you to send me an invitation, considering I reneged on the purchase."

"We always include folks who've shown a genuine interest in our homes," Susan said. "We know if that person came close to buying one of our homes, he or she recognizes quality construction."

"Oh, I recognize it all right. Being able to afford it is the problem."

"Peoples' situations change, right? Perhaps now is a better time for you to buy. We can take a second look and try to figure something out because we'd love to see you move in to our community. There are so many features..."

Rand's polite smile masked her inattention. She blinked quickly and looked everywhere except at Susan.

After she spotted her reason for attending the event, Rand looked at Susan once again and quickly excused herself. She walked so rapidly toward the other side of the large room, that she barely missed ramming a long table that sat right in the middle of the space. The table supported a miniature version of the development, replete with pretend houses, painted streets, fake bocce courts and artificial trees. Rand was so focused on arriving at her destination, she was oblivious to a second table covered with napkins, small paper plates, condiments, and a wide assortment of plastic platters that an hour earlier had held a copious assortment of small sandwiches. She zoomed past the food display and confronted London. She thrust her hand toward her prey.

"London. It's good to see you."

"Hello, Rand. This is a surprise," London said. "Have you changed your mind about buying one of our homes?"

Rand grimaced. "No, I'm afraid I haven't. But I thought I'd explore the special offers I saw mentioned in the invitation you mailed."

"The invitation? Oh, the Open House announcement. Corporate sent those to everyone who's visited our models and filled out our guest questionnaire."

Rand's grimace deepened. She raised an eyebrow."And here I thought I was special. I figured you or Susan Rafferty had mailed it to me."

London shook her head.

"Sorry, but neither Susan nor I had anything to do with the announcements." London paused, "But it's good you're here. We're completing the final phase of the development and we're offering the models for sale now. They'll be sold as is, with all of their upgrades offered for free. Maybe you won't be able to resist the one you were interested in."

Rand narrowed her eyes. "Perhaps you're right. Once I'm interested in something or someone, I can't resist the pursuit."

London turned slightly away from Rand in time to see a handful of brochures flutter from a visitor's hand and fall to the floor.

"Actually, London," Rand continued. "I thought I might get lucky and have a few minutes to chat with you. After all, it's been a while since we saw each other at the writers' workshop in Wellfleet and I've had a chance to read both of your books. They're wonderful."

"Oh, thank you." London paused. "Uh, I'd love to catch up, but maybe some other time."

"I understand."

"Why don't you phone me some time and we can talk about writing." London said.

Rand sensed London was beginning to step away.

"And remind me to tell you about the message I received from Milagros Farrow," London added.

Rand nodded. She stepped forward and closed the space that had opened between them.

"I imagine it's easier for you to discuss writing and Milagros Farrow than it is for you to talk about you and me."

"What?" London asked.

"We need to talk about you and me." Rand touched London's forearm. "I know we're different, but I've been in a relationship with a black woman before. Don't you believe unbiased white people exist?"

Rand's voice climbed from its usual volume to a much louder one. She was aware others in the room had stopped talking but that didn't deter her.

"Don't you think some of us know what you experience when you face white peoples' low expectations and then surprise them by doing more than they estimated you could do? Don't you believe some of us understand what it's like to go through life in your shoes?"

Rand paused and waited for London's response. When none arrived, Rand continued.

"Tell me, London. Do you ever step out of your comfort zone and date women who don't look like you?"

"This isn't the place for that conversation," London said. Her voice remained low and controlled.

"Where would that place be? When should I call you?" Rand asked.

"Not any time soon, Rand. If you'll excuse me, I see two of my clients over there and I need to speak to them."

Like a battered and subdued bull who gazes over the top of his lowered horns as his matador glides gracefully away, Rand watched London cross the room and approach two of the sales event's guests. She strained to hear London greet them. Then she blinked quickly and willed herself to memorize the elegance of London's walk and the warmth in her voice.

Suddenly aware she stood alone and bereft of her original purpose, Rand felt searing heat burst from her chest and surge to her face. Desirous of invisibility, she made her way to the room's perimeter and then exited the building.

She slid into her car and began a rant of self-recrimination.

"Why did I think she'd be glad to see me? Why did I believe she'd be able to talk about us while she was working? Why did I accuse her of never dating outside her race?"

Rand dove off the cliff of her unrequited questions and landed in a quarry of recent memories. She recalled her last two ferry rides to and from Martha's Vineyard, her coffee shop meeting with Jonathan in Oak Bluffs, Jonathan's description of the woman who'd asked so many questions about her, the career shift she'd been forced to make against her will, and finally, her persistent need to be close to someone who might in some way remind her of Willa.

Chapter Twenty

An Open House of Possibilities: Part Two

THIS MORNING'S MIRACLE, a pair of male cardinals I saw perched on one of the lower limbs of the sugar maple, failed to protect me from the day's weirdness. As fortuitous as it was, the cardinal sighting didn't give me a clue about the bizarre experience I'd have during a conversation that had begun like any other normal discussion.

I had to co-host our final open house sales event for the Oak Hill Estates project. I'd organized and attended so many of these events, that by now I could do one in my sleep. I'd smile constantly, welcome our guests, offer them food and beverages, add the lures of cut rate prices, custom molding, and upgraded appliances, then reel in the buyers eager to sign their names on the dotted line. This sales event would be exactly like all the others, formulaic and unremarkable.

What I hadn't expected to happen today was my encounter with a poorly dressed and oddly fractious Rand Carson.

"Don't you ever date women who don't look like you?" she'd asked me.

Her question startled me. I took a step back from her as if putting a little distance between us would get rid of her question along with my discomfort in having to field it.

Although I wasn't about to discuss it with Rand, especially not at a work related event and in front of Susan and the other visitors, the truth was, I'd once dated a white woman for several months and we'd enjoyed each other's company. But after a while, both of us decided we'd be better friends than lovers. And when I took classes to earn my real estate license, I fell pretty quickly for the instructor, a Latina realtor whose petulant lips could have sold me a hut built atop an asbestos mound. Women are women, and I'd never been averse to following an interracial path if that's where my heart or libido led me.

When Rand challenged me today though, I was speechless. Thankfully I spotted a man and woman who seemed to be engrossed in the floor plans we'd posted. I grabbed the opportunity to leave Rand standing there with her question dangling in the air. I strode toward the refuge those two strangers offered.

"We have three premium lots we're offering at reduced prices and each of the model homes is for sale as is," I explained to them.

I positioned myself so I could view Rand. Since I couldn't have predicted her presence or her questions, the least I could do was know her location.

"Take your time and please let me know if you'd like to tour the models," I'd said as I watched Rand slink to the edge of the room and then quietly leave the sales event.

I exhaled and turned to find Susan at my side.

"What was that about?" she asked.

"I'm not sure."

"I wondered if she'd changed her mind and wanted to buy a house after all, but she said no. She told me she still couldn't afford it," Susan said. "So why did she show up? For a free snack?"

"I don't know." Actually, I suspected I did know why Rand had been present.

"And what about how she was dressed? She looked like she'd really hit the skids."

Images of Rand fluttered through my mind. Moments earlier she'd stood toe to toe with me, wearing a spot-dotted shirt, wrinkle filled slacks, and an ill-fitting jacket with a torn breast pocket. The woman who'd confronted me today was not the Rand Carson I'd first met in our sales office. She wasn't the same person whose journalism panel I'd attended at the writers workshop. Certainly, she wasn't the Rand Carson with whom Theresa and I had shared dinner in a Provincetown restaurant one warm summer evening a few months ago.

Since that evening Rand had phoned me a couple of times. I'd suspected, the way prey usually senses the hunter's approach, Rand wanted to spend time with me. She just hadn't created an opportunity to approach me. I hadn't done anything to encourage her because I sensed her intensity and it made me feel uncomfortable. She'd projected an instant familiarity that made me doubt her sincerity.

The other barrier between Rand and me was Lenah. I realized my imagination had created the blockade because reality hadn't. I continued to hope Lenah and I might play some role in each other's lives, and as long as I nurtured that hope, I didn't want to mislead Rand. I'd never been able to multi-task with women, not even when I was younger.

"All in all, it looks like we had a successful day." Susan rubbed her hands together.

"Did you talk to anyone who's ready to sign the paperwork?"

"Definitely. We have three appointments set for tomorrow, one in the morning and two in the afternoon. The models are a hot commodity."

"Great. A couple more sales and our work here is done."

"A couple more sales and I'm sure you're going to be awarded that new position." Susan patted my shoulder.

I smiled at the thought of a promotion and began to daydream how I'd best organize all the sales staffs at Roger Kensington's future developments.

"I know you're up to the challenge, London. It seems to me you know everything there is to know about residential projects."

"I still have a lot to learn, Susan. It'll be a challenge."

While that fact was true, I knew my more difficult challenge was to convince Lenah Miller we were more alike than different. My most difficult challenge though, was to understand why I felt it was so important for me to have a relationship with Lenah.

Chapter Twenty-one

The Viewing

LENAH STOOD IN front of the casket and examined the body lying less than one foot away from her. She looked at the woman's slipper encased feet and realized she'd never noticed them until today. So many times in the past, Lenah had been conscious of how quickly those feet always moved, but she'd never really focused on them.

Lenah guided her gaze from the dead woman's slacks covered legs to her small chest. She focused when she arrived at the woman's face, because she thought she could see a contented smile rest upon the woman's lips. Bangs curved gently over the woman's smooth unwrinkled forehead, and curls the size of small link sausages caressed her cheeks. Lenah stared in wonderment at those tendrils of hair. For as long as she'd known her, Lenah had never seen the vaguest suggestion of curls adorn the deceased's head. All she could remember seeing was the woman's hair brushed back from her face and swept into longer strands that she frequently wore corralled in a ponytail and fenced in with lariats of multi-colored rubber bands.

A moment passed and Lenah continued to stare down at the face that projected serenity and acceptance, expressions Lenah had seen the woman wear only those times when they'd promised each other they'd make plans to go out for a meal together. Usually the woman was the personification of the word harried. Lenah stole a glance at the funeral program she'd picked from the top of the pile near the sanctuary's entrance and wondered if she'd wandered into the wrong funeral chapel. Who was this woman lying here in the light blue satin-lined coffin? Why had the undertaker changed her appearance from how she'd been to this drastically different person?

The entire time Lenah had worked with Sally Winston, she'd known her to be a creature in constant motion. She was one of those people who never stayed still. Even during the slowest of times in the Emergency Department, Sally always found a reason to stay busy. She'd scurry into the waiting room, or shuffle the stacks of blank patient information forms, or verify the state of readiness of each of the unit's triage rooms.

Lenah couldn't recall ever seeing Sally's eyes calm and expressionless, or her lips without movement. She could still hear the opinion honed inflection of Sally's voice as it traveled from its end-of-the-workday alto to its high pitched treble of excitement each time she reported the agitation she felt when she'd worked with an uncooperative patient.

Lenah tried to imagine how Sally might have sounded three nights ago the moment she'd realized her heart was attacking her. Had she screamed or been calm when she placed the call to the rescue squad? Had her eyes darted about her surroundings as she prayed for relief from the vise of pain suffocating her attempts to breathe, or had she sat quietly and hoped for the best? Had her lips contorted themselves in unheard pleas for help, or had she kept her thoughts to herself? Was the peaceful expression Sally now wore her consent to dying, or was it the result of the mortician's artistry?

Sally had been too fussy and feisty to go without yelling at death, Lenah thought. She wouldn't be smiling like this. Or maybe she would if she knew it was me looking down at her.

Lenah took one last look at the woman with whom she'd worked so closely for the past few years. She bowed her head slightly. The muscles in her throat tightened and threatened to prevent her from whispering a good-bye.

"I guess I have to accept you're gone, Sally. Working in the ED is gonna be different without you being there. Who's gonna offer me coffee? Who's gonna take my bets about the patients? Who's gonna listen to my stories?"

She gazed affectionately at her deceased co-worker and then backed away from the casket. As she stepped outside into the sunlight, Lenah was mindful she hadn't shared very many of her personal stories with Sally. She reminded herself that she'd entrusted her stories to two people only, and one of them died several years ago. The other one had listened carefully to Lenah's stories, memorized them, and used the tales for her own gain.

Lenah squinted at the sun.

"I intend to put an end to that," she said, and then swore to do so in Sally's memory.

Chapter Twenty-two

Prelude to a Memory

"I'M SORRY TO break another date, but a friend of mine died and I don't feel like going out tonight." Lenah stared straight ahead as she spoke into her phone.

"I'm sorry, Lenah. Was she a close friend of yours?" London asked.

"You could say that. I used to see her almost every day."

"In that case, you're really going to miss her."

"Yeah, I am. I didn't go to the funeral, but at least I went to the viewing."

"Do you usually go to viewings and funerals?"

"No, I hate funerals. I avoid them whenever I can." Lenah paused. "I missed an important one years ago."

"Whose funeral was it?"

"A person who once saved my life and gave me valuable advice I failed to follow."

"Maybe I should come see you. We could talk about your sadness," London offered.

"No thanks. I don't want to talk to anyone right now."

London heard Lenah's deep sigh fill the empty quiet space.

"Honest to God. Those two cardinals I saw this morning gave me no clue as to how this day was going to turn out."

"What are you talking about?" Lenah asked.

"My daily miracle. I mentioned that to you months ago. Remember?"

"Yeah, I remember. I didn't understand you then and I don't understand you now. You say lots of things that don't make sense to me."

"Maybe you just need to listen more carefully," London said.

"And maybe you need to talk to someone who can understand, someone who's more like you."

"Someone who's more like me?"

"Yeah, someone with your classy background, good education, and important job. Someone who follows all the rules, like you do."

Lenah squeezed her phone and winced. She hadn't planned to hammer that particular wedge between her and London, especially now when she'd become increasingly interested in London, and certainly not during a phone conversation when she wouldn't be able to explain herself fully.

But it was too late to soften the blow. Her words were a hard piece of metal she'd set upright in the middle of their soft relationship. She'd wielded her message so powerfully, it threatened to split their tentative friendship wide open.

"Sometimes a person's background isn't as important as her foreground," London said. "It's where we are now and where we're headed that counts."

"London, I know exactly where we are now as well as where we've been. As for where we're headed, I'm not sure it's to the same place."

London offered no response and Lenah could intuit the anger and hurt thrumming through London's silence. All of that emotion was more than she was willing to handle.

"I'm hanging up now before you get more upset."

Lenah put down her phone. Then she trudged to the kitchen, pulled a chair away from the table, and slumped into the seat. A mug of cold coffee stared up at her. She pushed it to the center of the table. Lacking the will to invent a distraction, Lenah folded her arms on the table and rested her head on top of them. She drifted into the kind of sleep that would have been peacefully restorative, had she not been jolted into wakefulness by the sound of a fist pounding so hard against her door, she thought the wood would splinter before she could fling it open.

"Hello, Ms. Lenah."

Candace breached the threshold and marched into the living room. "Are you busy?"

"I'm always busy," Lenah said.

Candace peered past Lenah and into the room's long interior. "I didn't want to disturb you," she said.

"You always disturb me, Candace."

"Is that so? I didn't disturb you a few years ago when we first got together."

"It was downhill from there."

"It must have been one of those subtle gradual slopes because we stayed with each other for a long while."

"I just didn't leave you, Candace. You always told me I lacked ambition. Remember?"

The women glared at each other.

"Why are you here?" Lenah asked.

"It's that time of the month and I thought I'd save you a stamp," Candace said.

"You're too late. I mailed your payment yesterday."

Candace nodded.

"Good," she said. "Starting next month, I'm increasing the amount you'll be paying."

"What? You can't do that."

"I can raise the rate any time I please, Lenah. I'm the one who's running this show."

Lenah turned away from Candace and began to pace back and forth.

"Don't do this to me, Candace. I can't afford to give you another penny."

"Well, you know the alternative and you don't want to go down that road either."

Lenah spun around and faced Candace. "I could kill you."

"I know you could, Lenah. But it's not worth your effort, right?"

"It's worth my effort all right. But it's not worth being locked up for the rest of my life."

"See, Lenah? You've come full circle. The possibility of being locked up for the rest of your life is exactly why you're sending me money every month. You like to think you run your life. But the only thing you run is your mouth. And you don't do a great job with that."

Lenah glowered. "Shut up, Candace."

"Ever since I've known you, you've been afraid of one thing and then another. You've been scared to finish your college degree, scared of your supervisors at the hospital, scared to apply for a new position with a higher salary, afraid to look for a job elsewhere, afraid to talk to a counselor about the nightmares that tear through your sleep, and you're scared to death of intimacy. It's a wonder you got close enough to me to share the reason you were so scared of going to jail."

Lenah clamped her lips together and seemed to stop breathing.

Candace gulped a breath of air. "You know what, Lenah? The combination of your fears and my knowing all about them made you my easiest mark."

"Get the hell out of my house, Candace."

Candace turned her back on Lenah.

"With pleasure." As she pulled open the door and stepped outside, she added, "I'll let you know in plenty of time about next month's increase. And I'll try damned hard to not break you."

Lenah strode toward the door and slammed it shut. She stood there with her back against the doorway's frame and her chest heaving with the effort her lungs made to take in and expel the air along with her rage.

"Shit, shit, shit. Where am I going to get extra money? I'm already working all the overtime I can handle. Any more hours and I'll start making serious mistakes because I'm so fucking exhausted...so fucking exhausted."

Lenah sank into the living room sofa and started to calculate how much additional cash she'd earn if she worked an extra shift every other day. The third time she attempted to add the figures and then subtract the extra taxes she'd owe, she gave up. Her thoughts turned to the deed she'd done years earlier, the act that was responsible for her present predicament.

Chapter Twenty-three

That Which Remains Unforgotten

IT WAS AS if Miz Myjoy Henderson knew what happened before she saw it. She tasted the same metallic flavored adrenalin that spread through Roberta's mouth the whole time Roberta ran from her aunt and uncle's house to Miz Myjoy's front door. Miz Myjoy heard Roberta's feet alternately splash and then suck at the mud in the ankle-deep puddles, remnants of the night's rainstorm. She smelled Roberta's panic and she knew the girl didn't feel the raindrops that crashed upon her head and streamed past her eyes, nose, and chin. She figured, as Roberta raced through the darkness the saturated air barely left its impression on her skin. Miz Myjoy knew, felt, and tasted all of this moments before Roberta arrived at her door.

Miz Myjoy smoothed imaginary wrinkles from her cotton covered thighs. She waited for Roberta to climb the steps to the porch, two at a time. Steps that six years earlier had seemed as steep as Pike's Peak to a much younger Roberta, were a mere hillock now. Miz Myjoy listened as Roberta opened the frail screen door and banged her fist against the solid oak slab that stood between them. Only then did she move to the entrance of her house.

Roberta stood there, her shirt, arm, and hand bloody.

"Is he dead?" Miz Myjoy asked.

"I think he's still alive."

"Where's he at?"

"On the floor near the kitchen."

"Give me a minute."

Miz Myjoy stepped back and turned toward a table on the right side of a room that would have served as a parlor in anyone else's house.

"Bullet, razor, or knife?" she asked.

"Kitchen knife."

The fingers of Roberta's right hand curled against her palm involuntarily, in memory of the way they'd held the handle of the knife as she'd fought back for once, after all the times her uncle had touched her in her private places.

Miz Myjoy picked up a scarred brown leather bag and slung its strap over her shoulder. She probed the table until she found a particular fabric covered satchel.

"When we get there, fill this here bag with enough changes of clothes to get you where you're going. There's a little pocket on the side. It's got money for a bus ticket and a slip of paper with my cousin

Marva's phone number written on it. Call her when you arrive at your destination and tell her you're safe. She'll let me know you're okay."

"Thank you, Miz Myjoy."

"We'd better get a move on if we want to keep him amongst the living," Miz Myjoy said.

The healer woman and the young girl entered the night and headed to the house Roberta had inhabited for the past eight years.

"You got any money saved to add to what's in the bag?" Miz Myjoy asked.

"Some. I still got a little of the money my mother left me in her will, and I got my graduation present from Aunt Lizzie."

Miz Myjoy nodded her approval.

"Where'd you cut the nasty old fool?" she asked.

"First in his gut. Then clear through his hand. When I ran to get you he was bleeding real bad."

"Probably bleeding like the pig he's always been."

Miz Myjoy and Roberta matched each other's pace. They walked in silence until Roberta spoke.

"Are the police gonna come get me?" she asked.

"Naw. The police ain't gonna know nothin' about this," Miz Myjoy answered. "What's he gonna say? That he tried to rape you and you fought back?"

"He'd lie and say I wanted it to happen."

Miz Myjoy linked her arm through Roberta's.

"If he does, he'll be facin' me on the witness stand. I'll tell the jury how I seen him try to force hisself on you several times."

The two women sloshed through the puddles hidden under the tall grass that surrounded the rear of Roberta's aunt and uncle's house. Roberta paused outside the back door and dutifully scraped the thick mud from her shoes onto an old mat. Miz Myjoy ignored her opportunity to clean the sludge from hers. She stepped over the mat, entered the kitchen, and forced her vision to accustom itself to the room's semi-darkness.

"Roberta, go do as I told you."

Roberta's form faded from sight.

Miz Myjoy scrutinized the room. She heard a low groan ooze from the pantry and slither along the floor until it reached the spot where she stood. She gripped her leather bag and forged her way past the old stove and the lower cabinets with their abstract pattern of missing paint chips. The odor of whiskey and lard drifted past her nostrils as she peered into the kitchen's ante-chamber.

"Look what we have here," she said softly.

"That, that heifer...tried her best to butcher me, Miz Henderson," the grizzled man sputtered.

"No she didn't, Leroy. She's real capable. If she'd done her best, she would've castrated you for sure," Miz Myjoy answered.

"Can, can you help me?"

"I can. Or I can let you bleed to death right here on the floor."

Confusion clouded Leroy's face.

"I could let the blood drain out of you and then put the knife in your hand and make it look like you accidentally cut yourself. I'd claim your niece came to me for help, but it was too late."

Leroy cast his gaze downward and caught sight of the thick red trail eking rhythmically from his belly down to the floor. Then, in supplication, he looked up at Miz Myjoy and spoke, his voice hollow and distant.

"I ain't gonna turn that girl in," he said.

"I didn't expect you would."

Miz Myjoy opened her bag and extracted alcohol, packing, and her stitching kit. She knelt on her knees and tugged at the sides of Leroy's pants. Spurts of blood punctuated each of her rough movements.

"This isn't how you pictured takin' your trousers off for a woman, is it, Leroy?"

A pain-wracked "uh" was his only answer.

"How many times did you think you could have your way with that girl before she fought back?" Miz Myjoy asked.

Leroy's expressionless opaque eyes stared back at her. In resignation he let his head turn to one side a second before he acquiesced to silence.

Miz Myjoy bent closer. With her ear near Leroy's open mouth, she whispered.

"You still breathin', old man?"

Leroy's eyes remained open, but he didn't answer her.

Miz Myjoy extended her fingers and made her palm as flat as a board. She pressed Leroy's chest in the spot where she figured his heart would be, if indeed he really had one. She ordered her hand to feel the thump of life from deep within his body. She felt nothing. She gazed at the red pool on the floor. It was still. The blood no longer flowed. Leroy's inanimate expression told Miz Myjoy all she needed to know.

She stood and walked toward the living room. Squinting, she saw Roberta move toward the front door.

"Roberta," she whispered.

"Yes, Miz Myjoy?"

"Remember the directions I gave you. Don't tell anyone what happened here tonight, you hear me?"

"Yes, ma'am."

"You can't ever tell a soul. Not even the one you'll swear you'll love forever. You haven't met her yet, but you will. You'll want to trust her with all that you are, but don't tell her about this."

Roberta blinked when she heard Miz Myjoy pronounce the word "her." She swallowed hard and understood Miz Myjoy knew her biggest secret. Too afraid to ask how Miz Myjoy knew that which she'd guarded so closely all of her life, Roberta pointed to the other room.

"Is he gonna be all right?"

"Don't worry about him. The only times he gave you a second thought were when your auntie left him alone with you and he schemed how best to do whatever he wanted with you."

Roberta lowered her head under the weight of the terrible truth.

"You have to forget about tonight, Roberta, and all the other nights that led to it."

Roberta nodded slowly and held up the bulging satchel.

"Thank you, Miz Myjoy."

"You can thank me by livin' the rest of your life exactly the way you are. Ain't nothin' wrong with the way you love, Roberta, just like there's nothin' wrong with your name. Folks around here always wanted to change what they called you. But not me. You're fine by me just as you are."

Miz Myjoy watched Roberta draw in a lungful of air and step away from the house. She imagined that one deep breath would sustain Roberta during her five mile trek through the damp darkness. She would reach the bus depot and buy a one-way ticket to the big city near the only other place in the world Roberta had ever considered home.

Chapter Twenty-four

A Ferry to Mercy

CANDACE'S GREED-NOURISHED ego prompted her to accept the offer of the free trip to Martha's Vineyard. She'd break up the long drive to Cape Cod and stop to visit friends in Providence, Rhode Island. Very early the next day she'd leave for Woods Hole, Massachusetts where she'd arrive in time to take one of the earliest ferries to the Vineyard. Once she was on the island, she'd return to the bookstore in Oak Bluffs where she'd done some research some time ago, meet with Tanisha, and gather some valuable information from the doltish young woman.

Monday morning, November ninth brought with it a particularly obstinate fog that refused to clear. An hour before the ferry, *Martha's Vineyard*, was scheduled to push away from its mooring, Candace climbed aboard the jitney that would carry her from the Steamship Authority's remote parking lot to the dock.

The newish bus made the short trip past wooded home sites and intersections occupied by family-owned businesses, rather quickly. When the bus slowed out of respect for the road's deep curve, Candace took advantage of the decreased speed and gawked at the gray expanse of sea which lay a short distance away. The glare from the Steamship Authority's sign shone through the morning fog and diverted Candace's attention from the view of the water.

Two minutes later, the bus driver guided his vehicle into the terminal's parking lot and steered it through the tight loop of a turn.

"Ferry terminal, folks. Nantucket and Martha's Vineyard," The driver announced. "Step down carefully, and don't forget your luggage."

Candace clutched her umbrella and stood. She secured her handbag over her shoulder and descended three steps to the parking lot's surface. She'd done this before, so she knew exactly where to go. Oblivious to the heavy mist surrounding her, she kept her closed umbrella under her arm, crossed in front of the bus, and walked directly to the ferry terminal's ticket office. Once she was inside the building, she approached the *Will Call* window.

"My name is Candace Dickerson. You're holding round trip tickets to Oak Bluffs for me."

The ticket seller read the labels on several envelopes before she selected the one that bore Candace's name.

"Could I see a photo ID, please?"

"Of course."

Candace lifted the top section of her card case and revealed her driver's license.

"Thank you."

The ticket vendor smiled and handed the envelope to Candace.

"The *Martha's Vineyard* leaves at seven-thirty and docks at Oak Bluffs at eight-fifteen. You can board right away."

Candace opened the envelope and removed both of her tickets. She examined each one carefully. Satisfied she had everything she needed for her passage to and from Oak Bluffs, she wended her way to the long metal ramp that connected the pavement to one of the ferry's three levels. She climbed the ramp and then entered the ship's interior.

The cavernous passenger lounge looked even more so because there were so few travelers aboard the ship. Television monitors strategically hung on walls here and there blared the morning's latest news stories. The text of a message crawled across two electronic display boards mounted at either end of the room.

Candace preferred to witness the comings and goings of the other passengers, so she passed by the empty seats that faced the outside, and instead, selected a chair that provided her visual access to the interior of the room.

What few passengers there were all seemed to be engaged with one mobile device or another. No one paid any attention to either television.

Commuters. Candace speculated. Certainly not the tourists I saw up here last summer. Candace quickly studied each of the other female passengers she spotted in the lounge. She didn't need to spend a lot of time examining any of them because she knew Tanisha, the woman she expected to meet on the Vineyard, was black. And as far as she could see, Candace was the only passenger of color aboard the ferry this morning.

She based her recall of Tanisha on the single time one year ago when the two women encountered each other at an authors' event. Prior to that book signing program, Candace had read a lot about the writer, Milagros Farrow. That day, the moment it was feasible, Candace approached the author, solicited her signature on the inside cover of a newly purchased novel, and then engaged her in a long chat.

"Did you say you went to Oberlin in Ohio?" she'd asked.

"Uh, yes."

Candace recalled reading Milagros had attended Ohio State University, not Oberlin.

"And you worked in marketing for twenty-five years?"

"That's right."

Candace had read Milagros' first career lasted twenty years, not twenty-five. As Candace continued to question Milagros and listen carefully to her, she heard several other answers that contradicted what she'd read about the writer. Her curiosity piqued, Candace began to suspect the woman might not be who she claimed.

Candace invited the author to a women's bar where they could continue their conversation. They sat across the table from one another, ensconced in a cozy booth. After Candace plied the woman with a few cocktails, there was nothing she couldn't have asked her.

In no time, Candace possessed all the information she needed to be able to unravel the woman's subterfuge. She listened as Tanisha confessed that Milagros Farrow, the brilliant black lesbian author, was the invention of a skillful and very imitative white lesbian writer.

The seductive gazes Candace lavished on the inebriated woman were all it took for Tanisha, a willing but unwise writer wannabe whose desire for attention allowed her to be the white writer's stand-in, to recount the times she'd stood behind lecterns in bookstores, read from Milagros' novels, and signed false autographs for unsuspecting fans.

"I was good at it. No one guessed I wasn't Milagros Farrow in the flesh," she boasted to Candace.

At first enraged, then later titillated by the pair's grand deception of their readers, Candace perceived an economic opportunity for herself. She began to construct the foundation of her new income.

"I know what you've been doing. Tanisha told me everything. I believe we can all benefit from your fans' gullibility," she'd said during a telephone conversation with the white writer who'd invented the persona of Milagros Farrow.

The ferry's horn bellowed and for the first time since she'd boarded the vessel, Candace became aware of the constant vibration she felt coursing through the soles of her feet. The ship's engine had come to life as it persuaded the huge craft to back away from its birth at the dock.

"Right on time as usual," an older woman said as she sat herself directly across the aisle from Candace. She unbuttoned her raincoat and removed the scarf she wore over her head. "I thought for sure we'd be late with all of this fog."

Candace allowed her lips to stretch into a brief tight smile.

The woman pointed to the electronic message streaming across the closer of the two monitors.

"Look at that. It says this fog's not going to lift any time soon. And they're expecting rain this afternoon."

Candace barely glanced at the woman.

"I hope the bad weather won't disrupt your plans, dear."

The woman eyed Candace sympathetically.

"I don't expect it to."

"Oh good."

The woman sniffed the air.

"That coffee certainly smells good, doesn't it?"

"Yes it does," Candace said. "I believe I'll get a cup."

She gathered her handbag and abruptly stood. She peered toward the far end of the room and spotted a counter laden with coffee dispensers and trays of cellophane covered pastries. She noticed a man dressed in a gray shirt with navy blue epaulets attached to its shoulders was emptying a container of steaming coffee into a large urn. She approached him.

"Good morning. Some coffee to start your day, Miss?"

"Thank you."

Candace helped herself to a Styrofoam cup. She thrust it under the urn's spigot, and nudged the lever forward.

"The rest of the works are over there."

The Steamship Authority steward pointed to the other end of the counter where a collection of sweeteners and powdered creamers were arrayed, just waiting for customers.

Candace demurred the offer to make any additions to her beverage. She took a sip of the coffee and decided to stake out a different seat, one that would put distance between her and the talkative older woman. Before she could navigate away from the beverage counter, the woman barreled toward her.

"What a good idea! A cup of hot coffee on such a cold raw day. I think I'll do the same."

Candace glared at the woman.

The ship's foghorn filled the air.

"We're going to hear that noise often enough, but that's a good thing. It let's every other boat out there know where we are," the woman said.

Candace clamped her jaw shut.

"Dear, isn't that your umbrella over there? Better get it before someone steals it."

Candace shot a look at the seat she'd vacated. She'd left her umbrella propped between it and the chair next to it. She glanced at the cup she'd filled to its brim and decided she had no intention of spilling a drop of the coffee. She left the cup on the counter while she returned to her original seat to fetch the umbrella. Once there, she bent down to retrieve it. Because it was stuck between the two seats, and it took Candace several attempts before she was able to extricate it.

She returned to her coffee, more determined than ever to shake the talkative woman's presence and enjoy the rest of the voyage to the Vineyard in solitude.

"So are you headed to the island on business?" the woman asked.

"Excuse me. I'm going to watch the news on one of the monitors. Have a good day."

"You also," the woman said slowly. She sounded forlorn as she added, "Good-bye now."

Candace left the woman standing there by herself. She glanced back and noticed even the beverage steward had abandoned his station. She reconnoitered to the back of the lounge and sat in a row of seats from which she could keep one eye focused on the other passengers and the other trained on the television. She sipped her rapidly cooling coffee while she watched the CNN news reader drone on about the morning's headlines. One after the other, the latest tragedies from all corners of the world flickered from the screen.

Candace stared passively at the monitor. After a few moments she began to feel queasy. The queasiness morphed into painful spasms that alternately gripped and then released her intestines. The images Candace saw on the screen began to blur and she felt a surge of horror when she imagined the shame she'd experience if her stomach betrayed her and emptied itself right here in the passengers' lounge.

A few seconds later, the only sounds Candace heard were the news reporter's muffled voice folded within her own moans. She bent forward and covered her stomach with the palms of her hands. She grimaced and her contorted features telegraphed the tremendous pain that was overtaking her. She gripped the sides of the chair and arose with difficulty. Her head moved from side to side like a searchlight cutting through the darkness. Desperate to find a bathroom, Candace slung her handbag over her shoulder while she held one hand over her gut. She labored to stand erect long enough to walk to the closest doorway.

She left the lounge, stepped into the corridor, and braced herself against a wall. She took agonizingly slow steps until she reached a door with a female's silhouette affixed to it. Candace leaned against the door and forced it open. She stumbled into the first stall, where she collapsed against a toilet.

Fifteen minutes later, the *Martha's Vineyard's* engine thrusters reversed direction. The ship slipped into its designated birth at the dock in Oak Bluffs, and all the passengers, save one, tramped down the metal ramp and began their day on the island.

A week passed before two coroners, one from the mainland and the other from Martha's Vineyard, reached agreement. An autopsy revealed the female passenger whose body was found in the women's restroom of the *Martha's Vineyard* after the boat docked in Oak Bluffs, had suffered a fatal series of coronary arrhythmias. It was possible the victim's death was the culmination of a prolonged period of untreated arrhythmia. Further tests, including toxicology studies, were underway.

Chapter Twenty-five

Career Plans Can Change on a Dime

"LONDON, OAK HILL Estates is the Community of the Year, and you've been named, Salesperson of the Year."

Susan's words buzzed through my head as I sped away from our sales office to the meeting at Kensington Builders' headquarters.

"Every one of our units sold in less than sixteen months, London. This has to be a new record for the company and a big promotion for you."

My ever present superstition about the dangers of tooting my own horn clamped my lips together tightly. They weren't ready to acknowledge the joy of accomplishment and yield a confident smile.

"I'm not counting on that, Susan. Besides, it took everyone's efforts to sell these houses. I didn't do it all by myself."

"Don't be so modest, London. You were our leader."

Leader. I hadn't thought to give myself that label. What if Susan were correct? What if I were a leader and not the follower I'd always considered myself? In my heart of hearts I knew I'd earned a promotion. With all humility cast aside, I dared to believe I deserved to be promoted to Director of Residential Developments.

That belief and I arrived at Kensington Builders' headquarters and marched into the conference room.

"Hello, London. How are you?" Sandra Linton beamed at me.

"Fine and dandy, Sandra."

I pulled out a chair and sat down at the long polished wood table. I turned to my left and right.

"How's everybody today?"

"Okay." Jocelyn Vega's eyes flicked away from her computer screen long enough to acknowledge my greeting.

Mary Barnett nodded. "I'm well," she said.

Ken Green coughed loudly. "I've got a bad cold. Started not to come to this meeting."

"That might have been a good idea, Ken," Sandra said.

He coughed again.

"I have some throat lozenges," I said.

"Thanks." Ken took the pack of tablets from me. "*Semper paratus*, eh? Just like a Boy Scout."

"No. I'm only prepared some of the time, just like the average person."

"You're more than average, London," Sandra said.

"Actually, we're all more than average. Wouldn't you agree,

Sandra?" Ken asked.

"Most of us, but not all," Sandra said.

I thought I spied an expression of uneasiness flicker through Sandra's eyes as she watched Roger Kensington stride the short distance from the room's entrance to his chair at the head of the table.

"Hello, everyone. I know you have a lot on your plates, so this afternoon's sales staff meeting will be short and sweet. First, I was late with the agenda, so it's being printed as I speak. You'll receive a copy before you leave. I hope that's all right."

Surely no one seated at this table would say it wasn't all right.

"Included on the agenda are the upcoming assignments for all the project managers. Sales have picked up this last quarter, so we're moving ahead with three new developments, two age restricted communities and one new estate home project. They're spread out, located in three different counties. We're starting early, so there's plenty of time for me to schedule a meeting with each of the managers."

Ken sneezed into the crook of his arm. "Excuse me, everyone." He stood and took a few steps away from the table. "I knew I should have stayed in bed today," he said.

From the corner of my eye I saw him smother his nose and mouth with an industrial sized tissue. Then I watched Sandra struggle to suppress a sneer.

Roger Kensington cleared his throat.

"The second item on today's agenda is our heartfelt congratulations to Mary Barnett. Mary's current project, Concord Estates, is completely sold out. And, she has a wait list of clients eager to see our plans for the next estate home development. That kind of enthusiastic activity is unheard of in this economic environment."

Clearly pleased, Roger paused.

"One other detail concerning Mary. She's been promoted to Director of Residential Developments."

Roger began to clap his hands. Mary allowed herself a modest smile. Ken sputtered and coughed. Jocelyn Vega's eyes glistened with wonderment. Sandra watched me closer than the Secret Service guards POTUS.

I felt like I'd had my jaws wired shut, but I struggled to force myself to mouth "Congratulations, Mary."

"By the way, everyone," Roger continued. "We have another project manager whose development is one hundred percent sold. London Philips and her sales team at Oak Hill Estates have done a bang up job. So congratulations go to her as well."

I'm sure I uttered the appropriate sounds as my colleagues glanced my way and flew their verbal flags of "good work" and "how did you do that?" And I'm certain I spewed the correct amount of praise to our new Director of Residential Developments as I shook her hand and wryly wondered if her promotion was related to the romantic relationship she and Roger Kensington were rumored to have begun. I hoped I'd shaken my head mentally and not physically as I'd rejected that sexist and probably false notion.

All I really recall from that staff meeting were my attempts to figure out what it would take for me to rise above my current position at Kensington Builders. I'd stood at the helm of a new home project during a hurricane of a sales season, and spent hours composing sales copy for numerous print and online ads. What more could I do to prove my competence? Hadn't I played by the rules?

What really gnawed at me more than anything else was the possibility that I'd committed a foolish mistake after all when I left my previous employer. Had I screwed up when I jumped off the ship of one of the few successful, gay, African American builders only to find myself abandoned by this straight, white captain of the industry who seemed to have ignored my work ethic and my successes? More importantly, had I earned the criticism and hurtful inference of race betrayal Lenah had launched when she questioned why in the world I'd left Whittingham Builders?

My obvious discomfort probably made me an easy read for Sandra Linton. She followed me from the conference room to the hallway and spoke softly as she helped me shrug my shoulders and arms into my jacket.

"Mary's houses were estate homes, London. Each one sold for five times more than any of the units at Oak Hill Estates."

I nodded. "Thanks for reminding me of that."

"And, I have to say this to you, London. A few months ago Mary didn't defy Roger's requests and take a week away from work to go to a writers' workshop."

Is Mary defying any of Roger's requests? I wanted to ask.

Sandra smiled at me.

"Don't let this dampen your spirit," she said. "There'll be more opportunities for you to advance, I'm sure. Look, here's the new project schedule."

Sandra handed me a copy of the meeting's agenda along with the list of Kensington's new developments.

"Roger's put you in charge of the next estate development. He has confidence in your abilities, and remember, there's already a list of clients eager to see the plans."

Sure enough, I saw my name printed next to "Timberline Hills, An Executive Estate Community."

"Don't worry," I said. "I'm still part of the team."

But in truth, I felt not at all like part of the team. I wasn't the leader Susan proclaimed I was. I wasn't even a follower because I wasn't sure for which team I should play, Kensington's, or Whittingham's? I'd experienced this same feeling of alienation quite a few times in my life. While it was uncomfortable, it was also familiar.

Instead of returning to the sales office at Oak Hill Estates, I drove home. The moment I walked into my house, I phoned Susan and left a message for her.

"I didn't get the promotion, Susan. I'll be selling houses at a new project, and if I have any pull, I'll ask for you to be assigned there also."

The mid-November afternoon would soon fade into an even colder evening. I thought about the winter to come, and how difficult it would be to sell new construction once the leaden gray sky cracked opened and dropped tons of snow. Buyers would decide to remain where they were and not venture onto leafless lots studded with ice covered ruts and invisible property line boundaries.

I sighed and decided to pour myself a glass of wine. By the time I drained it, I hoped I'd find a dreg of wisdom lurking in the bottom of the glass. I sipped the dark red liquid and pondered my daily miracles, my home, my friends, my writing, all the things that brought me joy.

Maybe I needed to spend more time with friends, or busy myself with home projects, or become more focused on writing fiction. Perhaps I hadn't violated any of the rules for a successful career. I'd simply overlooked the career where my success might dwell. I swallowed another half glass of wine before I decided to turn away from my disappointment about the job promotion and fix myself a meal. The telephone had a different plan for me.

"Is this London Phillips?"

"Yes."

"Hello, London. This is Milagros Farrow speaking."

"Oh my. Hello"

"I'd like to meet with you sometime soon, and I'll tell you why," Milagros paused. "As you know, I'm no longer writing. But the decision to stop churning out novels hasn't isolated me from ideas for new characters and stories. You can imagine how difficult it is to turn those sorts of thoughts off, can't you, London?"

"Yes, yes I can." I said.

"I have a cast of intriguing characters who possess a story that must be written. And you, London, are the writer who must tell that story."

"But, Ms. Farrow, I would think it would be you who should write it."

"I was afraid you'd say that, London. And I know you have no reason to trust me. But I'm asking for your trust anyway. Please tell me you'll meet me for coffee and give me a chance to explain everything to you."

It was easy for me to say yes the same day the trajectory of my real estate career had come untracked. I'd whispered my need to devote more of my time to the written word, and I'd drenched that thought in a bit of good wine.

"Fine, Ms. Farrow. When and where would you like to meet for coffee?"

Chapter Twenty-six

All The News That Fits

WITH THE CLOAK of exhaustion draped over her shoulders, Lenah trudged into the hospital. She hung her squall jacket on a hook in the Emergency Department's crowded "break room."

"What's shaking, Lenah?" Carl, the newly hired intake person, asked.

"Nothing except my confidence, Carl. I don't know if I can keep doing these double shifts three times a week."

"Better you than me, Lenah. I know I couldn't do it."

"And you're brand new to the job. You should be fresh and full of energy."

Lenah looked quickly at her new workmate. She knew it would take a long time to get used to seeing Carl in the space Sally used to fill.

"Are we busy this morning?" Lenah asked.

"Not yet. We have two people in the Triage rooms. One's gonna be admitted. They finished with the other one and she should be out here any minute to pick up her discharge forms."

"Okay." Lenah studied Carl's profile. She took note of his unshaved jaw line, and she knew what Sally would have said about him.

"How could a young man come to work looking like that? I'll bet he hasn't shaved for three days."

Lenah knew how she would have responded.

"I'd wager he hasn't used his razor in four days, Sally. If I'm right, you owe me a coffee and a chocolate donut."

Lenah smiled at the sounds of her imaginary conversation.

"Now that you're here, I can make a run to the cafeteria," Carl said. "Can I bring you a cup of coffee or tea?"

"Thanks, Carl. How'd you know I was just daydreaming about a pumpkin latté?"

"Lucky guess."

With that, Carl was off.

Lenah came from behind the counter and walked toward the waiting room. She peered into the long rectangle of space. No one was there to absorb the sounds that caromed from the television onto the room's walls. Lenah entered the vacant sanctuary. She picked up the remote control and changed the program. A musician's image appeared on the flat screen and soothing music flowed through the air. Before she left the room, Lenah bent down and scooped up a newspaper from one of the end tables. She returned to the registration area, saw no one had arrived during her absence, and propped the newspaper atop the counter.

Might as well catch up with the news, she thought.

Moments of idleness sauntered by, moments without a single pain wracked person in evidence. The unencumbered time gave Lenah an opportunity to actually read a few news articles instead of simply perusing them. When she reached the death notice section, one name in particular seemed to vibrate on the page. Although the article's font was identical to those of all the other news items, the words jumped from the paper's surface and made everything else small and insignificant. Lenah was galvanized. A dozen people, all bleeding profusely and screaming for her attention, could have lined up in front of her at this moment, but she would not have heard nor seen them. She stood at that counter and read the article three times before she could begin to absorb its message.

The headline—City Insurance Executive Found Dead on New England Ferry—claimed a stake on Lenah's attention. The two paragraph description of Candace's demise shook Lenah to her core. She felt her heart beat in her throat. Her hand began to tremble as did the newspaper she was trying to hold still. A wave of nausea stirred itself swiftly in the depths of her stomach, and surged up to her chest. Silently Lenah counted to ten and then she forced herself to take deep breaths. The nausea ebbed as spontaneously as it had risen.

"A fatal coronary event," she whispered. "I warned her about that heart flutter a couple of years ago."

Lenah restored the newspaper's pages to their original order and closed it. Then she folded her hands and rested them on top of the paper, as if she needed to safeguard it.

"Here's your coffee, Lenah," Carl said as he handed the cup to her. "My treat."

"That's sweet of you, Carl. I appreciate it."

"Don't mention it."

"It'll be my turn next time. Don't forget," Lenah said.

The Emergency Department's doors gaped open to admit the quick moving figure of a man carrying a child in his arms. The small girl clutched at the lapel of the man's coat. Little cries arose from her throat.

Lenah shot a look at Carl.

"Okay. Here we go."

Carl pointed at the newspaper.

"And just as you were about to read all that good news," he chided.

"Oh, I already read the stories that interested me."

Carl positioned himself close to his computer.

"Anything positive happening in the world?"

"The usual, mostly bad news but a few good stories, too."

Their conversation halted the second the man with the whimpering child arrived in front of them.

"Can you help me and my daughter, please?"

"We'll do our best, Sir." Carl stood in front of his keyboard, poised to type. "What's your name?"

While Carl and the anxious man traded questions and answers, Lenah fixed her gaze on the child. She memorized the little girl's facial features and the color of her hair while she listened to the father reveal the child's age and the reason for her distress.

"You have everything covered here, Carl?"

"Yeah. I'm good."

Lenah picked up the folded newspaper and stepped away from the counter. She walked to the break room where she placed the paper on the shelf directly above the hook from which her jacket was hung. She turned to the large bulletin board tacked on the opposite wall and drew so close she was almost nose-to-nose with it. With much care and attention to the details, she scanned each face she saw depicted on the individual posters of missing children. When she was satisfied none of the little girls pictured on the display was the injured child awaiting care just yards away from her, Lenah left the break room and returned to her post behind the counter. She looked to her right and saw the entrance doors to the Triage rooms had opened automatically. She saw the vestiges of the man's shadow and heard the child's delicate voice speak words that ended with a question mark as they both followed a hospital worker and sought treatment.

That day, Lenah's shift alternately passed quickly and then slowly. Every time she visited the break room, she gazed at the shelf above her jacket. A couple of times, the sight of the newspaper made her knees feel like rubber and her head slightly disoriented. At other times, its presence suggested the kind of lightness that accompanies the probability that a change for the better is at hand.

When she left work late that afternoon, Lenah tucked the newspaper under her arm and pressed it firmly to her side. She planned to read the article about Candace's death again and again because part of her didn't believe it was true. Was the subject of the death notice the same Candace Dickerson she knew? Why had she been on a ferry headed to Martha's Vineyard?

Probably chasing after some upper class moneyed woman, she speculated.

Shortly after unlocking the front door of her home, Lenah marched to the kitchen, flung open her refrigerator, and uncapped a bottle of beer. She sat down at the table and reopened the newspaper. Now, Lenah had the luxury of unhurried time, so she perused every headline. She turned the pages slowly and delayed her eyes' arrival at the article about Candace. When the short piece came into view, Lenah read every single word and took note of every bit of punctuation the reporter had written. When she finished examining the story, she sat motionless and stared straight ahead.

Lenah thought if the dead woman found in that ferry's restroom was her former lover, perhaps that explained why she hadn't heard from Candace after missing a monthly payment deadline. The Candace with whom she'd once fallen in love wouldn't have harassed her about the late payment, but the changed Candace would have covered her with harangues.

Lenah shook her head in disbelief. The unfortunate victim of the fatal coronary event had to be the Candace Dickerson who'd engineered a plot to garnish the better part of Lenah's salary for the rest of both their lives. If the deceased woman was the same Candace who had staked a claim on Lenah's financial future, that claim was no longer valid. The illegal contract ended with Candace's death.

Lenah caressed the moist sides of the half empty beer bottle. She welcomed the realization that she was released from the unwritten contract Candace had imposed. Gradually, a smile spread across her lips and she arose from the chair with such little effort, she appeared to be weightless. She strode the distance between her kitchen table and the telephone near the sofa in her living room. Then she picked it up and dialed. She listened patiently as its ringing turned into an outgoing message. With a great deal of calm peace she spoke.

"Hello, London? This is Lenah Miller. I know it's been more than a minute since we last talked, and I know I've said a few harsh things to you, but I'd like to atone for that. Would you care to come to my house for dinner next Saturday evening?"

Chapter Twenty-seven

The Coffee Date

WITH MY NOTEBOOK beside me on the passenger seat, I drove from Oak Hill Estates to nearby Hopewell Village and parked my car in a lot across the street from the picture-perfect café where I'd agreed to meet with Milagros Farrow. I'd phoned Sandra Linton that morning and told her I'd need to be away from the development for a few hours. I didn't ask for permission. I simply stated my intention to be absent for a bit. Ever since I hadn't gotten the promotion, I'd found it difficult to be the perpetually smiling good natured diplomat. Where had that wishy-washy mincing behavior gotten me? How had my diligent work paid off? My bruised ego still smarted.

I'd picked a safe time to be away from the office as the usual hectic daily pace had slowed following the sale of each of the models. All that was left to do was arrange the details of the final settlements and move-ins, and Susan excelled at those chores. I'd never been a detail person. I preferred to deal with the larger picture.

I'd driven through Hopewell Village several times, but I'd never stopped there. Its Main Street looked more like a town's three dimensional model than a real place. A perfectly designed and installed landscape fronted each of the businesses. The streets and sidewalks were scrupulously clean of trash. A palette of American colonial era colors covered the shutters that outlined second and third floor windows. Electric candles flickered here and there. Even the pedestrians seemed to be a good match for the environment. Everyone walked purposefully enough to suggest they weren't moving without a destination, but no one rushed with the mind-numbing hurriedness of people bound and determined to reach their goals.

I crossed the street, aware of the order and quiet that surrounded me. The sky was thick with a cover of gray so solid and low it fit like a knitted cap pulled snugly over the ears of his little part of the world. The dense clouds muted the sounds of all traffic, vehicular and human. It was as if everyone and everything moved along in hushed secrecy.

I opened the café's door and entered.

"One for lunch?"

A young woman greeted me and clutched several menus to her chest.

"There'll be two of us. I'm meeting someone."

"Why don't I seat you and you can wait for your friend at a table?"

How do you know she's a friend? I thought, and then acquiesced.

"How about over there?"

The hostess pointed to a vacant table not far from where we stood. I nodded and followed her. I purposely circled the table so I could sit in the chair on its far side. From there I'd have a view of the entrance and I'd be able to see Milagros when she arrived. I was certain I wouldn't have any difficulty distinguishing her from the other lunchtime diners. When I perused the panorama of faces all around me, I didn't see any that looked like mine or hers. Apparently, no one of color who lived, worked in, or was visiting the peaceful little town of Hopewell Village was taking a lunch break today in this particular restaurant. Milagros must have been here before though, as she was the one who suggested where to meet.

I sat down, picked up the menu, and took turns reading about the day's specials and gazing at the café's front door where a constant trickle of customers was either entering the cozy eatery or leaving it. Just as I'd made a choice from the menu's beverage list, I caught sight of someone I'd never expected to see, at least not today and not here. Rand Carson, dressed more appropriately than she'd been the last time I saw her at Oak Hill Estate's Open House event, stood inside the café's entrance. She craned her neck and peered toward the back of the room.

The hostess greeted her and they exchanged words. A second later both women turned and looked my way. Rand smiled and the two of them began to walk directly toward my table.

I felt every muscle in my body tense. The last thing I wanted to experience was another weird and angry confrontation with Rand.

"Hello, London. May I join you?"

"Hi, Rand. This is awkward, but I'm meeting someone here for lunch."

"I know you are."

Rand smiled. She took off her coat and draped it over the back of the chair.

"It's really cold and raw, isn't it? Do you think it could snow?"

I stole a quick peek through the café's window.

"I suppose so. That would explain why it's so damp and gray."

"But it doesn't explain my being here, does it?" Rand asked.

"No, it doesn't," I said. "Is this just a coincidence?"

Rand shook her head.

"Not at all. You agreed to meet with someone here, right?"

"Yes, I agreed to meet with Milagros Farrow."

"And I know why the two of you are meeting."

"Really?"

"I'll explain," Rand said. "And before you leave here, you'll understand everything."

I looked down at my hands and noticed they were gripping the edge of the table. I loosened their hold on the worn wooden surface and stared at Rand as she opened the menu.

She looked over the top of it.

"I'm not really hungry," she said. "But please, if you'd like to order something, be my guest. Literally. I'm treating you."

"That's not necessary."

"I insist. Order whatever you'd like."

Without our summoning her, a waitress stood beside our table.

"Ladies, what can I bring you?"

"I'd like a cup of coffee, please."

"Is that all, London?" Rand asked.

"Yes."

"And for you, Miss?"

"Nothing for me, thanks."

The waitress turned away, disappointment tugging at the end of her mouth where a polite smile had been only a moment earlier.

Rand took a deep breath and pushed her chair back slightly. She lowered her gaze before she spoke.

"First, I'm glad you agreed to come here and consider an idea for a new book."

"I thought I'd agreed to listen to Milagros pitch a story."

"You did. I'll ask for your patience while I clarify the situation."

The waitress arrived and placed a mug of coffee and a saucer filled with small plastic containers of creamer in front of me.

I gazed up at her and wanted to apologize for our meager order. Instead, I offered only a "Thank you."

"As you already know, Milagros isn't planning to write any more books," Rand said. "But that hasn't stopped her from inventing new stories or characters. You're a writer, and a good one at that. You know how it is when a new plot enters your mind and characters begin to take shape."

I didn't want to smile at Rand, because I didn't trust her. But I couldn't stop the grin from responding to her comments about new plots and characters. She had described a very familiar phenomenon.

"So, you know Milagros?" I asked.

"I know her very well. That's why she entrusted me with this errand."

I continued to stare at Rand.

"May I go on?" she asked.

I nodded.

"London, Milagros believes, as do I, that you have such talent with the written word. She knows if she gave you the gift of a story concept, complete with characters' descriptions, and a general outline of the plot, you'd write a marvelous book."

"This seems very unusual," I said.

"Not at all. It's been done before by other writers."

"If the story and the characters are products of Milagros' imagination, wouldn't she want to take credit for the book?"

"She and I have talked about that very question, and the answer is no."

"I don't know what to say."

"You don't have to say anything. Just listen. Then, if you're interested, jot some notes."

I saw the waitress was nearby so I picked up my empty mug and pointed to it. She and her pot of hot coffee scurried toward us.

"Why isn't Milagros here?" I asked. "Why are you here in her place?"

"It was a last minute decision." Rand looked away for a second. "And she knows you and I have been in each other's company. Even though the last time you and I spoke wasn't a very pleasant experience, she thought that because you know me, you might give me a chance to lay out all of the information."

I didn't believe Rand was telling the entire truth, but I'd stayed here this long and I was willing to listen to more.

"Okay, tell me about this story," I said.

Rand scooted her chair forward.

"The story is about duplicity, blackmail, greed and identities."

Rand's laser-like gaze defied me to look anywhere else than at her.

"I'll be specific. I'm talking about racial identity."

I picked up the mug and blew across the top of it.

"Here's the plot," she continued. "One of the characters is a well-established lesbian writer whose books feature mostly African American characters. The writer is revered by the black literati as well as by mainstream black readers. Although her novels enjoy a crossover readership, she doesn't go out of her way to reach out to a non-black audience. She speaks eloquently to black gays and lesbians and they adore her for it. She does book signings and interviews all over the country, and she possesses a wonderful combination of wisdom along with a keen awareness of popular culture. Can you picture her, London?"

I nodded.

"She's been in a relationship with her partner for several years. She's close to her partner's family, and each year the two women spend part of the summer at her partner's family's cottage on Martha's Vineyard."

"So, I take it her partner is firmly entrenched in the black middle class," I said.

"The upper middle class. For several generations. But the writer comes from a different background."

"Is that a problem?"

"It's always a problem, isn't it?"

Rand barely paused, so there was no need for me to answer.

"A bigger problem rears its head when the partner feels she's been abandoned in favor of the writer's obsession with her work. One summer when they're on the Vineyard they fill each and every long hazy day with arguments. In the course of one particularly bitter discussion they decide to end their relationship. For a long while after their break-up, the writer feels abject emptiness."

"What happens to her upper middle class ex-partner?" I asked, although at this point I was only mildly interested in a story that seemed to lack tension and suspense.

"She encounters someone new, a business woman. That's when the plot becomes complicated."

I watched Rand's eyelids flutter as she looked down to her lap and then quickly back up to me.

"The business woman is the villain of the story," Rand added. "She's ambitious, cunning, and interested solely in her own welfare. She's not in love the writer's former partner. She doesn't even pretend to be. After they've engaged in several sexual encounters that include more questions and answers about the writer than orgasms, the business woman has been able to gather every piece of dirt about the writer that the ex-partner has spilled quite willingly."

"Why is she interested in gathering dirt about the writer?" I asked.

"Because the writer is harboring a career-ending secret, a secret to which only two other people are privy."

Rand leaned forward and spoke in whispers.

"It turns out the writer so many black Americans love so dearly is not black at all. She's a white woman, and she's fooled everyone into believing she's black."

I frowned.

"What about her signing events? Her interviews? How could a white woman do those and pretend to be black?"

"She hired a surrogate, a black woman who was willing to assume the identity of a successful writer and travel all over the country promoting her books. No one was the wiser."

I whistled softly and shook my head.

"Amazing, right?" Rand smiled broadly. She seemed pleased by how I'd been affected by the twists in the plot.

"But back to the writer's ex-partner," Rand continued. "She told her new lover, the business woman, all about the fraud the writer's been perpetrating. The business woman needed to corroborate the information, so she tracked down the surrogate and flirted with her until said surrogate admitted she was a participant in the hoax. At that point, the evil but ambitious business woman decided to blackmail both the fraudulent author and the surrogate."

I covered my mouth with my hand.

"Things grew worse, London. The writer didn't dare confess to the deception she'd committed. If she'd admitted it, she'd have no future as an author. The publishing world and her entire readership would forever doubt her credibility. On the other hand, if she didn't own up to what she'd done, and if she wanted to quit and start all over again, she'd have to begin a new writing career under her own name or a new assumed one, and she felt too weary to do that."

"What about the surrogate?" I asked. "Could she afford to pay the blackmailer?"

Rand's smile disappeared. Her eyes seemed to recede in their sockets.

"Neither woman could afford to pay those high prices. Trust me when I say that. The writer was not dumb, and she had connections. Somehow, she was able to find out exactly who was blackmailing her. She learned where the blackmailer lived and she got photos of her."

Rand's voice sounded darkly somber.

"You distracted me with your question," she said.

"Sorry."

I'd stood up to Rand's annoyance the day she'd publicly asked what kinds of women I date, but that didn't mean I cared to weather her pique again, especially since I suspected she was less than mentally stable.

"Let me finish the story."

"Sure."

"The writer became desperate. She no longer dared to write under the guise of being a black author. Her livelihood had been compromised and she felt trapped. She decided to use the only option she could imagine. She lured the blackmailer to travel to another state and there she killed her."

"The writer committed murder?" I asked. I hadn't seen this coming.

"Yes."

"How did she do it?"

"She poisoned the blackmailer with an overdose of a prescription drug."

"Which drug?"

"A drug that can cause cardiac arrhythmia, especially if the person given the drug already has an irregular heartbeat."

"How do we know the blackmailer suffered from an irregular heartbeat?"

Rand sighed.

"That's for you to devise. I'm just giving you the plot outline."

"You've given me more than an outline."

"Then writing the book shouldn't be a problem for you."

"Nor should it be a problem for Milagros. I don't understand why she doesn't write it."

Rand remained silent.

"So, how did the writer obtain enough of the prescription drug to kill a person?" I asked.

Rand smiled. She ran her hand over the surface of her hair.

"Maybe she has a health problem for which she takes the same medication. Or perhaps she has a friend who works for a doctor, or at a hospital. Maybe that friend has a reason to help her carry out her plan. Again, that's for you to figure out, London. Just use your writer's imagination."

I stared into the coffee mug I'd drained for the second time.

"Rand, I don't know if that's a book I want to write. First of all, I can't write someone else's story."

"Sure you can."

"No, I can't. It feels dishonest, like I'm shoplifting someone's creativity."

"Consider it a gift."

I shook my head. I couldn't accept the gift of someone else's story any more than I'd been able to accept the sailor's cap my aunt took from her employer's son years ago.

"The plot seems improbable, especially if the crime goes unsolved. And I don't like the suggestion that African American readers can be fooled by a clever wordsmith disguised in blackface."

Rand sat back in her chair and folded her arms across her chest.

"So you think a white author couldn't pull off the ruse?"

"Not any more than a black person could pass for white in the presence of another black person." I answered.

"What about all the black lesbians who pass successfully as straight women?"

Silence wedged itself between us. I had no defense for something I'd found to be true many times over.

"I know all about that, London," Rand said. "Willa taught me so much about black people."

Who was Willa? I wondered. And why in the world had she taught Rand about black people?

"Why don't you write the book, Rand? If you're so close to Milagros, wouldn't she want you to do that?"

Rand propped her elbows on the table and made an inverted vee with her arms. She rested her chin atop her entwined fingers.

"There's such a thing as being too close to someone, you know? The boundaries that once defined us as individuals have faded amidst all the familiarity. Milagros and I have forgotten where one of us ends and the other begins."

I wasn't sure I understood Rand's comments about her friendship with Milagros, but I was sure their relationship sounded less than completely healthy.

"So how about it, London? You'd get to figure out the story's ending."

"No thank you." I bowed my head slightly. "I'm declining Milagros' offer."

"That's regrettable. You're a terrific writer, and you haven't come out with anything new in a while. You can't tell me you're fulfilled selling real estate."

"It pays the bills and keeps me busy until the next book comes along."

Rand pulled her wallet from her handbag and withdrew a five dollar bill. She tucked it under the coffee mug.

"That should take care of the check," she said. "But there is one more matter between us."

"What's that?"

"You and I. It's a shame we never explored a relationship. We didn't go out together, not even once. I can't help believing you've let our racial differences stand in the way of what could be some really good times. You seem to be bound by a set of rules that died during the last century."

"I've never followed those rules, Rand. I've had friends and lovers of all colors. I believe attraction follows no rules and love happens when it's supposed to." I looked at Rand and steadied my voice before I continued.

"I don't have a way to say this without hurting your feelings, but the simple truth is I'm not romantically attracted to you."

Rand pushed back her chair and stood.

"Thanks for speaking your truth, London."

She slipped her arms through the sleeves of her coat and cinched the belt tightly around her waist.

"And thanks for meeting with me. I'm sorry you won't write a book that's practically already written for you."

I looked up at her.

"Thanks for the coffee and the fascinating story. Please say hello to Milagros for me." I paused. "I wonder if I'll ever get to meet her."

"Who knows? It's possible you've met her and you didn't realize it."

She turned and walked a few paces away from the table. Then she stopped and came back. She looked down at me.

"You remind me so much of my lovely Willa. If only she'd come back to me instead of taking up with Candace. That ruined everything."

Willa? Candace? I was confused but I chose to say nothing more.

I waited until I figured Rand had gotten into her car before I pulled on my jacket and exited the café. As I set out to walk across the street, big wet flakes of snow flew in front of my eyeglasses, haphazardly kissed my face, and landed softly upon my head. The afternoon's heavy overcast sky had opened and given in to the cold edged moisture that needed to escape and fall upon Hopewell Village.

"Well, that was weird," I muttered as I opened my car door.

That night, as I began my free fall into sleep, I replayed much of Rand's conversation. I remembered especially the last three sentences she'd uttered. Only then did a terrible possibility confront me like an uninvited character who bursts into a scene of an already-scripted play.

Although I knew the woman who had treated me to two cups of coffee was Rand Carson, I had every reason to believe she was also Milagros Farrow, and the story she'd shared with me was at least partially autobiographical. I had no idea how much of the story's plot was true. If there were a line that divided fact from fiction, where was it? As I recollected the last bit of Rand's narrative, I hoped to hell no one had been murdered, not even an evil blackmailer.

Chapter Twenty-eight

Dinner With An Old Friend

"THAT'S A WILD story, London. If Rand Carson is really Milagros Farrow, and if she killed her blackmailer, why would she want a book written about it? Why would she want anyone to suspect what she'd done?" Theresa asked.

"Damned if I know the answer to that question, Tee. You'd have to ask a psychiatrist."

Theresa shook her head.

"Let's suppose the murder really happened and she's told you about it in a round-about way. Does that make you an accessory to the crime? "

"I don't know. I guess I should ask a lawyer. Do you know anyone I could call?"

"Not off hand, but that sounds like a good idea. I don't want to have to visit you in prison."

"I don't want that either, Tee."

"So what are you going to do?"

"For starters, I'm not going to write that book. Aside from that, I don't know what my next move will be."

"Speaking of next moves, are you still planning to keep the dinner date with that Lenah person?"

"Sure. Why not? I had coffee with a bizarre woman who might have faked being a famous black author, and who has possibly poisoned someone. After all that, how perilous can it be to have dinner with Lenah Miller?"

Theresa sighed. "Let me try to understand, London."

"What's there to understand, Tee?"

"The two or three times you've seen this woman, she's hurt your feelings for no good reason, and now you're going to her house for dinner. Is that what you're telling me?"

"It seems like I'm either desperate, or I don't have good sense, doesn't it?"

"Good sense? It seems like you don't have any sense at all."

This was one of the few times I had no rejoinder for Theresa because I agreed with her.

"What are you after, London? What do you want?"

In the long run, someone who'll love me as much as she loves herself, I wanted to say, and I would have if I hadn't felt so vulnerable to Theresa's disapproval.

"Someone who understands who I am," I blurted.

"Well, based upon the few things you've told me about Lenah, it sounds like she understands who you are and she doesn't accept you."

"Maybe we tried to make a connection at the wrong time."

"I guess that justification for her rudeness is as good as any other."

I knew my attempt to explain Lenah's past behavior toward me was weak at best. Even as I tried to rationalize seeing her again, I knew agreeing to have dinner with Lenah was not the brightest thing I'd ever done, especially now when my self-esteem was still in need of repair because I'd lost the promotion at work.

I'd already flogged myself for resigning from Whittingham Builders to pursue what I'd thought were better opportunities with Kensington. I didn't need to suffer another one of Lenah's insinuations of ethnic disloyalty.

Why had I accepted her invitation to dinner as easily as I'd agreed to meet Milagros Farrow for coffee and a discussion about an unwritten novel? Surely curiosity had driven me to consent to the latter course of action. It was the chance to relate to someone who might have an inkling about the how and why of who I was that impelled me to see Lenah once again.

She might know how to tie my past to my present. She might listen to my childhood memory of the sailor's cap and understand why I hadn't wanted to accept the gift that hot summer day I spent with my aunt in her employers' big house in Garden City, New York. Lenah might smile knowingly if I told her I'd worn that little white hat only once, secretly when I was alone in my room. It was possible Lenah truly would get it. She'd grasp it to the bone. And I was willing to risk another contentious encounter with her in order to seek her compassionate understanding, not her approval of some of the choices I'd made in my life thus far.

A few nights later, I parked my car in front of Lenah's house, a dwelling whose porch was separated from its twin structure by a low bannister in need of a fresh coat of paint. The two outdoor lights that flanked the front door defeated autumn's early darkness. I approached, lifted the heavy circular knocker, and let it clang against the door.

"Hello, London. Welcome."

Lenah's voice was full of warmth. It held no trace of the ambivalence I'd heard the day I first saw her at the hospital. She opened her arms and I stepped forward to accept her hug. She pointed to the bouquet of flowers I held somewhat awkwardly.

"They're as pretty as the ones you brought to your injured construction worker the first time we met."

"I went to the same florist," I said.

I surrendered the flowers and my jacket to Lenah and then followed her to the living room.

"Have a seat while I get a vase."

Instead of moving toward a chair, I looked at my surroundings. The high-ceilinged room was long and narrow, as was the house. A tweed sofa and matching love seat, along with a pine coffee table and other comfortable furnishings softened the room's severe angles. The fireplace, which interrupted the expanse of a burgundy colored wall, was surrounded by fieldstone and capped with a mantle coated in white.

Two bookcases stood at attention on either side of the fireplace. While they didn't shelter that many books, they did provide a home for quite a few photographs. Frames of all sizes and shapes displayed pictures of more people than I could count.

Lenah entered the room. She had a bottle of wine in one hand and two glasses in the other. "Can I pour you some?"

"Thanks," I said. I tipped my glass toward Lenah's. "Here's to good conversation and new friendships."

"Here's to second beginnings, maybe even thirds," Lenah added.

I aimed a quizzical look her way.

"Let me know if you're cold. I turned up the heat, but it takes a while to get warm in here. This is an old house."

"There's a lot of charm in old houses."

"There's a lot of maintenance, too," Lenah replied.

"I've been dealing with new construction for such a long time, I tend to forget about things like repairs and maintenance."

"London, a house is like a relationship. Sometimes the oldest ones need the most care."

"Aren't you the philosopher?" I said.

"Not really. But I am a peace keeper and I'd like to get the difficult part of tonight out of the way early."

I remained quiet in anticipation of a message that seemed to be troublesome for Lenah to deliver.

"I owe you an apology for some things I said the last time we spoke to each other. I said I didn't understand what you meant when you referred to your daily miracles. I said you and I were different, and you needed to seek someone more like you than I am. I know I insulted you, and I'm sorry about that."

"I accept your apology, Lenah. But I'm curious about something. When we talked about my professional ambitions and my having left a black-owned construction company to work for a white owned outfit, you criticized me. Why?"

Lenah cast her gaze downward and paused.

"Maybe because it was easier to criticize you than try to understand your reasons for quitting the black-owned firm. Or maybe because I knew we really were different and I was afraid the differences might mean we couldn't be close friends."

"But we didn't know each other well enough to be able to determine how different we are."

Lenah took a sip of her wine and leaned forward in her chair.

"Maybe I wanted to have the choices I figured you'd always had since you were a child and knowing I hadn't had them made me angry," she said.

"How did you know I'd always had choices?"

Lenah averted my eyes for a second before she answered.

"I could tell by who you are now. And you remind me of an ex-partner of mine who always created her choices. She wouldn't stop striving until she got to the top."

"Was that such a bad thing?"

"It wouldn't have been if she hadn't stomped over everyone in her path."

I started to reach over and grasp Lenah's hand, but I didn't want her to misinterpret a gesture whose motivation even I didn't fully understand.

"It sounds to me like we both brought something negative to the table. You confused me with a former friend of yours and I couldn't take your criticism," I said. "To tell you the truth, I need to grow thicker skin."

"Are you easily offended?"

"From time to time, but I'm learning to handle it."

"And I'm realizing not every ambitious person has the same negative qualities."

I turned toward the bookcases and their treasure trove of photos.

"Are these pictures of your family?"

Lenah nodded.

"Some are. But mostly they're photos of friends. I have a small family."

"Mind if I take a closer look?"

Lenah shrugged her shoulders.

"Help yourself."

I stood and ambled over to the display.

"The first one there on the left is a picture of my parents when they were young, before I was born. And the next two are my mother and my aunt."

"Where is this? The background doesn't look like any place in Philadelphia."

"Those photos were taken in a little town in the south, Dumbshit Alabama."

I turned toward Lenah and grinned at her. "I know that wasn't the real name of the town."

"It might as well have been," Lenah said.

"Is your mother from Alabama?" I hoped my question sounded as light and neutral as I wanted it to.

"Yeah. She grew up there. My father's from Philly. They met when he was in the Service, got married and moved up here."

I stepped to the right and pointed to a photo encased in an ornate gilt frame.

"Who is this?"

The photograph looked professionally composed. Everything in the background was subdued and somewhat blurred. The image of the woman however, was clear and sharply delineated. She must have stood six feet tall. She was dressed in baggy pants and a floral tunic shirt. Her hair was stunningly gray and her bronze colored face bore such a peaceful, self-contained expression. Her eyes were all-knowing and they seemed to stare right through me. It was as if the woman in the portrait knew me, as if she knew every person who would ever hold this photo in their hands and rest their eyes on her countenance.

I sensed Lenah's presence standing beside me.

"That's Miz Henderson, Miz Myjoy Henderson. She was a friend of my aunt and my mother. She was my friend as well."

"Does she live in Alabama?"

"Not any more. She died years ago."

"I'm sorry."

I returned the heavy frame and its portrait to its place on the book shelf and continued to view the other photos.

"If you want to eat that dinner I invited you to, we'd better go to the kitchen so I can finish preparing it," Lenah said.

She cupped my elbow and attempted to lead me away from all the photographs.

"Okay, but not before you tell me how old you were in that school picture over there."

I pointed to a small black and white photo embellished with the words, "School Days" printed at the bottom of it.

Lenah stared at the picture for a second before she answered.

"I was in the eighth grade. It was my fourth year in that pitiful segregated school in Dumbshit."

I would have laughed at Lenah's name for the southern town but I thought I should remain quiet and honor the terrible anger and pain I heard in her voice each time she pronounced the place's name. I felt a fleeting tremor of déja-vu when I gazed at the portrait of the braid wearing eighth grader. The girl in that photo reminded me of someone I'd known or at least of someone I'd seen once. Maybe I'd seen her in a volume of Gordon Parks photographs or perhaps in an article about the south I'd read eons ago in an ancient issue of *Ebony* magazine.

Lenah tapped my arm.

"Come on. Let's go."

I tried to keep my eyes focused on Lenah's back as she guided me to the kitchen, but I gave in to temptation and took one last look at the four by six snapshot of the eighth grade school girl in Alabama.

I'd never before known anyone who'd actually lived in Alabama. In my Northern-bred mind I'd imagined no one black could have lived in that state and survived the experience with body and mind intact.

Places like Dumbshit, Alabama and Shall-we-lynch-em, Mississippi might as well have been the figment of someone's horribly demented mind, not anyone's reality, not even someone with Lenah's survival wisdom.

"Can I help you with dinner?" I asked.

"No, it's all under control."

I sat at the table and watched Lenah pour pasta from a pot of boiling water into a large bowl.

"I hope you like linguine," she said.

"I do."

"And crab meat in a cream sauce?"

"I like that also."

A moment later, Lenah spooned the seafood and cream mixture over the pasta. Then she carried the steaming dish to the table and put it down next to a wooden bowl filled with salad.

"Help yourself while it's hot."

We took turns putting the food on our plates.

"So, what was fifth grade like for you, London?"

"Much like the fourth grade. Nothing spectacular."

"I bet you had a lot of friends, huh?"

"No. I was shy. In addition to that, I didn't enjoy doing the same things the other girls did. I preferred to draw rockets and pretend I was going to be an astronaut."

"So you hung out with the little white nerdy boys?"

"What makes you think they were white? Why couldn't they have been little black nerdy boys?"

"Because there weren't more than a couple little black boys where you went to school."

"How'd you know that?"

Lenah touched her forehead. "I'm psychic."

I didn't believe she had telepathic powers, but I was enjoying myself and I didn't want to dispute her.

"How long did you live in Alabama, Lenah?"

"Too long for comfort."

"I've never been south, but I already know I wouldn't like it," I said.

"Some things weren't all that bad, like the school semester ending early and being allowed to help Miz Myjoy take care of sick people. She made me want to be a doctor, or at least a nurse."

"Was she a doctor?"

"Nope. But she knew so much about curing the sick, everybody black in town came to see her before they went to see the real doctor. And she didn't charge them as much as the real doctor did."

I could see happiness light up Lenah's face as she recalled that part of her childhood.

"When did you and your mother come back to Philadelphia?"

"My mother died the year before I came back to Philly."

Lenah bowed her head, perhaps to pay homage to the memory of her deceased parent.

"How old were you when you came back?"

"Seventeen. I'd just graduated from high school, so I got a job and I started earning my Associates Degree at night."

I put down my fork.

"You were right when you said we were different, Lenah. Compared to you, I had it so easy. High school, college, a career, even coming out was a breeze when I think about it."

"I'm sure you went through tough times too, London. Nobody gets a free pass from problems."

I blinked and tried to conjure up my harshest experiences, my father's death and Paula's leaving me.

"What about your mother?" Lenah asked.

"My mother?"

"Yeah. You've never mentioned her."

"She died in a car accident when I was young."

"See what I mean? That was one of your tough times. That must have hurt you real bad."

I nodded and found it curious that I hadn't thought about my mother's death when Lenah had asked me about my difficult times.

"My father did all he could to pick up the pieces and give me a good adolescence."

"What was life like for you before your mother passed away? What did she think of your playing astronaut instead of little miss black debutante?"

In a flash, I heard my mother's saber-sharp voice sever the air.

"And don't use that word 'black.' What's wrong with 'Negro?'"

"It's old fashioned and out of style, hon." My father had explained patiently more than once.

"I bet she didn't like your tomboy side, did she?" Lenah said.

For the first time this evening, I felt the uncomfortable remnants of Lenah's earlier critiques.

"She was less than thrilled."

"That doesn't surprise me. How did she feel about all your little friends from school, especially the ones who lived outside your neighborhood? Did she urge you to invite all of them over for dinner or for pajama parties?"

I stared at Lenah. I didn't know where she was taking us, but I suspected it wasn't to any place pleasant.

"Was it your mother or your father who advised you to grow a tougher skin?"

Maybe she is psychic, I thought.

"It was my mother. She told me I was much too sensitive for my own good."

Lenah leaned forward.

"Did you think she was right?"

"I didn't think back then. I just accepted whatever she told me."

Lenah nodded and smiled gently.

"I know. We were all too young to think for ourselves. And in your case, you didn't have to think in order to survive. You had both of your parents there to do the thinking for you, and neither one of them would have hurt you intentionally."

"What about you, Lenah? Did you have to think in order to survive? Did your parents hurt you intentionally?"

I watched Lenah's chest rise as she breathed deeply. She put both her hands on the table and spoke softly, slowly.

"Yeah, I had to think in order to survive. Especially with my father. He violated me repeatedly from the time I entered first grade 'til the night my mother packed two suitcases and dragged my little fourth grader legs onto a series of buses headed for my aunt and uncle's home in Alabama."

Lenah stared right through me as she recited her history more than spoke it.

"A year after we got to Alabama, my uncle started abusing me. He molested me from the first morning of summer vacation after the fifth grade to the night I stabbed him and went to Miz Myjoy Henderson's for help."

Both Lenah and I had stopped eating. She continued to speak and I became her confessor. "Miz Myjoy tried her best to stop his bleeding, but she couldn't. The only life she saved that night was mine. She gave me advice and enough money to get a bus the hell out of that state."

I leaned forward, reached across the table, and touched the backs of Lenah's hands.

Their warmth and softness surprised me, perhaps because there'd been so much bitter cold and sharp hardness running through Lenah's memories.

Lenah looked into my eyes. Her gaze had softened.

"When I said we were different and that I knew where we'd both come from, I spoke the truth, London."

"I believe you, Lenah."

"But you don't know the whole of it. You don't realize who I am, do you?"

I stared at Lenah and pretended my eyes could peel away an imaginary mask and reveal her true identity.

"I'm Roberta, your friend who used to ride the school bus with you. You lived in Coventry Village. You kept inviting me to your house on the weekends or after school, but I never accepted your invitations because I knew your mother didn't approve of where I lived, or my color, my ashy arms and legs, my hair, my clothes, or my laborer parents. You never cared about us being different, London, because you never noticed it. Your good heart had no need to notice differences."

I examined every centimeter of Lenah's face. I searched her eyes, nose, and mouth and looked for the Roberta who'd been so familiar to me so many years ago. I tried to match my memory of that girl with the pre-teen child in the School Days photo propped on the bookcase in the next room.

"London? Do you remember how I used to climb onto that rickety school bus, sit down and lean against you? Because I remember. I recall how warm your arm always felt all wrapped up in your winter parka those mornings when I could barely keep my teeth from chattering so furiously I thought they'd splinter."

"Ro, Roberta Baker?" I stammered.

"Yes, London. Roberta Lenah Baker. Except for Miz Myjoy, the people in Alabama never called me Roberta. They liked saying R. Lenah, you know, like "Our Lenah." Miller was my mother's maiden name. I started using it after I came back to Philadelphia. I got rid of the R because it reminded me of all the rotten pain I endured down there."

"Why didn't Miz Myjoy call you R. Lenah?"

"Because she paid close attention to me and she believed there was nothing wrong with who I was. She said she never wanted to change anything about me."

I peered at Lenah and tried to reconcile what she'd said with the reality of who she was. Before I could stop them, tears filled my eyes and coursed down my cheeks.

"I never thought I'd see you again," I said.

Lenah sat back in her chair and beamed.

"Look at us. Two very grown women who grew up living across the road from each other in Coventry Village and Grantville."

"When and how did you know who I was?" I asked.

"The second you told me your name the day we introduced ourselves at the hospital. In all my life I'd never met another person named London Phillips. It had to be the same you."

"Why didn't you say something?"

"I wanted to see what kind of person you'd become."

"What? You were giving me a trial run?"

"I was giving myself a trial run. I had to be sure I was worthy of your friendship."

For so many years my little school friend, Roberta, existed only in the outermost borders of my memories. Her disappearance had been so complete, that from time-to-time I'd questioned if she'd really existed at all. And now, here she was, seated across the table from me.

That night at Lenah's house, we didn't eat more than two forkfuls of her pasta with crab and cream sauce. We did spend the evening feeding each other pages and chapters of our lives, our loves, our hurts, our speculations about the world and our place in it. We talked until we felt satiated. We were full of hopes for subsequent times we'd spend together and simply appreciate that we'd both survived so many years without each other's shadow at our backs.

"I have so many stories to tell you, Lenah." I said.

"London, I'll bet you I have more."

I grinned at her. She returned my gaze, but her smile was not as wide as mine, not offered as freely or as generously. Its guardedness gave me some sense of how different our paths through life had been. I knew from that moment it would be difficult for Lenah to disclose all the experiences she might want to share with me. It would be far easier for her to sketch the bigger picture and not fill in the details of the hurtful episodes.

A bit of time would pass before I'd be willing to share my tale about Rand Carson and Milagros Farrow. For one thing, I didn't know how much of Rand's story was true and how much was fiction. For another, I needed to summon the courage to find out if I had any culpability after the fact simply because I'd been told about a crime Rand may have committed.

I didn't know if I could tell Lenah the final chapter of Rand's saga, the chapter Susan told me one day shortly after I'd arrived at work.

Susan summoned me to her side as she pointed at a news item on her computer's screen.

"London, isn't she the woman who almost bought one of the Oak Hill Estates homes? Remember when she showed up at the Open House event looking all disheveled and then caused a scene?"

I'd blinked at the boldface headline next to the flickering cursor, Local Journalist's Body Recovered from Massachusetts Waters.

"It says she jumped off a ferry into Cape Cod Bay," Susan said.

"What?"

"It says she may have been trying to kill herself."

A chill enveloped me.

"Maybe it was an accident. Maybe she fell overboard," I'd said, still in a state of disbelief.

"Nope. There were witnesses who saw her hurl herself over the side of the boat, and half an hour earlier, a security camera filmed her sitting in her car on the ferry's lower level. The car's engine was running. The video showed a guard knocking on the windshield seconds before she got out of the car and headed to one of the passenger decks."

I'd felt my morning coffee churn in my gut as Susan continued to point at the text on the screen.

"And they found a long rambling letter face up in her car's back seat. In it, she confessed to having poisoned and murdered someone months earlier on that same boat."

"Jesus," I'd muttered.

"It says she claimed she acted alone, with no one else's knowledge about the crime."

I heard my heart beating frantically inside my chest.

"I'm glad she backed out of our house deal, aren't you, London?"

"Yes," I said. "Definitely."

That day I'd worked like a robot on automatic pilot. Late that afternoon I phoned Theresa and asked her if she'd seen the news article about the woman with whom we'd shared a meal one evening last summer in Provincetown. I thought talking with Tee about Rand's death would be enough to quiet my discomfort, but I was mistaken.

Two evenings later, I sat in Lenah's living room and although I hadn't planned it, I found myself confessing all that I knew about Rand and her alter ego, Milagros Farrow.

Lenah looked down but listened carefully as I'd unfurled my narrative. She didn't ask me any questions when I described the novel Rand had offered me. She didn't interrupt nor press me for any details. And although she'd paid close attention to everything I'd recounted so far, she locked her eyes on mine when I added the post script about Rand's apparent suicide and the letter she'd left.

"How are you feeling about this woman's death?" Lenah asked.

"A little strange," I said. "Like I'm the secret repository of a bizarre knot of information."

"You don't ever have to talk about it, you know. Starting now, I won't ask you any questions."

I was eager for my memories of Rand Carson to blur and eventually fade away, so Lenah's lack of curiosity about her was fine by me. I wanted new memories to spring forth from the seeds of some of my oldest ones. And I needed a new friend. I had the feeling Lenah could use one also.

When the bonds of friendship failed to form after one or two attempts, most people would have given up and walked away. Roberta Lenah Baker and I gave ourselves two opportunities to be friends, once many years ago when we were third and fourth graders, and now as adults, when we'd sensed we were women who shared more things in common with each other than not. We had history, a brief one, but that in itself was enough to encourage us to forge ahead together.

Lenah had pursued our friendship awkwardly, with verbal barbs followed by the balm of apologies and her stubborn persistence to give us a chance to prevail. I'd been willing to absorb the barbs and recover from them. I'd been filled with the need for someone to understand me. I'd remained vigilant for small miracles, so I welcomed Lenah back into my life. I was sure I could trust her with my secrets. And if she'd trust me with hers, I vowed to keep them close to me, closer to me than my teeth and skin.

Other titles from S. Renée Bess:

Breaking Jaie

Jaie Baxter, an African-American Ph.D candidate at Philadelphia's Allerton University, is determined to win a prestigious writing grant. In order to win the Adamson Grant, Jaie initially plans to take advantage of one of the competition's judges, Jennifer Renfrew, who is also a University official. Jennifer has spent the past ten years alone following the murder of her lover, Patricia Adamson, in whose honor the grant is named. Jennifer is at first susceptible to Jaie's flirtation, but is later vengeful when she discovers the real reason for Jaie's sudden romantic interest in her. A lunch with an old cop friend reveals that Jaie may very well have ties to Adamson's death.

Jaie is confronted with painful memories as she prepares an autobiographical essay for the grant application. She recalls the emotional trauma of her older brother's death, the murder of a police detective, her dismissal from her "dream" high school, and her victimization at the hands of hateful homophobic students. She remembers her constant struggles with her mother's alcohol-fueled jealousies and physical abuse she had to endure. This wake-up call causes her to look at her life in new ways.

But Jaie is not the only student applying for the grant. Terez Overton, a wealthy Boston woman, is Jaie's chief competitor. Jaie is drawn to the New Englander immediately but is also unnerved by her. She has no clue that Terez is trying to decide whether she wants to accept an opportunity to write an investigative article about an unsolved murder. Writing that article could put her budding relationship with Jaie in jeopardy.

And just when the angst of old memories and the uncertainty of her future with Terez are complicating Jaie's life, her manipulative ex, Seneca Wilson, returns to Philadelphia to reclaim Jaie using emotional blackmail. Senecas actions serve to wound and break Jaie in many ways. Will Seneca drive the final wedge between Jaie and Terez? Who will win the Adamson grant? And what did Jaie have to do with the death of Patricia Adamson?

ISBN: 978-1-932300-84-0

Available in both print and eBook formats

Leave of Absence

Corey Lomax, a writer and English professor at Allerton University in suburban Philadelphia, continues to recover from the rupture of a six year relationship with Jennifer Renfrew, the university's Assistant Dean of Admissions. Jennifer has embarked on a new relationship with Pat Adamson, a Philadelphia police officer.

Kinshasa Jordan, a novelist and teacher on leave from her public high school position in Connecticut, accepts a writer-in-residence post at Allerton. When she relocates, Kinshasa leaves behind a secure job as well as an abusive relationship.

Corey and Kinshasa meet as colleagues, writers, and minority women who must navigate their way through the sometimes unfriendly territory of white male dominated academia. Corey is proudly "out." Kinshasa's sexuality is a matter of conjecture. What is clear is both Corey's and Kinshasa's determination to avoid any romantic entanglements.

As the story unfolds, so do secrets, betrayals, a murder, and the slowly smoldering attraction between Corey Lomax and Kinshasa Jordan.

ISBN: 978-1-61929-106-5

Available in both print and eBook formats

Re: Building Sasha

Sasha Lewis, the uber-competent manager of Whittingham Builders, finds herself drowning in a riptide of distrust as she struggles to maintain her relationship with Lee Simpson. A genius at balancing details, Sasha commits a career-derailing error while being distracted by Lee's threat to burn down their house and its contents.

Lee's flagrant sexual liaisons with a business client, Angela Jackman, and her escalating deeds of emotional cruelty rip apart Sasha. In self-imposed exile from most of her friends, Sasha recalls a brief encounter with Avery Sloan; an encounter destined to become more meaningful when Avery's social service agency hires Whittingham Builders to rehab an old Victorian house.

What hateful acts will Lee perform in an effort to degrade Sasha? How much damage will Sasha endure before she begins to rebuild her spirit? Will Sasha grab Avery's outstretched hand and accept the gentle yet exciting offer of love she sees in this woman?

ISBN: 978-1-935053-07-1

Available in both print and eBook formats

The Butterfly Moments

After a twenty-plus year career as a Parole Officer in Philadelphia, Alana Blue is more than ready to leave her job and move on to more rewarding work. Jaded and burned out, Alana is given the difficult assignment of supervising Rafe Ortiz, a renegade Probation and Parole Officer who arrives in Alana's office by way of a disciplinary transfer and with a reputation for accumulating meaningless sexual conquests.

Alana's life is more complicated by the frequent conflicts she experiences with her homophobic daughter, Nikki. Convinced that the transparency of her mother's sexuality doomed her first marriage, Nikki is obsessed with keeping her second union intact, even if it means constantly repudiating Alana. Nikki's husband, Owen Reid, doesn't always agree with his wife's opinions regarding same-gender relationships; nor does he always support their marriage by remaining faithful to Nikki.

As Alana is reaching for an opportunity to pursue a new career, the body of a brutally murdered university student is discovered partially hidden on a property very close to Alana's neighborhood. Detective Johnetta Jones, recently retired from the Philadelphia Police Force, and hired by a suburban law enforcement department, is assigned to the murder case. When the investigation leads her to one of Alana's parolees, Johnetta remembers having interviewed this particular Parole Officer once before. Although her memory of Alana is mostly pleasant, Johnetta remains more emotionally connected to her work than she is to any woman she's ever met. Vaguely discontent, she is reluctant to forge a romantic connection with anyone...until her path intersects with Alana's once again. Their renewed contact suggests the possibility of love and the end of loneliness for both women. As Johnetta and her work partner, Detective Harold Smythe, get close to solving the university student's murder, Johnetta realizes arresting their suspect will imperil her tenuous relationship with Alana.

Alana becomes caught in the war between her impulsive attraction to Rafe Ortiz's flirtatious pursuit and her realization that her feelings for Johnetta Jones are growing deeper with each passing day. Will everything in Alana's world disintegrate when lies are revealed, true identities are exposed, and the murderer is unmasked?

ISBN: 978-1-935053-37-8

Available in both print and eBook formats

Other Regal Crest books you may enjoy:

The Game of Denial
by Brenda Adcock

Joan Carmichael, a successful New York businesswoman, lost the love of her life ten years earlier. Alone, she raised their four children, always cherishing her deep love for her wife. Her memories of their life together come back even stronger as one of their daughters prepares to marry. Joan and her four adult kids fly to Virginia to meet the groom's family and attend the ceremony at the small horse farm owned by the mother of the fiancé.

Evelyn "Evey" Chase, also a widow, has secrets in her past, and her memories of her dead husband aren't pleasant. She's concerned about meeting her future daughter-in-law's family, certain that she and her three kids will have little in common with the wealthy New Yorkers. Besides, the thought of two women in a relationship bringing up a family together makes her uncomfortable, even though her daughter-in-law assures her that lesbianism is not hereditary or catching.

When the two women meet they are drawn to one another in a way neither anticipated, and the game of denial begins. Evey fights her attraction and doesn't realize the effect she has on Joan. Joan tries to shake off her feelings, seeing them as a betrayal to the memory of her wife. Besides, isn't Evey Chase straight? After Evey and Joan share an intimate moment at the wedding reception, they are both emotionally terrified and Joan flees. Will Joan overcome the feeling of betraying her former mate and stop denying her desire to be happy again? Can Evey finally face her past in order to accept the love of another woman and the desire to live the life she had once dreamed of?

ISBN: 978-1-61929-130-0

Available in both print and eBook formats

I Heard the Pastor's Daughter Is Gay
by Luana Reach Torres

Katie North breezes through high school as an undercover nerd helped by the fact that her best friend is the most popular girl in school. Katie has no clue that she's smokin' hot and the object of a few varsity athletes' drool. She's a pastor's daughter--Miss Goodie Two Shoes--and up until now, her number one priority has been graduating with the highest honors. But, everything changes when Katie falls in love for the first time - with a girl. Her world is blown wide open, and everything changes. Will Katie find her true self at the cost of her father's love?

ISBN: 978-1-61929-068-6

Available in both print and eBook formats

OTHER REGAL CREST PUBLICATIONS

About the Author

Renée Bess is a Philadelphia native, and she and her partner reside in a northwest suburb of that city. Renée taught Spanish and French in a city high school for quite a few years. At the age of six, she was captivated by the plot of Dr. Dan The Bandage Man. She subsequently became enamoured with Nancy Drew, the Hardy boys and years later, Celie and Shug. Books became a necessary part of Renée's life, and writing became the natural corollary. She expects that there are more stories eager to come tumbling forth.

Email: ecrivaine1@yahoo.com
Web site: www.reneebess.com

VISIT US ONLINE AT
www.regalcrest.biz

At the Regal Crest Website You'll Find

- The latest news about forthcoming titles and new releases

- Our complete backlist of romance, mystery, thriller and adventure titles

- Information about your favorite authors

- Current bestsellers

- Media tearsheets to print and take with you when you shop

- Which books are also available as eBooks.

Regal Crest print titles are available from all progressive booksellers including numerous sources online. Our distributors are Bella Distribution and Ingram.